# BLACK ORCHID

## Bill Culver

Print ISBN: 978-0-69238-200-4
Ebook ISBN: 9798614333034

Published by Wynnpix Productions
Cover Art Designed by WEBMARK

*Dedicated to my wife, Cheri, for her patience and assistance in overcoming computer glitches of which I have no understanding or tolerance, allowing me to finish this work; to my outstanding sister Marcia, without whom I would be an only child, to victims of crime forced to deal with their pain and the slow turning of the wheels of the criminal justice system; and, finally, to those who pursue justice with a good heart against any and all odds.*

# PROLOGUE

The cold water flowing into Collette's mouth and nose brought her momentarily back to a murky consciousness. Vaguely she sensed pain in her leg as she was dragged underwater and then lodged under a tree root that protruded down into the thick water of the bayou. She would never know that her last measure of value in this world was simply to provide nourishment for an anonymous creature that dragged her nude and abused body from the knees of a deformed cypress tree.

As she passed into eternity, the tearing of the alligator's teeth in her flesh was not the only pain she noted in her broken body. Her entire body was racked with exquisite pain. Pain caused by one man who would come to dread her name as it became the first clue to unraveling a series of his unspeakable acts and sordid lusts, secrets that had lurked for many years in the Vieux Carre, the French Quarter of New Orleans.

✝

"*Christ*. It's *already* one a.m." Detective Nick Saladino was in his favorite position; leaning on the end of the bar that was furthest from the door at The Catacombs, his back to the wall. This was the favorite hangout of the N.O.P.D.'s homicide bureau. He dreaded the idea of going home; in fact, he had come to dread it virtually *every* night for the last two years, but wasn't really conscious of dreading it.

The other patrons of The Catacombs were accustomed to seeing Nick in his position at the bar. In fact, whenever he came in, the regulars quietly gravitated to a different location as an acknowledgment of Nick's claim over that territory. No doubt his manner and appearance played some part in their acquiescence. He was dark-complexioned and wiry, with a receding line of still-black hair that was only slightly flecked with gray. Those who were confident enough to look into his permanent scowl and dark eyes were often surprised that Nick, at fifty-two, was actually older than he looked. Most people who encountered him professionally or otherwise demurred to his aura of authority and intensity without challenge.

Nick slugged thirstily on his double Crown on the rocks, no longer capable of sensing the burn of alcohol in his throat that even an experienced drinker occasionally feels. He thought momentarily of Sharon, his second wife of five years and mother of his three kids. *Christ*, he thought. The prospect of the approaching weekend at home drove him to empty his glass and pound it on the bar to catch the attention of Becky, the current barmaid of two weeks' duration. He watched her while she walked behind the bar, his eyes focusing on her face then drifting lazily off the curve of her blouse like a slow ski jump, refocusing on her face and her smart, classy little ass. She was one of those rare chicks who could project innocence and sleaze simultaneously. *Fuck. She could make a* fruit *go for broads,* he thought appreciatively, as he watched the frenzy of detectives vying for her attention, not unlike sharks at a feeding.

His wife Sharon had been an attention-getter when they first met on the sand at Pontchartrain Beach Amusement Park. Nick noted that she still turned heads on occasion, but he was unable to recall anything else that he felt about her after all this time. He couldn't say anything bad about her. She was a good woman. He just didn't *feel* anything more than that, and he never associated his lack of feelings for her with the emptiness that drove him from deep inside.

It was the guttural laugh, low at first then growing louder and more intense, that startled the other patrons of The Catacombs, more due to its source than its intensity. Nick was rarely known to laugh out loud, but he had become absorbed in the memory of "Little Melvin," a man he had arrested earlier in the day who had just popped into his mind. It was a case that was as pitiful as it was comic, but it took Nick's mind off of his personal life temporarily, and he was grateful for the relief as he had a flashback of those events:

*****

"*Aw, shit.*" The police radio sing-song, virtually unintelligible to non-police personnel, had just advised Nick, who was on his way to lunch that morning, of a "30," or homicide, in the area of the St. Mathias Project, one of the most dangerous collections of feral human beings in the city. He reluctantly swung the black Crown Victoria in the direction of the area and away from Matanza's, a seedy sandwich shop in the back area of the French Quarter on Barracks Street, his favorite lunch stop.

Nick rolled up to a camel-back shotgun double house on Piety Street that was obviously down on its luck; it was now a crack house. Its only visitors anymore were addicts trying to find whatever it is that addicts seek inside the remains of the once-proud home.

"What it *is*," Nick greeted Mike Faust, a longtime, much-decorated street cop who had turned down numerous promotions to remain on the streets of his beloved Bywater area.

Mike, with red hair and a red handlebar mustache, stood six foot three and weighed in at a little over two hundred ninety-five pounds. He simply blocked out light any time he passed through a doorway. He and Nick had separated many a bottle of alcohol from its contents, and had noticeably depleted the stock of many a local bar, as well, on their frequent binges throughout the various neighborhoods of New Orleans.

"Wher' y'at, Nick?" Mike looked at Nick, squinting his eyes at the sun that reflected off of Nick's lapel pin. Homicide detectives were fond of wearing a gold pin depicting a buzzard with the inscription, "Our day begins when yours ends."

"Man, dis one is kinda strange," Mike said in the accent of the lower Ninth Ward, virtually identical to that spoken by natives of the Bronx. "It's a ol' broad. Gotta be *sixty-five*. She's layin' up under dat house wit no cloze on. I don' see no injuries. She musta just made groceries, cuz dere's a bag dere wit some stuff in it."

"No shit?" Nick was taking in the scene. "Where'd you say she was at?"

"She's under da goddam *house*, man." Mike snorted. "Coupla crack-heads next door seen her go unda da house wit an ole black dude, an' he was da only one come out."

Nick walked over and peered under the house. The crime scene techs were already on their stomachs in the dirt taking photos and looking for physical evidence. He could see the form of an obese elderly black woman on her back, legs spread open, eyes staring up at the floor joists above her head as if checking out some evil menace lurking in the flooring of the old house. He turned to Mike. "Any shots reported?"

"Naw, man. Ain't nobody hoid *nuttin*. But, ya know how it is 'round here. Nobody nevva *hoid* no evil, nobody nevva *seen* no evil, and all da *rest* a' dat shit."

Nick nodded and took one last look at the body as it was being dragged from under the house. "Christ, maybe the old broad died of a heart attack while making a little grocery money under this damn shooting gallery." Nothing surprised Nick any longer. She had the look of any of the old prostitutes who lived around the projects, supplementing their welfare payments by providing sex to the old men who couldn't afford younger hookers. He made a mental note to check with vice when he received the crime lab photos to see if anyone recognized her.

Nick made his way over to the front porch of the shotgun next door to talk to the witnesses who called the police. Mike tagged along behind him, and recognized them as a couple of burnt-out gutter-heads he had arrested occasionally in the past.

"Dese guys are boint out, man," he muttered to Nick as they walked. "I've nailed dem in da past for sellin' click-ums and PCP in da projects."

Nick nodded acknowledgement. He had dealt with people on PCP and click-ums, which were marijuana cigarettes laced with PCP and popular because of their cheap price on the streets. People on that shit had the strength of ten men for a brief period, then remembered virtually nothing. They made lousy witnesses in court.

"Y'all heard anything?" Nick asked.

"Naw, bro. We seen her and an old dude climb under there and he done come out a little later. We never seen her come out!"

"Y'all ever seen the dude before?" Nick asked.

"Yeah, bro. He goes by 'Little Melvin.' He hangs over at Boogie's," the older of the two replied.

"Boogie's is dat jernt over on St. Claude by Desire. Ya know, da one dat boint out on da second floor. Dey're still usin' da bottom of it fer a bawr," Mike whispered, seeing the puzzled look on Nick's face. Nick grunted and returned to the Crown Vic.

A few hours later, Nick was sitting in the waiting room of the Coroner's Office wishing Alex—Dr. Alex Betancourt, that is— would hurry up. Nick could have watched the autopsy, but he had a weak stomach and had grown to hate the procedure. He still felt uneasy among the many bodies laid out naked in a row on cold steel tables, each awaiting its moment to reveal its secrets to the deft hands and unblinking eyes of the pathologist. One of the things Nick hated to see most was the lifeless form of a really attractive woman, beautiful in life, cold and unglamorous in death, laid out next to all the other corpses, many of them street people, she no longer a thing of admiration. The thought again stirred something dark in the pit of his stomach and made him fidget nervously in the plastic chair.

"Asphyxiation, my boy. Asphyxiation." Alex's deep voice brought Nick back to the present.

"Asphyxiation?" Nick's surprise was evident in his expression.

"Yep. She had advanced emphysema, to the point where she would have normally had a difficult time getting enough oxygen to sustain life. It wouldn't take much additional oxygen deprivation to terminate her life." Nick looked at the deep crevices in Alex's face, and the ice-blue eyes, almost hidden from view by the sagging deep furrows around his eyes caused by too many years of squinting at too many horrors staring up at him from the gleaming tables.

"So was she strangled?"

"Nope. No signs of violence at all. This is similar to having a pillow put over your face, but I understand she was found under a house. There is semen present, and we'll check that. If he was a secretor, I can get you a blood type from the semen." Alex went on, "First time I've seen such a dirty box!"

Nick stared, uncomprehending. "*Shit*, Alex. You, of all people, can't be surprised at people being unwashed?"

"No, Nick. You don't understand. Her box wasn't just *dirty*—it was *full* of dirt. It had *lumps* of dirt in it." Alex's eyelids had opened somewhat to emphasize his point.

"No *shit*?" Nick shook the pathologist's hand. "Thanks, Alex. That's a new one on me. I owe you a cold one."

Nick left the Coroner's Office through the door that opened into the Criminal Court Building and strolled down the hallway past the various sections of court, thinking about Alex's words. As he went down the front steps to Tulane Avenue, he radioed Mike to meet him at Boogie's with the two witnesses from earlier in the day. He sped off in the Crown Vic, noting with satisfaction that he should be able to pick up "Little Melvin," wrap up his paperwork, and be at The Catacombs by five.

Mike was already waiting in front of Boogie's when Nick arrived. The two witnesses looked uncomfortable in the rear seat of his marked unit. When Nick entered Boogie's he noted that the dark forms inside stiffened, then watched him intently. His eyes adjusted gradually, and he noted an old black man standing guard over an ice chest at the end of the bar. The bar stank of stale charcoal and electrical wiring from the burned-out second floor, and Nick guessed that the only cold beer was in the chest, as the place obviously had no electricity following the fire.

Nick sensed no danger from the dark forms inside; most appeared to be elderly. As he approached the guardian of the ice chest, a small voice drifted out of the dark to his right.

"I'm rite 'chere, officer." Little Melvin was waiving his hand and limping towards Nick.

"Man, she jus' stopped breathin'. Wudn't nuttin I could do. She jus' stopped breathin'."

Nick motioned the old man to stop talking as he escorted him outside.

"Wudn't nuttin' I could do." The old man was shaking his head from side to side slowly, as they were both temporarily blinded by the sun outside of the bar.

Nick cuffed him and looked towards Mike's unit. Both the witnesses pointed at Little Melvin and Mike nodded at Nick, indicating that the witnesses had made a positive I.D.

The old man muttered to himself as Nick headed for the homicide bureau.

A few minutes later, seated at Nick's desk in the bureau, the old man looked at Nick. "*Goddam.* It weren't wert' the five bucks I give her. Goddam ol' broad musta had so many kids she was stretched big as a bowlin' ball! Man, I cudn't feel nuttin. A man my age need *help.* I had to grab some a dat dirt 'n put it in her box ta get sum *traction.* Shit, man. *Dat* didn't even help."

"As if dat ain't bad enuf, I goes to crawl off her, and I gets stuck between her head and da flo' a da house! Man, da mo' she struggled, da mo' we got stuck. *Goddam.* Den she quits movin' and kinda sags, like. Dat's when I got loose and crawled out. Man, I looked back and she wudn't movin. I knowed she was daid, and I headed for Boogie's. *Goddam.* It ain't *fair.* I knowed you'd be lookin' fer me. I figgered I wudn't be drinkin' no mo' cold ones fer awhile. *Goddam it.* It jus' ain't *fair.*"

Nick hadn't had a chance to read Little Melvin his Miranda rights, and had given up trying to quiet the old man. He got up and walked out of the bureau to think for a minute. He sat in one of the interview rooms and stared at the peeling paint, momentarily absorbed, spotting shapes in the cracked paint just as one would do while staring at clouds. He had no doubt the old man was telling the truth. After a few minutes, he returned to his desk, typed up his report and told the old man to go home. He dropped the report off on the Captain's desk with a notation "accidental," and headed for The Catacombs. It was 5:30.

Nick was startled out of his reverie when a hand clamped down on his shoulder.

"Say, peckerhead. You keep sleeping on the end of the bar like this, they're gonna start charging you rent."

Nick noted with satisfaction that another Crown had been put in front of him, and that there was an upside-down cup behind that, indicating that someone had bought him an additional drink. He turned slightly sideways while leaning both of his elbows on the bar and looked up into the face of Steve Chaisson, one of his favorite drinking companions, an Assistant District Attorney for the Parish of Orleans. Steve had been in charge of homicide screening and prosecution for the D.A.'s Office for a number of years, and the two had worked many cases together, growing inseparable as the years had progressed. The amount of booze they had consumed together, if totaled, would give a Tyrannosaurus Rex cirrhosis of the liver. It was not unusual for them to chase the same female at the same time; sometimes knowingly, sometimes not, sometimes together, sometimes not.

Steve, a night graduate of Loyola Law School, had been a bank officer while attending law school. He was fond of telling anyone who would listen that he had been a banker, but had decided to go straight and become a lawyer. Tall and thin with silver-gray hair combed straight back and silver-rimmed glasses, he looked more like a high-priced lawyer from one of the city's big law firms than a prosecutor. His blue eyes were capable of a penetrating cold stare in any courtroom, or a mischievous twinkle when engaged in the challenge of separating some hapless female from her notions of abstinence and virtue.

"*Congrats* on your big collar today." Steve slapped Nick on the arm. "You oughta be on Channel 6 tomorrow with *that* one. By the way, I already refused it; I agree it was accidental. Little Melvin is scared enough—he ain't gonna climb up on top of *anything* that moves for a while."

"*Cute*, cocksucker," Nick snarled and stood to face Steve. "*Real* fuckin' cute. I'll remember you said that the next time you hang a jury on a nutlock homicide trial."

Steve groaned, as much from embarrassment as from the prospect of having to retry a simple homicide case he had tried the day before, where the jury announced they were unable to reach a verdict. "Gawd, trying a case for the second time is worse than kissing your sister."

Steve bounced back. "You gonna mildew in here all night or are we goin' rolling?"

Nick responded by slugging down the remainder of his Crown in one huge gulp: the ultimate insult to a whiskey meant to be savored. Steve popped a ten on the bar and told Becky to keep it. He looked at the barmaid as she approached.

"Fuck, I hope she doesn't get used up and spit out too fast around here," he said to no one in particular. "Man, she'd make ..." Steve didn't get to finish his sentence.

"*Yeah, yeah.* I know," Nick interrupted. "She'd make a *fruit* go for broads."

They laughed and slapped each other on the shoulder as they sped off on the night's installment of their continuing odyssey through the bars and broads of the "*City That Care Forgot*."

"*Shit.*" Seated at his desk in the bureau. Nick winced and opened his other eye as he spilled hot black coffee on his thigh. For a moment the murderous beat in his temples was forgotten. It was 8:30 a.m. Friday, and he had managed to sneak home and change clothes while Sharon was taking the kids to school. He had left her the usual terse note:

*Tied up with a case right now. Call you later.*

"*Saladino.*" The booming voice of Captain Morrison made his unsteady hand spill coffee again, close enough to his balls to swear that he would buy one of those stupid plastic cups with a lid and straw that people wore around their neck at Mardi Gras for protection during future hangovers. He fleetingly wondered why some nerdy government agency hadn't yet outlawed coffee in the workplace as too dangerous.

"Beautiful. You look fuckin' beautiful. Let me guess. Your old lady threw your ass out last night. About *time*. Let's go. We got a problem out in the east."

Nick groaned and belched one of those exquisitely vile alcohol belches, made even more vile by the Lucky Dogs slathered with chili that he had wolfed down at some point in last night's quest for the perfect Crown on the rocks.

"Jeezuz *Gawd*. I can't *see*. Nobody light a match." Morrison gagged as he got a whiff of the belch, and reeled back from Saladino, spinning and heading out of the bureau. "Come on, road kill. Let's go."

Nick groaned and stood up, swaying like the Sears Tower in an earthquake, and headed toward the door. As he plopped down into the passenger seat of Morrison's car, Morrison let out a slow whistle.

"Ka-*rist*, fuckhead. You musta *marinated* your butt in Crown Royal. That shit's oozing outta your pores." Morrison rolled the windows down as he swung onto I-10 and headed out to the area known as New Orleans East, the location of most of the swamp that still remained in the Parish of Orleans and the City of New Orleans. It was one of those weary gray days in February, when the fog was almost as thick as the coffee, and the skyscrapers were hidden by the mist, exposed only at ground level in order to lure the office workers inside.

"Fuck are we going?" Nick managed to ooze out, his words barely audible.

"Well, well. No shit. You *can* still talk." Morrison brightened up. "Got a call from Simoneaux. Wants us to look at something he found."

Nick knew Simoneaux, who came to New Orleans from down the bayou... Bayou Lafourche, that is. Alcide (Al) Simoneaux was a true coon-ass... Nick stopped himself, remembering that the Louisiana Legislature had spent almost an entire legislative session and a small fortune in tax dollars passing a resolution that the word "coon-ass" should not be used in referring to Cajuns. Alcide was a true *Cajun*, Nick corrected himself. Nick always enjoyed being around Al, who spoke natural Cajun—a soft and clipped though melodious language, totally unrelated to those apparently obligatory idiot accents in every movie about The Big Easy. Nick shifted awkwardly in his seat at the embarrassment of having the public think that people in New Orleans spoke with such a distorted accent.

Al was the perfect wildlife officer for N.O.P.D., considering that his duties included rescuing citizens from itinerant hungry alligators, rescuing hungry alligators from pissed-off citizens, and investigating bodies dumped in the swampy areas of the east, which likely had more bodies than St. Louis Cemetery No. 1, at any given time. Al's family made a living as shrimpers, operating their boat out of Port Fourchon, about a hundred miles from New Orleans. His father also did well selling crawfish to the restaurants of New Orleans. Like most Cajuns, Alcide was an excellent cook, and Nick looked forward to the times when his phone rang with an invitation to meet Alcide at his camp for a night of playing bourré and wolfing down rabbit or squirrel sauce piquante, accompanied by the booze of the day.

Morrison pulled up to the entrance to N.O.P.D.'s wildlife headquarters near Bayou Bienvenue in eastern New Orleans, and parked next to Simoneaux's battered Ford Bronco, which was painted in faded jungle camouflage with the traditional star-and-crescent badge of N.O.P.D. in white on its door. Nick opened his eyes to see Al standing near his door, grinning and shaking his head.

"*Comment* ça *va,* Nick?" Al bent over and stared at Nick, looking for signs of life.

"*Ça va bien, et vous?*" Nick responded, managing a weak smile.

"*Bien.*" Alcide opened Nick's door and pulled him up into a bear hug, almost simultaneously pushing him away as he got a whiff of Nick's left-over booze and Lucky Dogs.

"*Goddamn.* Nick, *mon ami,* you must have worked a detail at a *still* last night." Alcide laughed and opened the gate to the compound, revealing a long and narrow raised walkway consisting of four two-by-twelve boards laid side by side about three feet above the swampy ground, and snaking back through the cypress trees to Alcide's "office".

Nick's eyes widened. By this time the coffee was starting to get some traction in his system, and a little adrenalin was being called out as he realized he would have to navigate the walkway to reach Al's office, which was raised on stilts in the swamp about five hundred feet from the entrance. Nick brought up the rear as Al lead the way down the boardwalk with Morrison right behind him, cursing as an occasional damp drape of Spanish moss caught him in the face.

As they neared the office, Nick froze as a slithery shape dropped silently out of a tree not five feet ahead of him and stretched itself out across the boards, as if demanding a password before allowing Nick to pass. Nick fumbled for the chrome Smith & Wesson Model 19 .357 Magnum that he carried in a shoulder holster, but before he could unholster the gun, he was startled by the report of Al's shot, which practically severed the head of the large, extremely venomous cottonmouth moccasin. Al laughed, bent over and retrieved the carcass.

"I've got some pets that will enjoy this little snack." Al turned back to the office. "Come on, *mon*. Come see what I found."

Nick warily followed Al the remaining distance to his office, a small cabin with a wide porch completely around it, all on stilts. An airboat was off to one side awaiting its next assignment. As they walked around the back of the cabin, Nick detected a smell of rotting flesh which didn't set easily on his already queasy stomach.

At the back of the cabin, Al pointed proudly to a dead gator lying on its back with its belly slit open.

"Nice, Al." Nick wasn't impressed. "That skin should make some pimp a nice pair of shoes. But homicide doesn't handle alligator deaths." Nick turned away, putting his handkerchief to his nose.

"No, *mon*. It ain't de gator. It's what de gator had for dinner." Al bent over and spread the belly open. "Look at *dat*."

Nick sneaked up on the odor and peered at the inside of the gator's exposed belly. *"Holy shit."* Nick was able to make out what appeared to be a human arm neatly tucked inside the gator.

# IV

Nick sat on a bench on the back deck of the compound near Alcide's pirogue letting the damp, cold air revive him from his alcohol grogginess. He surveyed the foggy swamp scene that surrounded him, noting that it was a perfectly dreary day for such grisly findings. Watching the coroner's people remove the arm from the gator's belly, he marveled at their apparent indifference to odor.

"*Shit.*" Nick's stomach was wriggling. He never could have been a doctor, and hated the fact that he had a weak stomach at the sight of blood.

"I got dis call 'bout a gator in a backyard, near one a dem canals, you know?"

Nick smiled. Alcide was telling the story of the gator for about the fifth time. It got a little better each time.

"Me, I went over dere, and dis gator is sunnin' himself on de canal bank. What you t'ink he does? He look up at me and smile. He t'ink I'm dessert.

"I start to get near him wit' de noose, and he come after me so fast, he breaks de noose, him! Me, I make like a crawfish in double gear reverse to de nearest tree. W'at you t'ink? The bastard, he look up at me wit' love in his eyes. Me, I ain't got all day, so I shoot de bastard."

"Female, left hand." Nick's attention was drawn back to the arm by the shrill voice of the assistant coroner who was examining the limb, which appeared to be someone's forearm and hand. Nick dutifully jotted the information in his notebook, only superficially interested.

*Some poor broad musta fallen out of a boat*, Nick thought, wishing he had a cup of hot black coffee. Captain Morrison had returned to the office, and Nick muttered a silent curse for being left in this bleak, cold setting.

After another hour of photographs, the coroner took the limb away for further examination, and Alcide drove Nick back to town in the Bronco.

"Man, put the fuckin' *heat* on!" Nick huddled in the topless Bronco against the wind.

"W'at you talkin' about, heat? Dere *ain't* no heat." Alcide laughed. "Fuckin' pussy."

Nick cursed Alcide, then Captain Morrison. But it all came out garbled, due to the bumpy ride of the Bronco.

At the bureau, Nick went straight to the coffee machine and warmed his hands and insides with a cup of the thick black liquid, used by everyone in New Orleans to sustain life. He gave no more thought to the morning's events, which he assumed to be an accidental death.

"1251." The soft voice on the radio didn't catch his attention at first. Nick was on his way to Matanza's for a traditional muffaletta sandwich filled with cold cuts and heavy on the olive salad. His stomach was growling.

"1251." The voice was more urgent, but Nick was tempted to ignore it. He hadn't had anything to eat in two days.

"*Fuck*. 1251," Nick reluctantly acknowledged.

"Dr. Betancourt in the coroner's office is trying to reach you. He's called twice." The soft voice on the radio caught his interest. One day he'd have to pass by the communications department and scope this chick out.

"10-4," Nick grunted, making a note to call Alex after he had eaten.

Nick ordered his muffaletta and scarfed it down, then sat back and watched the locals come and go, winking at Alonzo Matanza whenever a good-looking girl came in.

Back in the Crown Vic, Nick cruised slowly through the Quarter, always appreciative of the sights and sounds afforded by tourists and locals alike.

"The greatest free show on earth," Nick mused. "Especially during Mardi Gras season." It was just a matter of days before normally conservative chicks would be running around flashing their tits for virtually anyone who took the time to start the appropriate chant: "Show us your tits!" It always amazed Nick that you could walk up to any broad on the street and try to get her to flash her tits without getting in trouble. Any other day of the year, she'd call the cops and your ass would be arrested. Go figure.

As he neared Canal Street, he called Alex Betancourt using his cellular phone.

"Nick. You need to stop by here today." Alex sounded like a kid that had just discovered he could use his dick for something besides peeing; the enthusiasm was unusual for a man who was normally quiet-spoken. "We need to talk about this arm that Alcide found."

"OK, Alex. I'll be there." Nick hung up, then checked with the bureau for messages. Mercifully, there were none.

# V

Alex came right up from the morgue when Nick arrived. "Looks like you're going to have to do some real detective work for a change. This lady seems to be a homicide victim." Alex grinned, pleased with himself.

*Lucky fuckin' me*, Nick thought, balking as Alex started to lead him down the stairs to the pathology area.

"Come on, Nick. There's no smell right now. We just gave everybody a bath." Alex chuckled. Pathologists, without exception, seemed to take great satisfaction at their ability to make anyone else queasy at the thoughts, sights or odors associated with their profession.

As they entered the room, Nick noted with relief that the many stainless steel tables were empty and clean, save for one with a small object covered by a drape.

"Rope burn marks," Alex exclaimed, removing the drape and revealing what appeared to be the same human limb Nick had seen earlier in the day. "Look at her wrist. She was tightly bound at some recent point in time. My guess at this stage is some of that yellow nylon braid used by boaters. What puzzles me, though, is that her palm appears to have been subjected to some type of device, kind of like the old torture screws. Interesting."

Nick looked. The skin had been torn in places where he could see rope marks. The palm did have an unusual mark, though faint.

"I'd say she struggled against the ropes, tearing the skin."

Nick nodded. He had seen similar marks before, in cases where victims had been bound before death.

"Some sort of tattoo, here."

Nick looked at the area of the forearm where Alex was pointing. He hadn't noticed it before. About four inches long, it appeared to be some sort of star-shaped design, maybe a flower. Either it was black, or had turned black, with an eerie, dark-reddish tinge to it. It looked vaguely like something Nick had seen before.

"The crabs did some damage before the gator got her." Alex was pointing to areas of flesh that had been eaten away, small areas. "The good news is that the thumb and index fingerprints were relatively well-preserved." Alex handed Nick a standard fingerprint card, inscribed with just the name "Jane." "Fluids will be about a week."

"Thanks, Alex." Nick returned to the bureau to write his report on Alex's findings and the day's events, stopping by the crime lab to drop off the fingerprint card.

Back at his desk, he recognized the telephone number on the top message. It was Steve Chaisson from the D.A.'s Office. Nick checked his watch. It was 4:30 p.m. Friday. Steve would be wanting to find out where they were drinking tonight.

# VI

Nick pulled up in front of the Empress Lounge on Canal Boulevard. Steve's car was already parked around the side. It was 6:00 p.m. and just about dark. The joint was packed with Broncos and Blazers and young people's cars. The pressure-cooker crowd, consisting of housewives indulging in booze and affairs during the afternoon, usually hung out there until about 4:00 p.m., and then rushed home to cook dinner in pressure cookers for their unsuspecting husbands.

"Bout fuckin' *time* your ass got here. It's time to go find a fuckin' *bar*. Nuthin' usable here." Steve was already carrying a load.

Nick ordered a Crown on the rocks and looked around for talent. "Man, you are asshole-lutely right. Somebody musta left the doors open on Japonica Street," he said, referring to the location of the New Orleans SPCA.

Steve nodded. "You got a fuckin' radio. Call in and see if the SPCA was burglarized. Tell them we found the ones that got away."

They got fresh drinks in plastic cups and headed for the Quarter. Friday was a good night to pick up tourists looking to escape their mundane homes, lives, husbands and kids for that one night in New Orleans—for that one memory of being alive; something to sustain them through their daily, deadly routines.

Nick parked the Crown Victoria in a police enforcement zone on Bienville Street, and they strolled slowly to Royal Street, drinks in hand. Nick peered through the windows of the Devil's Den and nudged Steve. "Two at two o'clock."

Steve looked in. "Look like possibles to me."

They entered the bar and took up a position next to a pair of decent-looking chicks at the end of the L-shaped bar. When they arrived, Dolly, the barmaid, had their drinks already waiting for them.

"Where y'at, dawlin?" Dolly winked at Nick. "I wuz hoping to see ya soon. My kid got a little traffic beef, needs some help."

"No sweat, babe. Call me Monday. I'll see what I can do."

Dolly nodded and moved off to another customer.

Steve nudged Nick. "They're both very usable, my man. *Very* usable."

Nick smiled. Steve had long ago decided to dispense with the normal niceties of describing people of the female persuasion with terms such as "cute," "beautiful," "attractive," etc. He had developed his own rating scheme, which would greatly distress the members of the NOW organization and most of card-carrying womanhood. It consisted of only four categories, of which the middle two were "Usable" and "Very Usable." At the bottom of the list was "Not Fit For Human Consumption," while the highest category was "Looks Good on Lettuce," which, loosely translated, meant, "I'd like to eat her."

Their tastes in women were fairly similar, so Nick didn't feel a need to turn around and look, having confidence in Steve's assessment of the chicks. Nick and Steve continued to talk to each other, ignoring the women until one of them decided not to be ignored any longer.

"You guys must be locals. Are you from New Orleenz?"

Nick and Steve winced almost simultaneously at the nasal whine of the standard Easterner. They turned to face her and marveled at such a shrill sound coming from a chick who was actually quite attractive: dark-haired, with a chest that massaged the bar whenever she reached for her drink.

"Yeah, dawlin. We're from N'awlins." Steve made a point to accentuate the pronunciation. "What part of New York are y'all from?"

The dark-haired one was a little offended at first, but relented.

"Manhattan. My husband and I have an apartment in Manhattan. I'm Marcie. I'm in computer sales."

"And I'm Cass. We work different regions for the same company. I'm from Boston." This other chick was fine as wine, a redhead with a luscious milky complexion and deep blue eyes. She flashed a smile that lit up the dim barroom for an instant. She, too, had a rock on the fatal finger.

"What do you guys do in this town?" Marcie looked at Nick.

"Mostly, we drink," Nick responded, looking around for Dolly.

Both women laughed easily. Nick looked at Steve. "*Bingo*. A couple of *players*." The thought passed between the two men through eye contact, without verbalization.

"Cute," Cass laughed. "But what do you do to earn your keep?"

Steve moved a little closer. "He works for the city. I work for the state. We're paid to keep an eye on each other, and to protect tourists."

Nick chimed in. "Yeah, we run around the Quarter and inspect tourists. *Female* tourists. We may need to check your tourist visas and search you for hidden souvenirs."

Marcie started laughing. "Pay up, Cass. I told you when they walked in they were cops."

Dolly appeared, and Nick bought a round. They made small talk for a while, then left the Devil's Den after a few more rounds and, carrying their drinks in cups, headed for the Lagniappe Hotel on Conti Street where the two women were staying.

The elevator, small and dimly lit, was a perfect enclosure for four agreeable people with a nice buzz on. It was a slow ride to the third floor, and none of the four moved away when their bodies brushed against one another.

The room was well-appointed, a small suite with bedrooms on either side of the living room, and a wet bar. Marcie called room service and ordered a bottle of Crown and a bottle of J&B, plus mixers. Nick walked over to the tube and switched it on, noting that the hotel offered a selection of adult movies, all soft-core. He picked one from the menu and sat on the carpet with his back against the sofa, drink on the coffee table. Marcie plopped down on the sofa next to Nick, her tight skirt riding halfway up her thighs.

"These goddam movies are a lot better with the sound turned off. The fake moaning and dumb conversations are distracting," she said.

Nick started to talk to Marcie, but was cut short by a knock on the door. Steve got up and opened it, and the bellman placed the booze and glasses on the coffee table in front of Marcie. He, too, paused as he bent over and caught the view down Marcie's legs as she shifted to sign the check.

When he left, Marcie noted, "I shouldn't have given him a tip. I should have charged him for the peek."

Cass agreed. She was sitting on one of the bar stools and her legs were crossed, revealing a long pair of symmetrical, milky thighs clad in the lightest of hose. Steve noticed that freckles were visible through the hose. He looked at Marcie and Nick across the room. They seemed to be doing well. She was relaxed on the sofa, and Nick was sitting on the floor next to her, rubbing her calves, slurping down his Crown.

Steve sat down next to Cass and turned his stool toward her.

"Y'all always travel together?"

Cass looked at him dreamily, the booze starting to take effect. "When we can. It's nice to get away with someone you know. Provides safety and companionship."

The more mellow and sultry Cass became, the louder and more boisterous Marcie became. She and Nick, still watching the movie, had started to grope each other, and Marcie was commenting on the action on the screen.

"*Christ*. A cow could move better than that." Marcie was getting up, imitating the movement on the screen. Steve watched Marcie's gyrations until she flopped onto the carpet next to Nick; both propped against the sofa, their knees in the air, watching the action on the screen, until they embraced and rolled over on the carpet.

"Ooh, are they going to do it in front of us?"

Steve's attention was drawn back to Cass, who was also watching the action across the room.

"You mean y'all haven't done this before?" Steve was surprised.

"Never in the same room. Never where we could see each other."

"Gonna be a long night," Steve said to no one in particular.

Afterward, Steve got up and headed for the bathroom, returning to find Nick sitting up making drinks.

It was daybreak on Saturday when Nick stumbled out to Conti Street and headed for his car. It was another foggy, fugly day in February. He found the Crown Vic on Royal Street and cursed as he noticed a piece of paper under the windshield wiper.

"Goddam meter maids." He got in the car and sat down, then realized it was an envelope, soggy from the overnight dew. There was a note inside from Sharon. *Never marry someone who teaches poetry*, Nick thought, as he noticed the form of the note:

> *Nick:*
> *The house is mine,*
> *The kids are, too.*
> *I just can't take*
> *Another day with you.*
> *I'll file the papers,*
> *You'll get served,*
> *We'll be divorced,*
> *You're a JERK!*
> *—Sharon*

Nick sat for a few minutes, and let it sink in. He got out of the car, cursing to himself and slamming the door, and then headed for the Devil's Den. Dolly was still working.

"Hey, Nick. Long time no see. I figured you wuz good for the weekend when you and Steve left with those babes."

"Yeh." Nick managed a weak grin. "We wuz *definitely* had by a good time. Gimme a tequilaclear."

Dolly looked up. "Oh, *shit*. One of *those* days, huh?" She hated when Nick ordered his favorite combination of Cuervo Gold and Everclear, one shot of each mixed together. She didn't even like the smell of it; it almost made her puke.

Nick showed Dolly the note from Sharon.

"*Yep*. Tequilaclear it *is*." Dolly stacked two on the bar.

Nick shot one down and took the other with him. When Dolly looked up again, he was gone. He had written her a note on a napkin.

*Be careful. It's getting drunk outside.*

# VII

Monday morning, Nick was at the office early; rumpled, but at the office. He was reviewing the work schedules for Mardi Gras Day, which was the next day. *Everyone* worked in uniform on Mardi Gras Day. Everyone but those assigned to work undercover. Nick, like most cops, always dreaded Mardi Gras Day. There were plenty of entertaining sights, hundreds of tits flashed, but there were always a few assholes to deal with, made more difficult by the crush of the crowds.

When the phone rang, he answered it reluctantly, as his mind was still dealing with Sharon's note.

"*Saladino.* It's Hall from the crime lab."

Nick recognized the voice of Alan Hall, the crime lab's fingerprint expert. "Yeah, man. What it is?"

"Pay attention, motherfucker. Gonna be a pop quiz. We got a make on the prints. Didn't even have to go to the FBI. Saladino, are you there?"

"Yeah. Fuck, yeah. I'm listening. The alligator case. What about it?"

"We got a make on the prints, man." Alan was undaunted. "It's a chick named Collette Prejean. Twenty-one years old. She's a hooker from Abbeville. Convicted three months ago on a second offense prostitution in front of Judge Waldrip. He gave her one year suspended, one year active probation."

"No shit?" Nick perked up a little. "Thanks, Alan. I'll stop by and pick up the fingerprint card. You got her rap sheet?"

"Yeah. It'll be on my desk. And I did check her FBI records anyway. These prostitution charges are all she's got." Alan clicked off and Nick sat back, thinking about Collette Prejean. He had no idea that Collette would soon lead him on the most insidious, shocking case of his career.

Nick checked his notes on the "alligator incident," and realized he had forgotten about the photos of the arm. On his way to Alan's desk, he stopped and picked up the glossy 8 x 10s, then picked up the rap sheet and booking photos of Collette at Alan's desk. Back at his office, Nick reviewed the photos. Although mug shots are rarely complimentary, Collette obviously had been a good-looking chick. Blonde, blue-eyed, perky face. Nick shook his head and turned to the photos of her arm, all that was left of her. He noted that the rope burns were visible, and pulled out one that showed the tattoo, making a mental note to check the local tattoo parlors for possible leads.

"Well, fuck. Might as well start with the easy shit first." Nick dialed Probation and Parole. "Her probation officer oughta be able to provide something."

"Just my fuckin' luck," Nick muttered when advised by the secretary that Collette Prejean's probation officer was Jeremy Claiborne, a squirrelly, whiney little bastard who held his job primarily... no, scratch that... *only* because his daddy was a federal judge, and his sister was a judge in Criminal District Court in Orleans Parish. Thomas "Mr. Contempt" Claiborne had been a federal judge for a quarter century and was now on retired status, much to the relief of most of the attorneys in town. Charysse Claiborne, the judge's daughter and sister to Jeremy, was in her mid-to-late-forties, with jet-black hair and blue eyes, never married, with a disposition like her father's.

*Hard bitch. No fuckin' wonder she never married,* Nick thought. *Probably never been laid. It's kinda like that* Catch-22 *crap. She's got a bitchy attitude because she never gets any, and she never gets any because she's got a bitchy attitude.*

Nick was somewhat aware of the family history. Thomas Claiborne laid claim to being a descendant of William C. C. Claiborne, who was the first governor of Louisiana and a prominent statesman. William Claiborne was supposedly married three times; twice to Creole ladies, raising some question as to Thomas Claiborne's racial heritage, if his claims of descendancy were true.

Nick hung up and headed for the probation office, halfway across the city. He didn't have much time before everything shut down for Mardi Gras the next day, and traffic was already screwed up. As he headed the Crown Vic for the intersection of Tulane and Broad Streets, some little foreign car blew through the red light, causing Nick to brake and swerve, and sending all the papers on his front seat crashing to the floor.

"Hope you *fuck* better than you *drive, asshole,*" he yelled. "Goddam *Isuzu*. Probably means *dogshit* in Japanese."

He pulled up in front of the probation office a few minutes later, and entered the shabby building. He was greeted by a metallic voice and a two-way mirror. A camera poked out at him from the ceiling. There was just one door, steel with a small window protected by a metal grille. He flashed his I.D. and pushed on the door when he heard it click.

"Claiborne," he responded to the receptionist's raised eyebrows. She nodded and directed him to a small office down a corridor that smelled vaguely like body odor; it was narrow and poorly lit. The door to Claiborne's office was open, and a small, pale figure sat behind the desk, feet propped on a desk drawer, a telephone in his ear. Nick picked a chair and sat down, his nostrils flaring at the smell of whatever cheap cologne the little creep had bought at K-Mart. Nick shook his head at the sight of the handcuffs and the Smith & Wesson Model 10 .38-caliber revolver on the creep's belt, and wondered if it had ever been fired, even in practice. There were no windows, and Claiborne's pattern-bald head was bright under the fluorescent light.

As Claiborne swung around, Saladino almost laughed at the sight of the tight little mustache clinging to Claiborne's upper lip, which itself was almost non-existent.

*Definitely* not *a womb-broom,* Nick thought to himself. He noted the name of the file on the top of Claiborne's desk: Collette Prejean. He reached for it, and Claiborne snatched it away, obviously agitated.

"They told me you called about this file, Saladino. What do you want?"

Nick's skin crawled at Claiborne's effeminate but hostile voice. Claiborne's dark ferret-like eyes were his most arresting feature. They were almost venomous, and seemed to lack warmth or feelings of any type.

"I'd like to see your file," Nick responded.

"What's the little bitch done now? These miserable prostitutes are all the same. I don't know why the goddam judges give them a break." Claiborne sniffed.

"When was the last time you saw her?"

Claiborne looked through his file. "She was convicted of second offense prostitution on November 15. I interviewed her the same day and I've talked to her on the phone on December 15 and January 15. She's supposed to report in person on February 15, next week."

Nick nodded. "Where was her *first* conviction?"

"Here. Where else?" Claiborne sniffed again.

Nick made notes on his memo pad. "How about an address?"

"Desire Street. Isn't that appropriate? Corner of Desire and St. Claude Avenue. That 'boarding house' that *everyone* knows about." Claiborne sounded indignant when he emphasized the word "everyone."

"Physical description?" Nick was tired of the creep's attitude.

"She was twenty-one, five feet six-inches, blue eyes and blonde hair, 125 pounds. But if you ask me, she could pass for forty."

Nick had a strong picture of this poor girl trying to deal with her asshole of a probation officer. *Christ,* he thought to himself. *She's just a fuckin'* hooker. He wished somebody would legalize prostitution. It would be a hell of a lot safer. Save all these poor bastards from getting rolled or killed looking for a piece of ass. Probably save a lot of hookers from the mental and physical abuse they suffered at the hands of their pimps. He hated the times he had had to arrest hookers when he was in vice. Most of them were running away from something—usually childhood sexual abuse.

Nick was about finished with this interview. "Any distinguishing features; scars, tattoos, shit like that?"

Claiborne looked up at him. "I don't *examine* these goddam sluts. I just interview them."

Nick got up and headed for Claiborne, a snarl on his face.

"I've had about enough of your fucking *attitude*, you little cocksucker," he said in a measured tone. As he sat on the corner of Claiborne's desk, he grabbed the file away. Flicking through the report, he was surprised to note that it stated that Collette had *no* identifying marks, and he flung it back on the desk. He didn't look back at Claiborne as he left, glad to be out on the street again.

Heading back to the office, he swung by the intersection of Desire and St. Claude Avenue, and went inside the building described by Claiborne. It was, at one time, home to a family of some means, but had been cut up into a number of small rooms for hire by the hour, day or week, as the sign at the entrance proclaimed. He went to the door marked "manager" and knocked.

"Ain't no vacancies," a hoarse voice yelled from within.

Nick wasn't surprised at the sight of the toothless hag who answered the door. The strong odor of booze and sickness made Nick step back.

"*Po*-lice." Nick emphasized the first syllable and produced his I.D, then showed her the photo of Collette.

"So what?" The old lady turned to re-enter the room. Nick was reluctant to follow her due to the stench, but stepped slightly inside the door.

"Have you seen her?"

"Upstairs. Apartment 'D'. Lives with her pimp. Upstairs." The old lady was engrossed in some TV show that featured people screaming at each other about doing each other's boyfriends.

"What's the pimp's name?" Nick asked.

"What the hell do I care? I just collect the money." The old hag kept watching the set.

"Do they still live here?"

"He pays the rent, but he ain't always here. Sometimes he's gone fer days. He ain't been here since the weekend."

Nick was writing in his notepad. "You said apartment 'D'?"

"'*D*'. Like fuckin' *dogshit*. And close the fuckin' door on yer way out."

Nick had to chuckle at the hag's use of the word. He left a card on the table near the door and returned to his office, still pondering the significance of Claiborne's information. If it was correct, then the tattoo on the arm must be new. At least since the original probation interview of November fifteenth. *If* the little bastard's information was correct.

Nick checked the phone book for tattoo parlors and found twenty-two of them. "*Great.* Just fuckin' *great.*" He knew they would be doing a booming business during Mardi Gras, with all the kids in town boxed out of their minds.

He put the file away and headed for The Catacombs. It was 4:00 p.m., and he'd have to be on the streets at 7:00 a.m. Fortunately, he had been assigned to work undercover in the Quarter for Mardi Gras, which was easier than uniformed duty, but he still would be on the streets until after midnight when the cops swept the hordes from Bourbon Street, officially ending Mardi Gras. Of course, all that did was move the crowds into the bars where they continued to drink until sunrise and beyond. People had been known to emerge from the Quarter three and four days later, still in costume.

Mardi Gras morning, Nick hit the streets at 7:30. Still foggy, still fugly with a forecast of rain, but the temperature was in the 50s and expected to rise into the 60s. By that time, parades were forming all over the city and in the suburbs, but the first parade, Pete Fountain's Half-Fast Walking Club, wouldn't hit the Quarter until around noon. None of the other parades entered the Quarter, so Nick strolled leisurely around, wearing jeans and a loose-fitting jacket to hide his radio and revolver, which he always wore in a shoulder holster. He liked the snugness of the straps around his shoulders and in his pits.

There were stragglers from the previous night still on the streets and in the bars, and a number of vendors made emergency deliveries to restock the bars and restaurants for the day's onslaught. The gutters along the sidewalks stank from food, booze, vomit, and trash abandoned by the last night's crowds, all of which was marinating in the heavy dew that had fallen. The concrete surfaces were slippery from the sweat produced by heavy humidity. An occasional tired jukebox could be heard through the doors of a bar.

The police had set up holding tanks every few blocks which consisted of police barricades on a side street positioned in a semi-circle against a building wall, where drunks could sleep it off and minor offenders could be held until they could be transported for processing. Nick shook his head at the thought. In the city where virtually anything goes during Mardi Gras, you really have to *try* to get arrested, but there's always some stupid bastards who succeed. Their reward is to be removed from the party.

By about 11:30 a.m., Bourbon Street was packed butt to butt with people in various stages and forms of intoxication, from families wearing identical costumes to the body-piercing freaks with rings in their nipples, dicks, and Christ knows where else. Nick always had to overcome the strong temptation to walk between the ones who had rings in their dicks and were being pulled along by their handlers, who had attached leashes to the ring, leaving a distance of three or four feet between them. So far, Nick had successfully overcome the temptation.

Every part of the human anatomy was available for viewing, and even for fondling, for the price of a pair of cheap plastic beads. Even the professional, conservative chicks would lift their shirt for a pair of beads offered by the grossest zithead on the street, on Mardi Gras Day. Chicks who would slap or call the cops if you asked to see their tits any other day of the year thought nothing of showing their floppies to hundreds of people on Fat Tuesday.

A few feet away, a couple of fine little girls occasionally raised their shirts when the crowd started to chant *"Show us your tits."* A little further down the street, Nick came upon a still-foxy older woman with a couple of pre-teenagers in tow. She was flashing her tits at the balcony overhead, trying to get some dork up there to throw her a strand of beads. Her kids were laughing.

"*Fuck.* To think they laughed at the Indians for trading Manhattan, or wherever it was, for some goddam beads." Nick shook his head. He watched the broad's class-A tits being fondled by various passing strangers every time she flashed them. "*Nice.* She could make a motherfucker outta me."

Around on Bienville Street, some guy was standing in the street showing his dick to some broad who was up on a balcony with her skirt raised; she had nothing on underneath. It reminded Nick of childhood days: "I'll show you mine if you show me yours."

After noon, Nick headed for the "Fruit Stand" on the corner of Bourbon and St. Ann Streets to take in the show and watch for pickpockets. The Fruit Stand had become tradition on Mardi Gras Day. The Chalice Club, one of the gay bars, erected a wooden platform and walkway above the crowd, and sponsored a contest for the most elaborately dressed. The contest had grown to such an extent that drag queens from around the world worked all year and spent countless sums of money on elaborate dresses and costumes to compete at the Fruit Stand each year, which always drew a huge crowd. As the crowd cheered and jeered, the contestants flounced their way along the walkway, hoping to win the grand prize, reputedly a vacation trip for two.

The contest was well underway when Nick forced his way through the crowd and positioned himself with his back to a wall, on the corner. He watched the contest, unable to understand the announcer over the noise of the crowd.

After an hour or so, one contestant caught his attention, although Nick wasn't consciously aware of it at the time. Something about him-her-it seemed oddly familiar. The costume was pink, almost a pearlescent pink, with dark flower-like designs on it. The headpiece was shaped like the designs on the costume. Nick had the impression that the person behind the mask was staring at him, almost menacingly, but couldn't tell for sure due to the mask covering the contestant's face. Nick made a mental note to check with the bar later to try to determine the identity of the masker.

He wandered off towards Royal Street but was stopped by a gutter punk who offered to show him her tits for a dollar. She was dirty, with rings in her tongue and navel. Nick brushed her off and continued on his way, muttering to himself. "*Fuckin' skank.* Bitch would probably put something on you *Clorox* wouldn't take off. Probably fucking *douches* with Janitor-In-A-Drum."

A little after midnight, Nick knocked off and headed for the Devil's Den. The next morning, Ash Wednesday, he would have ashes on his forehead; it was an annual ritual, the meaning of which he had long ago forgotten.

Steve Chaisson had spent Mardi Gras at his apartment in Metairie, the suburb located in Jefferson Parish between the airport and downtown. It was a perfect apartment for a bachelor: large, with a loft overlooking the living/dining room and hidden cameras in the bedroom. There was a well-stocked bar and an amateur wine collection. The artwork in the bedroom consisted of a couple of exotic nudes in oil, tastefully done. The loft contained a small glider with a number of large and small pillows strewn on the floor, and a small table holding a few board games, decks of cards, and a container of plastic poker chips.

He was expecting company, female company, and was excited. He knew she would be in good form that day. A bottle of merlot was waiting near a tray of cheese and crackers, and he had made a remoulade sauce which sat on the table, surrounded by boiled, peeled shrimp. Steve wore only a robe, tied at the waist.

Julie Landry was luscious, or, in Steve's vocabulary, *edible*. Perfect high cheek bones, porcelain skin, almond-shaped dark eyes, a statuesque five-foot-eleven, and a proud 36D on a 26-inch waist. The kind of well-stacked tall chick you'd have to use grappling hooks to climb up and hold on to. An extremely intelligent professional, Julie was exquisitely creative in her quest for sexual gratification. Chicks like Julie were the reason men were grateful to Mr. Polaroid for providing them the opportunity to become home pornographers.

Steve and Julie had been an item for a couple of years, with regular weekly sessions. Steve believed there was no romantic love between them, but they shared an honesty and lust that was without equal. Julie was separated from a doctor she had married ten years earlier and had no kids. As a result, the two were able to share unusually open moments during the interludes between their marathon bouts of sex, and there were none of the usual hang-ups, such as jealousy or possessiveness.

Steve heard a car door outside and footsteps on the stairs. His pulse started to pound as he opened the door. Even after two years, he was still breathless at the sight of her, and he pulled her inside. She was wearing a black leather mini-skirt with a silk blouse deeply veed at the neck to reveal her deep cleavage. He shoved his tongue down her throat as soon as the door closed.

"Well, I'm glad to see *you*, too," Julie managed after her heavy breathing subsided somewhat.

"Goddam car wouldn't start. Cheap bastard won't buy me a new one."

Steve shrugged. "It's not like you're really still married to him. How'd you get here?"

"Goddam cab. Goddam driver kept staring at me." Julie snickered. "Of course, I did kinda flash him once."

Steve had a strong picture of some poor cabbie married to some fat, ugly grunge of a woman, getting a shot of Julie's bald kitty under her skirt.

"Fucker's probably parked somewhere right now choking his chicken over it."

Steve took a sip of merlot and leaned over Julie, putting his lips to hers and letting her suck the wine slowly through them.

"Mmmm. Great stuff." She liked the intimate method of sharing wine. It was only minutes before they were consumed with each other, then spent, stretched out on the bed.

"*Fantastic,*" Steve panted. "*Fan-fucking-tastic.*" They lay on their backs staring at the ceiling. It was an hour before either of them talked.

"Christ, I hate to go to work tomorrow." Julie stretched luxuriantly.

"I don't mind. It'll actually be pretty interesting tomorrow, what with the wackos processed through the system on Mardi Gras Day. Magic Court is always entertaining the day after Mardi Gras," Steve mused, referring to the city's Magistrate Courts, which were the first courts of appearance for persons arrested the day before.

"I was in Magic Court last week for a probable cause hearing on a homicide, watching the case before mine. A film company executive from out of state, arrested while he was getting a blow job in Pirate's Alley next to the St. Louis Cathedral. He was standing in court next to the black female who was sucking his dick, and the Magistrate called the courtroom deputy to the bench, whispering to him and pointing at the black 'female.' The deputy nodded, walked over to the black 'female,' and pulled her wig off. The executive looked over at what was left, realized he was getting a blow job from a transvestite, and fainted right there in front of the whole courtroom. The judge felt sorry for him and dismissed the charges. It was pitiful, but really pretty funny."

"You really enjoy all that shit, don't you?" Julie looked at Steve, who was grinning. "What about all those victims you have to deal with? That doesn't bother you?"

"No. Not really." Steve was thoughtful. "They actually provide the motivation that keeps you going as a prosecutor. When you listen to the pain and anger inside of them, it kind of transfers to you, and you ride off on your white horse to get revenge for them in the only manner provided by society. It's really the only thing that can almost make them whole again."

Julie nodded. "Maybe. But don't you think *God* will punish the criminals and reward the victims in some way?"

Steve snorted. "In a lot of ways, I hope God *doesn't* exist. I think it's great for those who need to believe, kinda like Santa Claus, but, if He really exists, He's a seriously vindictive bastard. When you deal with the crap that people do to each other, especially to innocent people, to innocent babes, you don't have much choice but to believe that either we're already serving our term in hell, or that God is a serious prick."

Julie thought about that for a moment. "Yeah. I've had some thoughts about that myself." She turned over and dozed off. It wasn't long before Steve too, was asleep.

# VIII

The next morning, Ash Wednesday, Nick visited St. Joseph's Church on Tulane Avenue for his cross of ashes on his forehead, then headed for the office. As he passed a rundown building on Tulane, he noted new graffiti on the walls.

*Some miserable little slug crawled out from under its rock during the night and left a trail of graffiti slime*, Nick thought. He had always thought that graffiti was actually kind of pitiful. To him, it was like a homeless dog trying to mark off some territory by peeing on a fireplug. It seemed to him that one gang graffiti was indistinguishable from the next, none really stood out.

Back at his desk, he reviewed the photos of Collette Prejean's arm, trying to decide what the tattoo represented. It was an outline of something, not filled in. "*Some kinda flower, or maybe even some fucking gang symbol.*" To Nick it sort of resembled the *fleur de lis* emblem worn by the Saints football team, but it seemed unlikely that a young girl from a rural parish would be that enamored of a New Orleans football team.

It was hard to make out the actual lines of the tattoo, which seemed to have no definite outline and was rather fuzzy in appearance. He supposed it may have been due to the acid in the alligator's stomach, or maybe even the lousy handiwork of some no-talent tattoo artist. Nick played with the design a while longer, trying to reproduce it freehand on a piece of paper. In the color photo, the tattoo appeared to be black or maybe even a dark red sort of color, but he couldn't tell if that was the actual color or just a result of the tattoo's exposure to stomach acid. He kept pondering Jeremy Claiborne's information that Collette had *no* tattoos in November, less than three months ago. His instincts were aroused over the tattoo; he felt it might actually be the most significant lead he had about the mysterious Collette Prejean.

He ripped the page that listed tattoo parlors from the telephone book, and, armed with the photos of Collette and her arm, set out to interview the local tattoo artists to see if any recognized either her or the tattoo. He had decided on his first stop, chosen for its location: only a few blocks from Collette Prejean's address.

St. Claude Avenue was one of those streets teaming with life. As it meandered through New Orleans, following the course of the Mississippi River, it passed through the most colorful parts of the city's heritage. To the north, it formed the outer boundary of the French Quarter where it was called North Rampart Street. At Esplanade Avenue, St. Claude penetrated the Faubourg Marigny, named after the Duke d'Marigny who originally owned most of the Faubourg but lost it piece by piece due to his unfortunate lack of gambling talent.

From the Faubourg it passed through Bywater, established in the eighteen-hundreds on land comprised of French and Spanish grants. Heavily ethnic, Bywater was a heavy mix of Creole cottages and Victorian and shotgun-style houses. After Bywater, St. Claude crossed the Industrial Canal and ran down into St. Bernard Parish. Throughout its length, St. Claude was a super-saturation of ethnic mixture: retired Irish and Italians with a smattering of other European cultures mixed with blacks and Creoles, along with an assortment of straight and gay professionals restoring some of the century-old architectural gems still standing. St. Claude has always been one of the most heavily lived-in streets of the city.

Nick pulled up in front of Silky's Tattoos, an old shotgun with the front painted flat black, and a large plate glass window also painted black and covered by wrought iron bars. Some decorations were painted on the front, but they looked more like graffiti than tattoo designs. An old chopper was parked out front: a pan-head, the chrome and black paint exquisitely maintained.

He went inside, feeling like he had walked into a t-shirt shop, designs everywhere on the walls. One wall in particular was used to display Silky's prowess as a tattoo artist. Rows of Polaroids were lined up neatly, and a few instantly caught Nick's attention. He gazed at a few, amazed at the number of well-groomed yuppie-looking females who bared various parts of their anatomy for Silky to leave an indelible souvenir. Apparently, Silky was also skilled at body piercing, as another group of photos attested. Nick winced at the nipples and dicks pierced by "jewelry."

As he reviewed the photo gallery, he was startled by movement caught in the corner of his eye. A figure had been watching him from the rear of the shop. It was a chick, seated on a stool with bright blonde hair pulled behind her head and held with one of those plastic butterfly-type clamps that women seem to think are fashionable. She wore biker's leathers and no make-up; fuck, *she didn't need any.*

Nick whistled to himself, *"In your face, tomato paste.'" This* was a fuckin' *fox.* Webster would put a picture of this chick in his dictionary as a perfect illustration of the word "fox." This was the kind of chick you wanted to run away with, anywhere! *"Un-fucking-believable."*

"I'm looking for Silky," he finally managed, not taking his eyes off her.

She stared unblinking at him. "Why?"

"You a friend of his?" Nick hated people who wanted to be cute.

"Why?" The broad hadn't dropped her cold, ice blue stare.

"I need some help," Nick replied, moving closer to her. Her gaze remained fixed on his face.

"Fucking Salvation Army's around the corner. I don't loan money." She spoke in a flat monotone.

This fucking chick was getting on his nerves. He flashed his I.D. and she laughed, which pissed Nick off even more. She got up, lit a cigarette, and looked right at him.

"*I'm* Silky."

"You?" Nick let that sink in. "*You're* Silky?' He turned and looked at the photos of various body piercings. "*Christ.*"

Silky took a drag on her cigarette.

Nick was still thinking about this fox making a living punching holes in dicks and nipples. Nipples and dicks. *Fuck, sounds like some kind of fuckin' breakfast cereal*, he thought to himself. "*You* did all these?" He pointed to the photos.

"If the fuckheads pay for it, I do it." Silky's eyes flashed, defiant. "Who the fuck are you to ask?"

"You're right. You ain't nothin' *but* right," he conceded. This wasn't what he was here for. He took the booking photos out of their envelope and laid them in front of Silky, watching her intently as she focused on them. "Ever seen her?"

"Cute kid. What's her problem?"

"She's dead." Nick scowled.

Silky showed the slightest hint of relenting on her attitude, but then froze up again. "Tough. I didn't do it. And no, I don't recognize her."

Nick showed Silky the photo of Collette's arm. She stared for a minute and lit a new smoke.

"Recognize the tattoo?"

"No. It's pretty fucking bad. Nobody could have sold one that bad. That's some amateur kitchen-table botch." She shook her head, almost sadly.

"You don't think one of the shops in town did it?"

"Anybody that fucking bad wouldn't be in business very long. You're looking at *no* technical skill combined with *no* artistic talent. This isn't much better than that crap the kids in the projects do to themselves with plain needles."

Nick gave it a last shot. "You ever seen a design like this before? Any idea what it's supposed to represent?"

"I've never seen it. My guess is it's some kind of flower. Some kinda weird tropical shit." Silky looked at the photo again. "Too fucking bad."

"Yeah, she didn't have much of a life."

"I mean the tattoo. I hope she didn't pay for it."

Nick started to leave and noticed a diploma hanging on the wall next to the door. It proclaimed that one Shannon Katherine Harrington had been awarded a Master of Fine Arts degree from Louisiana State University in Baton Rouge.

"Is this you?"

"Yeah. In my more boring days." Silky maintained the monotone.

Opening the door, Nick said, "And *your* Harley?" He knew the answer and didn't wait for it, closing the door behind him.

*That was one fine bitch. She could make me write bad checks,* he thought as he got back in his unit.

On his way back to the office, Nick stopped again at Collette's last known residence, but no one was in apartment "D," and the landlady didn't appear to be in, or at least not capable of answering the door.

Returning to the office, Nick thought about his kids, whom he hadn't seen or talked to in days. He resolved to contact Sharon and try to set up some type of joint custody arrangement, although he had no idea when he would be available to stay at home long enough to have them come over. Come to think of it, he had no idea where he was going to live. A friend had let him stay in a boathouse on Lake Pontchartrain, but that couldn't last much longer. It wasn't much better than a camp; it wasn't one of the boathouses that had been made into a home, some of which were quite elaborate. The entire first floor was simply a dock, while the second floor had only the barest essentials.

The tattoo continued to bother Nick. He still had the feeling he had seen something like it somewhere before. Silky had also thought it looked like some type of flower, so he headed for the city library. At the information desk, he asked for directions to the books on flowers. The librarian, thin and humorless, began to direct him to the correct stack, then apparently thought better of it and led him to a small area of ominous-looking volumes. *God, I hope they have pictures*, Nick thought, smiling and thanking the librarian for her help.

"Some of these have photographs, if you need them." The librarian gave a superior glance, as if reading Nick's expression.

*Smart-assed bitch*, Nick thought to himself, turning to one large book that looked promising.

After about a half an hour of flipping through the books, he gave up.

"Shit. These fuckers all look alike after awhile." He had at least learned that the study of flowers was not called "flowerology," but "botany." He returned to his office.

*"I'm sorry. The number you have dialed has been changed. The new number is not listed."*

Nick slammed the phone down. Sharon had changed to an unlisted number. This was gonna be nasty. Not that he couldn't get the number. He was a cop. Shit like that was easy. But Sharon had apparently made up her mind. Which was the same as saying that whatever course she had decided upon was set in stone. That was OK, too. He was willing to let her have everything because he knew she would use it to take care of the kids, which were his only concern. Besides, to fight it would only make the fucking lawyers rich.

He put those thoughts out of his mind and became determined to track down the type of flower that the tattoo represented, if in fact it was a flower. He called the main number of LSU in Baton Rouge and asked to be put through to the botany department. The receptionist was female with a young and flirty voice. He asked for the name of someone who was an expert at identification of flowers and was informed that most of the faculty was proficient in that area. After all, they were *all* botanists.

"Sweet-*hawt*, I'm looking for the *best* damn botanist you got." He put on his best southern accent and the girl giggled.

"Oh! Well. That would be Dr. Cameron Vodanovich." Her tone became more reverent. "He's the head of the department."

*Now we were getting somewhere.* "Super. Will you transfer me?"

"I'll transfer you to his secretary. Hold on." The girl clicked off before Nick could answer.

A few seconds later, a deeper and obviously older female voice came on. "Dr. Vodanovich's office."

"I'd like to set up an appointment to come see Dr. Vodanovich."

"He's not in," was the terse answer.

"I understand, ma'am. I'd like to schedule an appointment when he's available."

"You and fifty *other* people," the voice huffed. "His schedule is booked for the next two months. And these people are all too important to reschedule."

That did it. "Look, lady. My name is Nick Saladino. I'm a homicide detective in New Orleans. I need Dr. Vodanovich's help in examining a piece of evidence in a murder case, and I need it *soon*."

There was momentary silence on the other end, then the flinty old bitch said, "You don't need to be so *nasty* about it. Dr. Vodanovich will be in in the morning and I'll see what I can do. Give me your phone number."

Frustrated, Nick gave up for the day and called Steve. He needed some advice about divorce, and he needed a drink.

It was already dark when Steve reached Izzy's in the uptown area of New Orleans, off Prytania Street. It was a great old neighborhood bar where the bartender had to push a button behind the bar to activate the electric door lock so you could enter. If he didn't know you, you didn't get in. It was, as usual, full of regular neighborhood faces, mostly blue collar workers, some professionals. Dingy, but the beer was always ice-cold. He was surprised that he had arrived ahead of Nick, who normally had at least a two-drink head start on him.

Luigi, the bartender, greeted him by putting a frosty Miller Lite in front of him, no glass. Steve knocked down a long, thirsty guzzle, returning the bottle to the bar half-empty, then looked around to see what was shakin'.

"What's up, Steve?" Luigi asked after delivering a couple of other orders.

"A little bit here, a little bit there," Steve replied, his traditional answer.

"T'aint it the truth." Luigi grinned and returned to the other patrons.

Steve saw Nick come up to the door and reached over the counter to buzz him in. He looked tired.

"What's the issue?"

"Don't *even* fuckin' ask," Nick responded. Luigi returned with a Crown on the rocks for him. It didn't last long. He banged the empty glass down on the counter, and Luigi made another. "You know, my old lady kicked me out? Now she's got a fuckin' unlisted phone number. I can't even talk to the kids."

Steve nodded. He was surprised that Sharon had waited this long.

Nick looked at Steve. "Can you represent me if this goes all the way?"

Steve thought briefly about interposing himself between Nick and Sharon, but instantly realized it wouldn't work. "No shot. I can advise you from the sidelines, but I'm not gonna represent you. I'm too close to it. Besides, you don't really need a lawyer if y'all can work out the child support and visitation schedules. Louisiana is a community property state. Half of everything is yours, more or less."

"I don't fuckin' want it." Nick slugged the second Crown down. "I don't fuckin' *want* it. I ain't contesting *nothin'*."

"No big deal, then. All you got to do is waive service, let her take a default against you, and it's over."

Nick nodded. "I'd just like to be able to see the kids occasionally. She's a better parent. She'll raise them right."

"Listen, buck. I don't think you're really surprised at all by this."

Nick was working on his third Crown. "I didn't think she would go this far. I guess I didn't know what she would do." The booze was starting to feel warm in his stomach. "I got to say that the only loss I feel right now is towards the kids. I haven't really felt anything strong towards Sharon for a long time."

Although he had never heard Nick talk like that before, it hardly came as a surprise to Steve. For as long as he had known him, Nick's home life had always taken a back seat to his work. In fact, it had also taken a back seat to Nick's carousing.

They both scouted the bar for talent while they talked, almost like two synchronized radar units. There was only one chick in the place, but definitely of the "not fit for human consumption" variety. *Christ, they didn't make enough Scotch to crawl up on top of that old lounge lizard.*

They drank up and left. It was time for a pub crawl and they headed for their favorite chippy joint, Trinity's. It was dark inside. No: it was *dark* inside, with a few booths along the back walls, and tables surrounded by sofas and love seats, a small dance floor, and an "S"-shaped bar. The booths were great if you were with somebody else's wife. Steve rode with Nick, who had a good buzz on.

"What's your fuckin' hurry?" Steve yelled when Nick flipped on the blue lights hidden in the grille of the Crown Vic and set the siren to wailing. Steve breathed a sigh of relief when Nick finally turned off the lights and siren about a block from Trinity's.

"Didn't want to lose my buzz," Nick laughed, and slapped Steve on the back as they entered the bar.

After a few hours, Nick returned Steve to his car and screeched off. Steve stood for a few seconds, watching Nick's taillights disappear, and then he headed for home.

# IX

Thursday morning. It was 9:00 a.m. Nick was in the Devil's Den in the Quarter, where he had ended up after dropping Steve off. He was pissed-up but still capable of walking. When he finally realized it was daylight, he put on his shades and headed for the door.

"Gotta go to work," he mumbled. He found his car parked at a meter on Decatur with a parking ticket already under the wiper. He reached over, cursing, and threw the ticket on the street. "Fuckin' meter maids."

"For *shame*." A male voice from behind him.

Nick turned slowly around, fighting to see into the sun.

"*Congratulations*, sucker. You've been sued. For divorce." The stranger pulled Nick's suit coat open and stuffed a wad of papers in the inside pocket. "And you've now been served."

Nick stood motionless, stunned. After a few minutes, he opened the door and fell in behind the steering wheel. He pulled the papers from his pocket and looked at them.

"Bigger'n shit." That was *his* name on them. Sharon's name was there, too, as plaintiff.

"Here we go." The gates were open and Nick knew it wouldn't take Sharon long to cross the finish line.

He started the car and drove to the office. *Coffee,* was all he could think of, hoping it would clear the fuzz in front of his eyes, and in his brain.

"Hey, *fuckhead*. Some old broad's been calling for you all morning. I didn't know you were into the old stuff nowadays." It was Cody Mitchell, whose desk was next to Nick's in the bureau. "I guess that's cool, though. You can try a new wrinkle every night." Cody laughed at his own joke.

Nick ignored Cody and sipped his coffee.

"Say, man, this chick's persistent. Says she's at LSU in Baton Rouge."

Nick cursed as the balled-up message popped him in the head and landed in his coffee, then he spun around and pointed his revolver at Cody's head, all in one motion.

Cody's eyes widened briefly, then he turned back to his paperwork. "Fuck you very much," he muttered.

Nick flicked the spilled coffee off of the message and looked at the name and number. *Selma Henderson, in Baton Rouge.*

"Appropriate name," he thought, envisioning some dowdy, fat woman.

He dialed the number and got the same flirty receptionist from yesterday.

"Daw-*lin*." He laid it on thick, pronouncing it in his best ninth ward accent, a practiced art. "Let me talk to Selma." There was a brief giggle, then Selma's voice rasped into his ear. *Christ, the old broad must chew gravel with her food for digestion. Oughta make for a great hum job*, Nick thought.

"Nick Saladino," he identified himself.

"*Mr.* Saladino. *Where* have you *been*? I've been trying to reach you for *hours*. Dr. Vodanovich can see you this afternoon at 3:00 p.m. Please don't be late."

Nick's answer was met by the dial tone as Selma hung up. He held the receiver away for a minute. He was still holding his revolver and pointed it at the receiver.

"*Pow,*" he said softly, then returned the gun to its holster and turned back to his coffee.

"*Three* o' fuckin' clock!" He looked at his watch. It was already 11:30. Baton Rouge was an hour's drive; no, better allow two hours. He didn't know where to find Dr. Vodanovich on the LSU Campus, so he needed to allow time to locate the doctor's office. He thought about Collette's home town of Abbeville. Nick took out the map he kept in his desk. There it was. A small town on U.S. 167, about twenty miles south of Lafayette, Louisiana. Take I-10 west to Lafayette and turn left.

Nick estimated it to be two hours beyond Baton Rouge by way of I-10. He put the map away and organized his file on Collette Prejean, then headed for lunch at Matanza's.

It was drizzling as Nick swung on to I-10 and headed for Baton Rouge. He crossed the Bonnet Carre Spillway at the northwest end of Lake Pontchartrain, and noted that the water and sky to his right blended together on the horizon, one solid mat of gray. As he continued on, the water was replaced by swamp and dense thickets of trees—cypress and a variety of hardwoods. All of them bare.

"Winter *sucks,*" Nick said aloud. "Winter is just fuckin' *ugly.* Trees are ugly. Sky is ugly. The fuckin' *sun* ain't even right. It comes out of a different section of the sky in winter and casts weird-assed shadows. It's even got a different color to it—it's not bright like in the summer. It just fuckin' *sucks.*" Nick couldn't understand how people voluntarily lived in cold climates. "It's no wonder the suicide rate is *higher* in the winter. Fuck, that's probably why they put so many goddam *holidays* in the *winter.* To take people's minds off the total fugliness of it all." The whole crappy winter scene was depressing to him. He saw absolutely no reason for it. Obviously, the person in charge of the weather had become senile, or simply walked off the job, letting the weather lapse into chaos.

Nick's attention was caught by a highway sign that announced he was nearing Baton Rouge, and he opted to take Highland Road to the LSU Campus, which was somewhat south of the city. A two-lane country road, Highland was full of curves and dips with occasional ravines on the sides. It was a beautiful drive, but its serenity was being destroyed by over-development.

He drove through the arch that signified the entrance to the campus. Nick had always been impressed by the LSU Campus. Sprawling, huge, with a group of small lakes at one end and the Mississippi River at the other, the campus was impressive. A few of the huge Japanese magnolias were in bloom, their fallen lavender leaves creating puddles of color at the base of the trees. He headed for the Student Union in the center of the campus, and parked the Crown Vic in front of the Campanile bell tower.

Inside the immense building, Nick paused for a minute in the lobby to soak in the atmosphere, which was vibrant. Students in all forms of dress were hanging out or bustling about their business. Nick envied their lack of concern and responsibility. He had never known that luxury. Some of the coeds were un-be-*fucking*-lievable, their tight little butts wiggling a pattern as they walked. Some of the other coeds were unbelievable, too, but in a much different, less attractive way. Nick watched a couple of earth-mother types, with their amorphous dresses and unkempt hair.

*Christ. Their fuckin' dorm rooms must have industrial-strength mirrors.* Nick shook his head at the thought. He couldn't imagine the earth-mothers looking in their mirrors each morning and thinking, "I look *good*."

Nick went to the cashier at the book store and asked for directions to the botany department. The cashier pointed him to a studious-looking woman with a neat bun on the back of her head. Her hair had been pulled so tight, her eyes were pulled up at the side corners almost like an oriental. She looked at him quizzically and he felt uncomfortably out of place. He inquired again for the location of the botany department, and she smiled.

"You mean the plant biology department." Nick felt even more uncomfortable. "They're located in the Life Sciences Building, across the street from the Student Union parking lot." She continued to grin, and Nick couldn't tell if it was a smile or a smirk. He just thanked her and left.

He had no trouble finding the building. It looked to be one of the newer ones on the campus.

"You must be Mr. Saladino." It was the flirty receptionist. She sat behind a small wooden desk at the entrance, her satiny-brown ponytail flopping as she turned and spoke. There was that giggle. "Are you *really* a detective?" Another giggle. Her brown eyes stared at Nick. He thought about that ponytail flopping around while he pounded her from the rear, doggy-style, but didn't have long to savor the thought.

"*Mr.* Saladino."

*Jesus.* That voice could only be sexy to a piece of sandpaper. He looked up and was surprised to see that Selma Henderson was not what he had pictured. In the doorway was a tall, shapely woman in her mid-fifties with red hair neatly coiffed in one of those simple, purportedly elegant styles that matrons think gives them a chic appearance. Her face had aged into a handsome set of lines that were authoritative yet comely. She was wearing the uniform of the executive secretary—a dark blue suit and a blouse with a bow-tie at the neck.

*Nice legs*, Nick noted to himself after his quick scan. He nodded and walked towards the woman.

"Dr. Vodanovich will see you *now*. Please follow me."

He looked at the receptionist, who favored him with another giggle, and followed Henderson to the office of Dr. Vodanovich.

The office wasn't what he had pictured in his mind. He had thought of Dr. Vodanovich as an old man with flowing white hair, walking around in khaki shorts with his knobby knees wobbling, and Nick had figured the office would be some sort of musty greenhouse with a worn safari hat hanging on a peg. Instead, he found a young man, late thirties with curly blond hair and a large muscular physique, wearing a white lab coat. The office was almost sterile, with books lining the walls and a computer terminal on one side.

Dr. Vodanovich looked at Nick through horn-rimmed glasses. "Not what you expected, right?"

Nick nodded. He focused on photos on the wall of what appeared to be Dr. Vodanovich in an LSU Tigers football uniform. *Definitely* not what he had expected.

Nick stuck out his hand. "Nick Saladino, New Orleans Police. Thanks for seeing me on such short notice."

The man's handshake was crushing. His hands were huge. Nick found it hard to believe that those hands were capable of dissecting flowers, or whatever it was that plant biologists did.

"No problem." Vodanovich looked at Nick and winked in a conspiratorial fashion. "I was supposed to meet with some graduate students, but it sounded a lot more interesting to talk to you. I don't get homicide detectives every day." The scientist leaned forward in anticipation. "What can I possibly do for you?"

"Doc, I'm working on a very strange case. So far, my leads are almost non-existent." Nick went on to provide a quick summary of the events that had brought him to Baton Rouge. He embellished the tale a bit to capture the doctor's attention, which was really unnecessary, as Dr. Vodanovich stared at him wide-eyed, barely blinking, an almost boyish enthusiasm creeping into his face.

"Oh, *neat*. I get to help solve a *murder*. That'll make grand conversation at the faculty club lunch table! Some of those conversations do get so *boring*."

Nick had a strong picture of those conversations. "Look, Doc. What I need is for you to look at this photo of a tattoo and tell me if it represents any kind of flower you know of. I don't know if it will make any difference to my investigation, but I need every lead I can get."

Nick took the photo of the arm from the envelope and passed it to Dr. Vodanovich. He noted that the doctor cringed at the grisly sight.

Dr. Vodanovich stared at the photo for a minute. "I've never seen *anything* like this before." The scientist was shaking his head negatively.

Nick was crestfallen. He had hoped that the tattoo design would produce *some* information. "Oh, well, back to square one, as they say."

"This is amazing." Dr. Vodanovich continued.

"You don't recognize the design, huh?" Nick asked, ready to leave.

"No, no! That's not what I mean. I mean that I've never seen anything *like* this. A detached human arm that has been through *so* much trauma. But with a still discernible tattoo. This is fascinating. Who did you say it belonged to?"

Nick perked up a little. "A young girl from Abbeville. A hooker."

"Wow, poor kid. And you never found the rest of the body?" The scientist was captivated.

Nick shook his head, growing impatient. He hadn't meant for this to turn into a *freak* show. "What about the tattoo, Doc? Ever see anything like that?"

Vodanovich pushed his glasses down his nose some distance, holding the photo away from his face. "It's not a very well-defined image. But I do believe that it may be some type of flower. Let me see... could be... *nope*." Vodanovich rubbed his cheek as he pondered the photo. Nick could almost see detailed information flickering through the man's head as he sorted, classified and reclassified his knowledge.

"Whaddaya mean, *nope*?" Nick was down again. "Shit, doc. If this thing isn't a flower, I don't know where to turn with it."

"I mean nope, it's nothing local. Yep, I think it's a flower. Nope, it's not common. But, yep, I might be able to help here."

Vodanovich got up and removed a ponderous volume from a shelf of ponderous volumes. Nick looked at the title. To his surprise, it was written in common English. *Exotic Plants of the Tropics*.

"I believe it's a form of *orchidaceae*. The orchid family, to you." Vodanovich flipped the pages slowly, then looked up at Nick, who was leaning forward to see the book's photos. "Of course, there are as many as thirty-five thousand different species out there."

Nick sat back and let his breath out slowly until he was forced to again inhale. Thirty-five thousand was an intimidating number.

"A fascinating family of plants. Each singularly beautiful, each exquisitely different. The varieties of these plants extend throughout every form of plant known. Some are evergreen, some are deciduous." Vodanovich was on a roll.

"Deciduous?" Nick replied.

"Lose their leaves each year." Vodanovich smiled tolerantly.

"Oh." Nick leaned forward again. "Of course." He shook his head in agreement.

"They can be terrestrial, growing in the ground, or they can be epiphytes, growing from a perch in a tree. Some are even parasites on fungi."

"So what are you saying, Doc? You think this tattoo is some sort of orchid?" Nick was hopeful.

"I believe we should find something quite similar." Vodanovich was still patiently flipping pages, occasionally muttering something under his breath. Nick watched, waiting to see how much longer the man's glasses could remain in their precarious perch at the end of his nose. Vodanovich couldn't possibly be breathing through his nose with the glasses squeezed down on it as hard as they were.

"*Yes.*"

Nick was startled. Dr. Vodanovich was like a kid who had found the prize in a Cracker Jack box.

"Yes." Vodanovich was becoming more scholarly now. "Of *course.*"

Nick was worn out from the roller coaster ride of emotions he had just gone through.

"What? What'cha got, Doc?"

"I suspected as much." Vodanovich was comparing the tattoo to a photo in the book.

"For Christ's *sake*, Doc. What are you talking about?"

Vodanovich pushed his glasses a few inches back up his nose and put the book down. "*Trichoglottis*. That's *it*. It's *Trichoglottis*, detective!" Vodanovich's face had lit up like a Christmas tree. "Actually, this specimen appears to be

*Trichoglottis Brachiata*, sometimes called *Trichoglottis Phillippinensis Brachiata*." He seemed bubbly.

"Calm down, Doc! What the hell is *Tricho*...whatever the hell you said?" Nick had tried to write it down, but didn't get very far.

Vodanovich's tone became softly reverent, almost hushed. "It's the *'black orchid'*."

"The black orchid?" The thought of a black flower wasn't very appealing to Nick. "A *black* orchid?"

Vodanovich had returned to a somewhat more professional manner. "Of course, it's not really necessarily black. A true black orchid is virtually legendary. It actually comes in a variety of shades, from a pinkish-red to a dark wine color. Gorgeous. Just gorgeous. It's a tree-grower and it's evergreen. It has a yellow throat..."

"Dammit, slow *down*, Doc. I can't write *that* fast!" Nick was trying to keep up with Vodanovich and he knew he wouldn't be able to decipher his scribble later.

"Oh, sorry." Vodanovich waited for Nick to catch up, then continued when Nick looked up and nodded. "It's monopodial. That is, it usually has one stem and one flower per stem. Normal height is about two feet. Blooms in the spring and summer." Vodanovich sat back with a satisfied expression, almost smug.

Nick was still writing. "Anything else?"

"It's mildly fragrant and relatively long-lived. You might say it is sort of star-shaped." Vodanovich continued reading.

Nick looked at the photo of the black orchid in the book and compared it to the tattoo. To even his untrained eyes, the similarity was unmistakable.

"Doc, I think you got something here." Nick was beginning to catch some of Vodanovich's excitement. He finally had something he could call progress on this damned case, although he had no idea what it meant or what to do with it.

"You said these things aren't from around here?" Nick knew that would have been too good to be true.

"Well, they are sometimes grown here, but are not indigenous. They're actually from the Philippine Islands."

"*Great*." He could imagine submitting an expense report to the captain outlining a visit to the Philippines, wherever the fuck that was.

"But these plants are easily grown around here. They like medium humidity and warm night temperatures, so it's fairly easy to please them in south Louisiana. I'm sure there are quite a few collectors who have them. I am aware that there are orchid clubs, possibly some with local chapters," Vodanovich added.

Nick was feeling more positive about the case now, even though he had no idea where to go next. "And it's called a black orchid, but it's not really black?"

"Right. Actually, there are other species of orchids that have been called black orchids, also, but this tattoo seems to me to most resemble the particular species most commonly referred to as 'black orchids.'"

"There is also *Dracula Vampira*, native to the forested slopes of northwestern Ecuador, which is a different shape and basically a green color, although it has an intense black area and streaking. Then there is *Coelogyne Pandurata* which comes from Sarawak and was discovered by a fellow named Hugh Low in, oh, 1845 or so. It is a tree-dweller, with clusters of greenish-yellow flowers that have black ridges on the lip. Of course, there is no orchid that is actually *all* black."

"That's wonderful, Doc." Nick had had enough. His span of attention had overflowed ten minutes and three orchids ago. He reached over and slapped Vodanovich amiably on the arm. "Can you make me a photocopy of the page with the picture of the Trich-whatsis on it?"

"Oh, certainly." He pushed a button on the desk and Ms. Henderson appeared, took the book, and left. When she returned, it was with a color copy. "There are some nice benefits to working under federal grants," Vodanovich said, laughing quietly at Nick's expression of surprise. "Color copiers are just one of them."

"Wow! No *wonder* I can't afford to pay my taxes." Nick thanked the scientist profusely and left, throwing one last admiring glance at the receptionist. He was rewarded with an expression that made him sorry he wouldn't be returning to Baton Rouge any time soon.

# X

Back outside, the campus was bustling with the typical traffic jams leading off campus. Nick, rather than get mired in the traffic, took advantage of the situation, deciding to walk around the campus and take in the sights, both movable and immovable. After a half-hour or so, he returned to the Crown Vic and headed west on I-10, across the Mississippi River Bridge to Lafayette and then on to Abbeville.

As he crossed the bridge, he looked back over Baton Rouge, comparing the old State Capitol Building to the "new" Capitol Building. He had always favored the old one with its turrets on top, but he understood the need to build something with more capacity, and, of course, he appreciated the need to erect a monument to Huey Long's ego. He laughed at the thought of the new building appearing as a phallic symbol to some of his female friends and colleagues, although it was an impressive building. Its office tower loomed tall over Baton Rouge, topped by an observation deck high above the wings for the Senate and House of Representatives, which balanced the tower on either side.

As Nick crossed the twin spans over the Atchafalaya Basin at Whiskey Bay, the sunset played out its last cards for the day in a deep orange panorama tinged with pink. The sun stared at him blindingly on a perfect horizontal plane as it sank down to see what was going on on the other side of the planet.

He pulled into the outskirts of Lafayette in less than an hour and turned south towards Abbeville. He had made an appointment to meet a sergeant with the Vermilion Parish Sheriff's Office. His partner Cody Mitchell had worked a case with ties to Vermilion Parish a year ago, and had developed a friendship with this deputy, coincidentally also named Prejean. In twenty minutes he was in Abbeville, a neatly laid-out, sleepy town in the heart of French-speaking (Cajun French, that is) Acadiana.

The sheriff's office was on the main drag, and Nick pulled the Crown Vic into the area marked "law enforcement only." He was greeted at the front door by Sergeant Prejean, a burly, dark-haired man. He was casually dressed and well-fortified against the cold.

"Detective Saladino." The man spoke with a Cajun accent, but, surprisingly, not a very thick one. "I'm Prejean. Norval Prejean."

"Nick," Saladino said. "Just call me Nick."

"I can't say I'm surprised at what happened to Collette," Prejean began, as they returned to his office.

"You were related to her?"

Prejean nodded. "All Prejeans in this area are related. She was a cousin. Distant cousin."

"Man, I'm sorry."

"You need be sorry only for *her*. The kid had a miserable life here, and it sounds like it wasn't any better in New Orleans. She had the fucking misfortune to be born the daughter of Pearly Prejean."

Nick could see it coming. It was a story he had seen and heard all too often from hookers on the streets of New Orleans.

"Pearly never worked a day, except for occasionally trapping or fishing or raiding traps that didn't belong to him. He beat his wife, and when they were old enough, he beat his kids. Collette's mother worked as a barmaid in one of the roadhouses out on Highway 90, and Pearly occasionally made her turn tricks with his friends, or with anyone else who had a little cash, for that matter. When Collette became a teenager, he 'broke her in,' as *he* called it, and turned her out to support the family."

*How did I know,* Nick thought to himself. He shook his head slowly. "Let me guess, so she ran off to the big city to live on the streets."

"You got it. She was eleven the first time I saw her get picked up for prostitution. After that, she was booked a number of times but I was usually able to pull a few strings and get the charges dismissed. Of course, considering the fact that she was picked up a few times with one or two of the local married politicians, it was easy to make the charges disappear." Prejean smirked. "Looking back, maybe I didn't do her any favors helping her beat the system. She finally ran off to New Orleans when one of the charges stuck and a judge threatened to put her in a foster home. That judge was one of the politicians she *hadn't* been in bed with."

Prejean looked at Nick. "I understand she was living with a pimp?"

Nick nodded. "It's not hard for them to make the transition to a pimp. Low self-esteem, accustomed to being beaten and used as a sexual receptacle. Add in some type of drug addiction courtesy of the pimp, and it's pretty much the end of life as most people understand it. Although there was no evidence of any sort of drugs in her system, I suspect that's only because there was literally no system left to examine."

Prejean finally bordered on revealing some emotion at that point.

"Sorry," Nick offered.

"It's alright." Prejean recovered his façade.

"Sergeant, I need you to look at a photo for me." Nick placed the photo of Collette's arm in front of Prejean.

"Jesus, is that really *all* that was left?" Prejean was now visibly shocked, his mouth open as he gazed at the photo.

"Fortunately, the fingerprints were still relatively intact. They're the only reason I'm here now talking to you. Take a look at that tattoo." Nick pointed at the design in the photo. "Did Collette have anything like that when she was living here in Abbeville?"

"I don't recall anything like that." Prejean's mouth was still open. "You found this in an alligator? No shit?" He was incredulous. "Gators like their meat gamey. Dead or alive, they like to drag it underwater and lodge it under a submerged tree root to let it really get flavorful."

Nick nodded. "Does this design have any significance to you? Ever seen anything like it before?" Nick knew it was unlikely that Prejean would recognize the tattoo, but he couldn't let the question go unasked.

"No. I've seen a lot of tattoos, but nothing quite like that comes to mind."

"Any chance of talking with any of her family?" Nick was about finished with Sergeant Prejean and possibly with Abbeville.

"Séance, maybe. Pearly was drowned about a year ago when he went out in a stolen pirogue, drunk. Too drunk to swim when the boat turned over. Coroner's report said .0275 blood alcohol, almost three times the legal limit."

"How about the mother?" Nick knew it was a useless question.

"Nah. Stabbed to death in a bar down in Intracoastal City by some drunk who had been sleeping in the bars since getting off his crewboat two days earlier. She stole his marijuana stash

while giving him a blowjob in the parking lot behind the bar."
Prejean anticipated Nick's next question. "And Collette's
brother, he just up and disappeared. Hasn't been heard from in
a couple of years. I suspect he's in jail somewhere."

Prejean stood up. "And to complete the story of the family,
their miserable houseboat sank in the bayou last year. It was so
filthy inside, it damn near poisoned the marine life. Come on, I'll
buy you dinner."

A welcome idea. Nick had just realized he was starved.

# XI

It was late when Nick finally headed back east. He had chosen to return to New Orleans via old U.S. Highway 90 for a change of scenery, and enjoyed the feel of the small towns as he passed through them. Berwick, Morgan City, Houma. He thought about Collette Prejean and the miserable life she had endured. In some strange way, maybe it was better that she was no longer so afflicted. What Nick had heard that night made him more determined than ever to find out what had happened to her.

A dimly-lit bar on the side of the road on the outskirts of St. Charles Parish caught his attention an hour or so later, and he pulled over to get a cold beer. The tattered sign near the door optimistically proclaimed the place to be the "Stardust Lounge," although the hand-painted red letters had faded to the point where Nick could barely make them out in the dimly-lit area. The seediness of the joint's exterior was exceeded only by the grossness of the interior. It was one of those places where the air is *so* musty and thick, the air particles themselves were forced to fight with each other for space.

"What'cha need, dawlin'?" The barmaid was short, chubby and dirty. Mannish in appearance, with close-cropped hair and an obvious lack of much-needed make-up. She wore Kelly green hot pants and a sleeveless shirt open halfway down the front, stained. She had *huge* tits, forcing the helpless shirt to gape wide open; unfortunately they were the type of tits that were anything *but* sexy, the kind that hung past her navel—so low you'd have to get on your knees to lick the nipples. They were the kind of tits you'd seen closing around you in those nightmares where you always suffocated to death.

"Beer, whatever kind you've got. A bottle." Nick wasn't about to trust the glass sterilization in this place. He had a strong image of the cleaning process.

She waddled off and returned with a beer and a glass.

"No glass, babe. Bottle baby." Nick took a slug. It was cold. He was grateful for that.

She put the glass back, carrying it with her fingers on the inside. She watched him for a while, bored. There wasn't anyone else in the joint. *Big surprise.*

She waddled back and stood in front of him. "How about a little champagne party, sweetheart?" She was smiling now, revealing teeth that had seen no dental care since entering this world. It didn't add to her charm any.

"Champagne party?" Nick had noticed about a half dozen splits of cheap champagne on the back bar, clustered together for protection against the dinginess of the joint as if they had been kidnapped en route to some gala event.

"Forty bucks." She was still smiling.

Nick looked back toward the door, anticipating what was coming with some revulsion.

"Forty bucks for a bottle of champagne and *me*." She picked up a split and held it next to her cleavage proudly, pulling the shirt away to reveal enormous tits shaped like plastic bags with grapefruit in the bottom.

"Such a deal." Nick almost gagged. "Sorry, babe. Maybe next time." He poured the rest of the beer in a plastic cup and didn't look back on his way out.

"Kee-fuckin'-*rist*." He shot the rest of the beer down. "That could almost make me turn celibate."

# XII

Friday morning. It had been a week since Collette Prejean had entered Nick's life. He still had no suspects, except possibly her pimp. He looked at the file, dismayed at the paltry amount of information he had accumulated so far.

The tattoo was beginning to piss him off. He had a nagging feeling that he had seen it somewhere before. He pulled out the color copy of the black orchid he had received from Dr. Vodanovich, pinned it up on his bulletin board next to his desk, and leaned back in his chair with a cup of coffee, studying it intensely.

"It's really just a fuckin' *tattoo*," he thought. "Christ, there doesn't have to be *anything* significant about the fuckin' thing. Just some poor gutter hooker stoned out of her tree, letting some other gutter snail put it there, probably in exchange for a blow job. It actually doesn't *have* to mean a fuckin' thing. But I hope it does. It's all I've got."

Nick worked on other cases for a few hours, but the damn thing kept creeping into his thoughts.

"Say, lover. It's for *you*." Cody had answered the phone. Nick hadn't heard it ring. It was late afternoon. "*Another* old broad! This one sounds like the Crypt Keeper. You must be drinking over at Club Dead since your old lady threw your ass out on the street. How *are* those gum jobs? Do they make you hold their teeth while they're going at it?"

Nick raised his fist under Cody's chin. "Smell *this*, cocksucker. Fuck, with friends like you, who needs enemas?" He picked up the phone. "Saladino."

The voice was hoarse, rasping, with an occasional heavy cough that smokers are reduced to when trying to cough up a spoonful of phlegm.

"You still lookin for that goddam pimp, he's here now."

Before Nick could respond, the dial tone had replaced the voice, but it was apparent to Nick that it was the landlady from Collette's boarding house.

"Take a ride, Cody? I might need some back-up. I'll fill you in on the way." Nick adjusted the shoulder holster and put on his coat before they headed for the garage.

"*Crap*. Motherfucker. *Piss*."

St. Claude Avenue traffic was at a standstill for a train shunting back and forth across the street, trying to make up its mind which cars to take with it. Nick swung around on the neutral ground and sped down Royal Street which ran parallel to St. Claude, managing to cross the tracks a hair or two before the train arrived.

"Hope that mother fucker is still there!"

As they squealed to a stop in front of the boarding house, a light-skinned black male was opening the door, about to exit. He burned them instantly and ran back inside, slamming the door.

"Fuck, fuck, *fuck*." Nick was cursing as he raced up the steps with Cody at his heels. At the entrance to the building, they paused on either side of the front door with guns drawn. Nick reached down and grabbed the knob, pushing the door slowly open. It was clear. They proceeded upstairs to apartment "D" and knocked, again standing to either side, guns drawn.

No answer.

"It's the fucking *po*lice. Open the fucking door!" Nick shouted.

No answer.

"OK, here we go!" Nick kicked the door. The rotten old door frame gave instantly and completely, and the entire door fell flat on the floor of the apartment. They scanned the room. Nobody. The only window in the room was open, ragtag curtains flying in the cold breeze. The door to the next room was ajar, and they peered in cautiously.

A naked mattress was on the floor. Nothing else was in the room save for a naked white female on the mattress and a couple of syringes resting on a flattened beer can. She was sitting upright staring at them, making no attempt to cover herself. She was barely fifteen.

Cody spun around and sped downstairs in time to see the black male turn the corner in a raggedy-assed Olds Cutlass, orange with a green vinyl top, or what was left of it. The car's engine was desperately in need of a transplant; it sounded like a rod was about to go through the block, and the smoke from the tail pipe likely eliminated most of the mosquitoes in a two-block radius. Slow as it was, it was faster than Cody could run, and Nick had kept the keys to the Crown Vic.

"3-8-7 x-ray 2-5-6." Cody was at least able to get a look at the plate, which was also in piss-poor condition, likely stolen. He wrote it down and went back upstairs.

Nick was sitting on the floor talking to the girl, who had put her clothes back on. What there was of them. A halter top, hot pants and sandals. She didn't seem to feel the cold, which didn't surprise Cody, looking at the filthy needles and syringes next to her. He noted her black hair and blue eyes. Sort of what they call "Black Irish" coloring. She had some nasty tracks on her arms and legs.

Cody cursed. He had a sudden urge to strangle the bastard when they found him. This was somebody's daughter.

"Says her name is Carla Wayne." Nick had gotten the girl talking, if you could call it that. She was on the nasty side of sobering up.

"From Mobile. Ran away from her family six months ago. Our boy picked her up at the bus station."

"I didn't know what to do." Carla was slurring her words. "I only had twenty dollars. All these scary people were staring at me, so I just sat on a bench for a while. This guy comes up and he's real nice to me. Bought me some food and a beer. I passed out after I drank it and woke up here. He brings me everything I need, but I didn't know it would be like this."

Nick and Cody looked knowingly at each other. "What's his name?"

"All he told me was 'Cueball'. That's all I know."

"Come on, sweetheart. Let's go." Nick was lifting the girl to her feet.

"I don't *want* to go to jail. I haven't done *anything*. I just want to stay right *here*." Carla was whining like a child.

"God, I hate fuckin' *whining*. I hope you don't have fuckin' AIDS. Your arm is still bleeding."

"We're not taking you to jail. I know a nurse at Charity Hospital who will clean you up and help you get into some kinda treatment." Nick and Cody supported the girl down the stairs and into the Crown Vic. "After you get cleaned up, you're gonna look at some photos."

The next day, Cody pulled up at the emergency entrance of Charity to pick Carla up and take her to the office for a photo line-up. He was relieved to see that she had cleaned up fairly well and was coherent, but she had refused placement in a treatment facility. He was always amazed at the Charity ER. Beds in the hallways, nurses and doctors moving in a frenzied dance, albeit a well-coordinated one. It was the place to be if you had traumatic injuries.

At the office, Nick had already called down to vice to see if anyone recognized the name "Cueball." No one did, and he ran the moniker through the computer, coming up with no less than three "Cueballs." He pulled their mug shots. Only one was black. That made it a lot easier. He selected mug shots of six other similarly-featured black males and headed back to homicide. He had become wary of setting up the photo line-up process after one dumb-fuck judge had thrown out the line-up in a prior homicide case, ruling that the line-up was "suggestive," and therefore tainted, on the grounds that the other photos were too dissimilar.

"Christ!" Nick grumbled to himself. "It's not like I put a photo of the asshole in with a photo of a nun, a refrigerator and a duck, and told the witness to pick out the *man* she saw commit the murder!"

Cody joined Nick back at his desk. He had run the plate. "Stolen. From uptown. Couple of months ago. Surprise."

"So what's fuckin' *new*?" Nick was spreading the photos in front of Carla.

"You shoulda seen this junker he was drivin'. Oughta be easy to spot. There can't be too many orange and green Cutlasses around. Looked like a fuckin' pumpkin! Asshole must think it's *Halloween*."

"No shit." Nick turned to Carla, who was looking at the photos. "See anybody you know?"

Carla was talking better than the last time he had seen her. Maybe the coffee had hit home. Nick hoped he wouldn't have to depend upon this I.D. procedure in court. He could see some capable defense attorney asking Carla when was the last time she had had a fix before reviewing the photos.

She looked at Nick and Cody, then returned to the photos. After a few more minutes, she picked up one and handed it to Nick.

"Him?" Nick was elated. She had picked the photo of "Cueball." For once, he had a tangible suspect in this case who could be tied to Collette Prejean.

Carla nodded.

"Sign and date the back of it," Nick said, handing the photo back to her with a pen. She scratched something that looked illegible, and Nick gathered up the photos, tucking them into an envelope and initialing it before placing it into his case file. He checked the name he had written when Carla selected the photo. Leroy Johnson, aka "Cueball," aka "Pumpkin Man." He laughed, thinking of Cody's description of Cueball's getaway car.

Nick got a rap sheet on Cueball. *"Bingo."* The sheet reported four arrests and two convictions for pandering, one for inciting prostitution, one for molestation of a juvenile, and one manslaughter conviction. There was also a warrant for failure to pay his child support, issued out of Juvenile Court.

"Lovely, just lovely. This asshole's got a *warrant*. That's perfect. We got a reason to get him."

Nick noted the long list of addresses on the rap sheet, mostly in the area of the Ninth Ward around St. Claude Avenue. He called Mike Faust, who knew the St. Claude area better than anyone, and ran the story down to him.

"Yeah, I've seen dat bastid! I know what he looks like. Lemme look around some. I'll let ya know. I can tell ya right now dat ya can't *miss* his fuckin' car. Looks like a fuckin' *pumpkin*."

Nick returned to Carla, still sitting where he had left her.

"What are you going to do with me?" she whined.

"*Christ*. Don't fuckin' *whine*. If you want to go back to Mobile, I'll buy you a bus ticket. I suggest you get the fuck out of New Orleans."

"*No*. I can't go back to my family. They've put me in the hospital a couple of times already."

"Well, you're not gonna live long on the streets here. How about an older sister? Brother?" Nick asked.

Carla shook her head, negatively. "They won't talk to me. My sister's husband tried to grope me and she caught him, so she banned me from her house, saying it was my fault. I don't have anyone else."

Nick sighed. He was getting tired of hearing this kind of shit, day in and day out, victim after victim. "Then you gotta go to some type of treatment program, but you already refused the one offered to you at Charity. Let me think... I'm taking you to Annunciation House. The director is a friend of mine. After that, it's up to you."

The director was someone Nick had taken off the street five years earlier and helped into treatment. He was one of very few success stories, and he went on to establish a treatment center in a rough area of town.

Nick called Steve from his car phone. "I'll be at Izzy's." Nick left the message with Steve's secretary. He wanted a quiet place where he could think about Collette's case. Steve showed up an hour later and they both propped themselves on the bar with their elbows. Nick had decided to bring Steve in on the Prejean case, as an additional source of ideas.

"Steve, this fuckin' case is buggin' the shit outta me!" After Nick had run it down to Steve, Steve stood straight and motioned for Luigi to bring them another round.

"Interesting. I'm surprised the media hasn't gotten hold of it. At least, I haven't seen anything on it." Steve liked an unusual case. Even in the bizarre world of crime and criminals, a lot of things become routine, almost rut-like; only the names changed. The people upon whom society depends to deal with such things as the dirty underbelly of society inevitably become jaded and cynical, giving birth to some of the deepest forms of "dark humor."

Nick snorted. "Shit! Fuckin' media assholes. Can't do anything else in society, so they become TV or newspaper reporters. Lowest form of life on the planet. Nothin' but arrogant, self-righteous snails who'll sell their mothers for a headline or to push an agenda."

"Yeah, you right," Steve chimed in. "*Wow*. Didn't mean to start you off on a roll. So what's the big deal with the Prejean case? Sounds like all you got to do is find your pimp and you ought to be able to just about wrap it up."

Nick wasn't so sure that it would be that easy. With as few pieces of the puzzle as he had, his instincts told him that this puzzle was somehow larger and more complex than that.

"So, you think Mike Faust can find him?" Steve asked.

Nick nodded. "If he can't, I'll lay odds this asshole isn't in the St. Claude area. But I'm betting he is. He's a homeboy. Every time he's been arrested, it's been at an address in that neighborhood."

Steve left at about seven-thirty p.m. Nick kept drinking. He thought about his kids for a while, then shook himself free of the thoughts. He knew that at least they were in a safe environment, and he still didn't feel that he really had anything to give to them. That thought made him drink even more. He decided he needed a livelier atmosphere and headed for the French Quarter and the Devil's Den, where he switched from beer to Crown on the rocks.

*Damn, even some of the losers are starting to look decent.* Nick surveyed the crop for likely prospects. He hadn't had time to finish his reconnaissance, though, when an old doll sat down next to him.

"Have a drink, sweetheart. And whose grandmother are *you*?" Nick let a little sarcasm drip out.

"Nobody's, you *asshole*. And I look a hell of a lot better than *you* will at this age!"

The woman was feisty, early fifties, well-groomed and well-proportioned. Nothing to write home about, but then, he didn't exactly have a home to write to. She definitely wasn't something to turn your nose up at, especially in Nick's mental state.

"You're right! You are asshole-lutely *right*. In fact, you ain't nuttin' *but* right!" Nick was slurring, the booze finally absorbing some of his pain. "In fact, you are *so* fine, sweetheart, you remind me of my favorite Beatles song, *I Wanna Hold Your Gland.*" Nick tried to sing the song to himself but couldn't remember any of the other lines, which didn't stop him from repeating that one line over and over as he leaned back down on his elbows on the bar.

The woman sneered. "Well, I can see you're not going to be doing much else tonight!" She turned away from him, spotted another likely-looking candidate, and moved off down the bar.

"Good shot, lover-boy!" Dolly put another drink in front of him. "If you're not opposed to the idea, I get off in two hours. Take me outta here and I'll cheer you up. I owe you one for helping with my kid."

Nick looked at her through half-closed lids. "Deal." Then he turned back to his new drink.

"Let's get the flock outta here!" It was one a.m. Dolly put a go-cup in front of Nick and headed for the door with her own drink. Nick tagged along. They got into the Crown Vic where Nick had parked it on St. Louis Street.

"Where're we going? Where's your place?" Dolly asked.

"I don't remember."

"Christ! I should have guessed!"

# XIV

Monday morning, Nick sat down at his desk and wrote Sharon a brief letter. He had purposely avoided trying to go to the house, other than one visit right after being served when he retrieved the major portion of his clothes. He was still living in the boathouse, on the second floor. In the letter, Nick told Sharon that all he really wanted out of the divorce was a reasonable visitation schedule with the kids. Noticeably absent from the letter was any offer of reconciliation, or even any thoughts about missing her. He ran the letter to the post office, then returned to his desk.

After staring at the professor's orchid photograph on the bulletin board for a few minutes, he returned to his only two leads: the black orchid and the pimp. He grabbed the list of tattoo parlors and hit the streets to visit each one in alphabetical order.

By one o'clock he had knocked off seven of them, with no results. Not even a glimmer of recognition in anyone's eyes when they were shown the photo of Collette and her tattoo. Most of them made basically the same comments as Silky Harrington concerning the poor, kitchen-table quality of the work. Nick headed for Matanza's. His stomach acids had begun working on his stomach lining out of revenge for not being fed in a while. He didn't make it.

"*1251*," his radio crooned. That sultry voice again. He still hadn't checked this chick out.

"Jesus fuckin' Christ! Goddam people must be watchin' me to see when I'm trying to eat! Fuck!" Then Nick acknowledged recluctanty, "1251."

"Mike Faust in the fifth district is trying to reach you."

"*No shit*. 10-4." Nick was elated. "I *knew* that crazy bastard would find him!" He switched his radio from the detective bureau channel to the channel monitored by the fifth district. He knew the number of Mike Faust's unit. "531," he mumbled into the radio. No answer. He tried again. "531." No answer. "Shit, he must be in the bacawza."

"*To the unit calling 531.*" The radio had snapped to life. "Faust is 10-7 at the district with baggage."

Faust had gone off the air at the station when he brought in someone. Nick gave up the idea of lunch and headed for the fifth district station on St. Claude Avenue next to the Industrial Canal, a short but vital water route that connected Lake Pontchartrain with the Mississippi River through a small set of locks.

Mike was at his desk with the same bright-skinned male Nick had seen run from Collette's boarding house on Friday. Mike had him seated at the side of the desk in cuffs, and his eyes moved just enough to acknowledge Nick's presence. Nick sat on the desk next to Mike's.

Faust resumed his interrogation. "My man. I know yer Cueball Johnson. Now if ya want me ta fingerprint ya to confoim it, we ain't gonna be on real good toims here. Ya know I got ya on a warrant for child support, over twenny-five grand woit. Dat's a helluva lotta *Pablum*, bro. Ya wanna cooperate, I'll try ta help ya out wit' da judge; ya don' wanna cooperate, I'm sure da judge'll be more 'n happy to help out wit' a moida investigation by holdin' ya in da pokey until he can set a hearin' date fer ya. I'm sure ya ol' lady'll be happy ta have a chance ta rip ya nuts in court. An' who knows how long it'll take fer da hearin' to be scheduled? Afta cop time comes D.A. time, if ya git wut I'm talkin' about."

"Aw, man! What you talkin', murder investigation? What's up wit' dat shit?" Cueball whined.

"Another fuckin' *whiner*." Nick stood up menacingly. "Christ on a crutch! I fuckin' *hate* whiners! The only thing worse than a child whining is a goddam *pimp* whining."

"Dis is Detective Saladino, homicide," Faust said, introducing Nick, who just glared at Cueball. "I already did his Miranda crap, Nick."

"Look, bra! Ya got me right, ya got me wrong. Ya get it? It just might be I ain't paid that fuckin' bitch for getting' knocked up, but that's on her. It ain't mine. Ya get whut I'm talkin' about? She wadn't nuttin but a fuckin ho, and she cain't make no fuckin' jack when she be knocked up! Ain't nobody gonna pay to ride on a basketball! Know whut um sayin'? Yeah, I'm Cueball, and yeah, I knows dat charge is against me. But my little black ass ain't got nuttin' to do wit' no fuckin' *murder*. I don't *even* know whut *dat's* all about. Know whut um sayin'? Don't *even* knock on d*at* do'!"

Nick and Faust exchanged glances. Nick leaned toward Cueball. "Let's you and me talk like it is. I got to tell you, bra, that you are behind the eight ball on this one, my man. I am happy to tell you that I like you a lot."

"Yeah, ya see? *Everybody* likes me." Cueball puffed up.

"Jesus! You're dumber than your fucking nickname! I like you a *lot,* alright. *As a prime suspect in a murder I'm investigating.* You also need to know that I don't like pimps. I especially don't like whiney pimps. In fact, I *hate* them. And you, you sorry fuck, are a two-time loser with me. You're a whiner and you're a pimp!"

"Now, I'm gonna assume that you're gonna talk to me like a man, instead of a pimp, and we're gonna take it slow so you can follow along. Ready? This is a photo." Nick shoved the picture of Collette in front of him. "Paw the ground once with your foot if you recognize the chick in it, twice if you don't. Got it?"

"Aw, man, whut you talkin'?" Cueball whined. "You dis'n me, but you expect me to help you?"

"Naw, bra. I don't expect you to help me. I expect you to save your worthless ass by giving me what I need."

"I'm tellin' ya. I ain't got nuttin' to do wit' no murder."

"*Super*. Then you won't mind doing your civic duty and assisting the *po*-lice with solving a murder." Nick put Collette's photo in front of Cueball again. Cueball was silent for a few minutes, obviously trying to put a story together.

"Yeah, well, I seen her around some. On the streets. You know. Dey all alook alike."

"On the streets? Is that the best you can do? You're jackin' us. You know that's not a nice thing to do with your friendly local officer who patrols your district every day." Nick was starting to lose control, thinking about Cueball's reference to the young girls who were living on the streets, thanks to assholes like him. "How about in your apartment? Maybe you were kind enough to let her stay with you for a while?"

"Man, I don't remember," Cueball whined.

"Yeah, well, I guess you got so many women coming and going it's real hard to remember any *one* of them, right? Women are just kind of a fungible commodity to you, is that it?" Nick was boiling.

"Say whaaa? Whut dat mean?" Cueball sensed the intensity in Nick, but unfortunately chose to stall again.

"Don't strain that marble you got for a brain. Your landlady puts you and this girl together in her boarding house. You know, you already got one manslaughter conviction for stabbing some poor bastard that tried to climb up on top of one your dog-eared hookers for sloppy seconds without paying extra. This ain't gonna be no manslaughter rap where you walk out in a couple of years. A nice little conviction for second degree murder is life in Angola without parole, my man. You'll need to pack a few tubes of K-Y Jelly to accommodate the big boys up there. They do like pimps."

Cueball started to show some agitation.

"In addition, it would be just terrible if someone dropped a nickel to the other inmates and told them that you raped and killed a child. Even a scag like you knows what that would mean. Some shiv up your ass or in your heart while you're in the showers. Wouldn't hurt much though, and you'd probably never know it was coming."

Cueball was sweating profusely.

"Yeah, bra. Yer nickname at Angola would be 'mattress-mouth.' That huge mouth of yours would become a landing place for guided muscles." Nick and Faust laughed.

"OK. So the bitch stayed wit' me for a while. She was jus' some little ho' that I met at the bus station. She came to town lookin' to make money, an' I tol' her I'd help her. You tellin' me the bitch is daid? I ain't seen her in weeks. I sho' as shit ain't *kilt* her!" Cueball's shirt was drenched.

"Cueball, Cueball, Cueball. Can't you just picture yourself taking two of your brothers on at a time? You know, those huge dicks like you see in the porn movies? Maybe some of your whores can teach you the technique before you go." Nick knew he had touched on a fear deep inside Cueball.

"C'mon, man," Cueball whined at a higher pitch. "I ain't seen the bitch. She went out one day and fuckin' never came back. I figgered she hooked up wit' some other businessman, or she fuckin' left town. I never seen the bitch after that. Know whut I'm sayin?"

"So what *are* you saying, cocksucker? Or should I say, soon-to-be-cocksucker? You put her on a john? She never came back? That's bullshit! Pimps don't ever let their ho's out of sight! That's supposed to be your *job*. Protection! You tellin' me you ain't no good at what you do? Bullshit!" Nick was beginning to realize he'd have to put a little physical pressure on this dumb fuck.

"Naw, man. She was on probation for prostitution, know whut um sayin? She was told by this li'l dude that she had to meet him, you know? She went to the probation office like she was supposed to, and this little dude tol' her to meet him a couple nights later, you know?" Cueball was almost crying.

"Well, I gotta tell ya, Cueball. That's a new one on me." Nick slapped Cueball hard on the left cheek. He raised his hand to slap Cueball on the other cheek and Cueball put up his hand for protection.

"Bra! I swear on my kids, dat's da trut'"

"You swear on your *kids*? The kids you won't pay child support for? That's pretty funny. *What* little dude? Who are you talking about?" Nick was still poised to strike.

"The fuckin' probation officer, man! Dis bitch...." Cueball didn't get to finish before Nick kicked his chair over, dumping Cueball on the floor.

"*Collette*. God damn it! *Not* 'dis bitch', you fuckin' *dildo*. Jesus *Christ*. The best part of you musta dripped down your old man's leg."

"She ain' never *tol'* me her fuckin' name, bra. I don' never ask. Bad for business. It don't make no difference, anyway. Long as she got all three holes. It don' make no difference." Cueball cuddled up in a ball, waiting for the kicks to come.

Nick heard the noise before he realized anything was happening. Faust, who had been sitting next to him throughout, had jumped up, pulled Cueball up off the floor, and thrown him up against the wall, holding him almost a foot off the ground. There was no sound. Mike said nothing. He just held him there for almost a minute, then let go. Cueball dropped like a lead balloon and crumpled back onto the floor.

"What'cha do *that* for? You tol' me to tell it like it is, now ya don' wanna hear it?" Cueball whined.

Faust started for Cueball again, but Nick put his hand on Mike's shoulder. He stopped. Nick could feel that he was trembling. Nick shook his head slowly from side to side and Mike sat back down.

Nick looked over at Cueball, still on the floor. "Crawl back to the chair." Cueball did as he was told. "*Now*. Tell us again. Collette. Say her name, goddamn it! Collette." Nick was determined to give her some dignity. Christ knows she never had any in her life.

"Collette," Cueball said.

"Good boy. Now tell us again about where Collette went," Nick said.

"She tol' me she was gonna see her probation officer. She had to meet him at a bar in the Quarters. It was at night. About eight o'clock. I dropped her off at the bar and waited 'til she went inside. I ain't never saw her agin'."

Nick stood up as if to leave. "You might as well book him in and let the system have him. This hairball is still jackin' us. Next he's gonna be tellin' us the probation officer was looking for a piece of ass. I'm through! Meet me for a beer when you're finished with him."

"Wait, bra! Wait! Dat's da trut'! She had dis probation officer. He was inta like… *strange* shit! She…"

"*Collette,*" Nick reminded Cueball menacingly.

"Yeah, yeah. Collette. She was *afraid* a' dis dude. She seen him at his office when she was supposed ta, and he tol' her ta meet him at dis bar a couple nights later. She said he was talkin' stuff she didn't understand. Shit like 'original sin' and how all women were natural sluts when they were born and needed to be punished. Shit like dat. She was afraid of him. She didn' wanna go, but he tol' her if she didn't, he'd yank her probation."

Nick had sat down again and was listening intently. He was beginning to believe Cueball, and didn't like where this was going.

"So where did she go to meet him?" Nick asked.

"I tol' ya. Some place in da Quarters. One a' dem gay joints, got a stupid name. Dey call it da 'Slip It Inn.'"

Nick knew the place. It was on Dumaine Street. Rough joint. Combination of bikers, fags and anything else looking for trouble. The gays that hung out there were the rough type.

"When was this?" Nick asked. He was thinking about what Cueball had said about Collette's probation officer. That was Jeremy Claiborne. Strange. Why would Claiborne have Collette meet him at a bar? As for that shit about women being sluts, that fit in pretty well with Claiborne's attitude when Nick had visited him a few days earlier. It was pretty obvious the little creep didn't like women. Nick knew he had a piece of the puzzle; he just didn't know where or why it fit in.

"Man, I don' keep no calendar. It's been a few weeks. I don' know." Cueball was looking relieved.

*A few weeks. Back in January,* Nick was thinking. What was it Jeremy Claiborne had said? She had been in for an interview on January 15. She was due for another report on February 15. *Interesting,* Nick thought.

"Let's see, *bra*. Since your memory is getting so good now, tell me if you recognize this." Nick put the photo of Collette's arm in front of the pimp.

Cueball paled and looked away. "Gawd, whut *dat* is? Whut you show me *dat* for?"

"That, my man, is all that is known to be left of Collette. Take a good look. Do you recognize that tattoo?"

Cueball looked again and quickly looked away. "Naw, she ain' had *nuttin* like dat! She ain' had no tattoos, not *nowhere*. An' believe me, I seen it *all*. Nuttin' like dat. You musta got the wrong ho."

"You telling us that Collette didn't have this tattoo?"

"Naw, man. I'm tellin' ya. Da bitch... Collette... she didn' have *no* tattoos *anywhere*. Man, she had perfect white skin, not a mark. Da johns loved her." Cueball winced instinctively, waiting for the blows to come. "Ever time she was in my crib, she got right outta her clothes and stayed dat way 'til she went out agin. She ain't had *no* tattoos, nowhere!"

Nick and Mike got up and left the room.

"Whaddaya think?" Mike asked.

"*Smegma*." Nick said. "This asshole is snail vomit!"

Mike chuckled. "I meant whaddaya t'ink 'bout his story? I gotta say I t'ink dat bastid's tellin' da trut'. Whaddaya make 'a dat probation officer shit?"

"Her probation officer is Jeremy Claiborne. 'Nuff said."

Mike let out a low whistle. "No shit! *Dat* dude is pretty fuckin' strange. If it woin't fer his connections, dat l'il shit cudn't get a job at a jewelry store cleanin' da boid shit out da cuckoo clocks!"

"Yeah, I know. That's why I backed off him when I did. I need to go think this thing out." Nick filled Mike in on his interview with Jeremy Claiborne, including the fact that there was no tattoo mentioned in Jeremy's file on Collette.

"*Muth-a-roo*. Ya don' think da l'il bastid got somet'in' ta do wit' dis?"

"I don't know what I think right now, bro. I just know I got to do some thinking. It's kinda like I might be about to open Pandora's Box and find out that Pandora don't douche. Ya know?"

"Anyt'ing ya need, ya let me know," Mike said, as they walked back into the room with Cueball.

"Pay attention, motherfucker. Me, I wouldn't do this, poissonally," Mike said. "But Detective Saladino here, he says ta give ya a break! So I'm gonna put a "NAT" on dis fer now. I'm gonna write it up as 'necessary action taken', and let yer miserable ass go fer now. Yer ass better let me know where yer at every day a yer life, in case I need more info on dis case, ya got dat? Ya wanna change yer address, ya check wit' me foist! Now *beat* it."

Mike turned to Nick after Cueball left. "Let's go get us a col' one."

They headed for the Worm Hole, a seedy joint on Royal Street near Louisa, in the upper Ninth Ward. A favorite of longshoremen off the wharves a few blocks away, the draft beer there came in huge frosted mugs. Even the bottled beer had ice slush in it. Occasionally, when the proprietor was in the mood, there would be salted peanuts in the shell for patrons to snack on. By ten p.m. the floor would be covered with crunchy empty shells. The only other food the joint served was homemade hot sausage po' boys. The sausage as it came from the kitchen would burn like hell when you ate it, and just as bad when you took a dump the next day. Some of the longshoremen liked to tell the owner to "turn the temperature up a few degrees," meaning to add more red pepper to it.

"Man, I'm hungry." Mike was sloshing down his first draft. "Wanna split a hot sausage?"

Nick had just about finished his first beer in two long slugs. "Naw. That stuff will tear up your insides."

"So what's da deal wit' you and yer ol' lady? I hoid y'all split," Mike asked. "I'm sorry ta hear dat."

Nick shook his head. "Yeah, it's true. I feel bad for the kids, but I can't say I'm sorry it's over. We didn't have anything to say to each other any more, you know? It's just the right thing to do. There's something sinister about marriage. It's the strangest fucking thing. You take two people, they're getting along great. I mean, everything is great. You spend a lot of time talking to each other, you know? So you say 'This is great', and you put yourself into the institution of marriage. You know—ceremony and all. And so help me, I don't care if you've been an item for two weeks or ten years, the minute you sign that fuckin' piece of paper, it all goes to shit. Almost instantly, there are no more quiet conversations. You never have time to talk, even though you're together more than you ever have been before. Sex suddenly reverts back to what the Pilgrims thought was appropriate— strictly the missionary position, and then only on certain nights. Blow jobs are suddenly something performed by whores for money. *Fuck. You* go figure it."

"Shit, I've been married so long, I can't ever t'ink in those ways any more. I see some cute little split-tail on da street now, it reminds me I'm a grandpa... I t'ink some people are better suited for marriage den others, an' den some people make luckier choices. Me, I ain't got but a high school education, but it seems ta me dat people jus' react to what's put in front of 'em. Dey don' look no farther dan da end'a dere noses, ya know? I mean, some people are jus' lucky cuz da goil nex' door is poifect fer dem, jus' like some people know from da minute dey born what dey gonna do fer a livin' da rest 'a dere life. Dey da ones ya hate! Other people, dey gotta keep tryin' cuz dey too impatient ta wait fer da right one. Fer some, dey ain' never gonna be a 'right one'."

Nick sat back listening to Mike. Those were the kinds of concepts everyone with any experience in life knew and understood but that, unfortunately, few people drew upon in love and marriage.

"Yeah, you right. All I can say is that every time I got married, it seemed like the right thing to do at the time. For my first divorce and for this one, all I can say is it seemed like the right thing to do at the time. It ain't nothing more complicated than that to me. No hard feelings. But women don't feel that way. They make it into some huge complicated emotional deal. *Women*. You know? They're always bitchin' about how you gotta kiss a lot of frogs before you find a prince, right? But, *fuck*. There's some pretty nasty stuff walking around out there disguised as females. I guess when one comes along who seems to have decent values, a fine body, isn't bad looking and speaks English, you decide it might be a good idea to hold onto her. Unfortunately, that in no way is related to the idea of whether you're right for each other, if in fact there *is* any such thing."

"Me, I been lucky," Mike replied. "I fucked aroun' a coupl'a times, but I lost interest after a while. What really got me, I didn' have nuttin' ta say afta we finished humpin'. It was like, da moment ya shoot off, ya wish dey wud jus' get up and leave, wit'out havin' ta say nuttin' else. It was kinda like, 'wham, bam, don' let da door slam!' I know ya been dere, too."

Nick nodded.

"I'm'a tell ya, it seems ta me dat yer attracted ta someone 'cuz somet'in inside a ya knows dey can take care a yer needs. Den, afta ya been wit' dem fer a while, dem particular needs ain' botherin' ya no more. Dat's when other needs come to da top, ones ya didn' know ya had. An' ya get attracted to someone else becuz ya feel like dey can fill da *new* needs dat's botherin' ya right then, da ones dat ain' bein' satisfied by da one ya still wit'." Nick had never seen Mike so philosophical before. It was a new side to his friend.

"You're probably right about that. I know I've been through more then I can count. Some I try to remember, most I try to forget. I'm always amazed by the people who run around saying that the *worst* piece of ass they ever had was *wonderful*. Any asshole that says *that* ain't had much! Fuck! The worst I ever had was *horrible*. Enough to give you nightmares that you are about to do her again." Nick chuckled softly.

"I been dere, too," Mike agreed. They both laughed at the thought.

After a few more rounds, Mike headed for home. "If I can do anyt'ing fer ya, ya know where ta find me."

"Thanks, man, I know it," Nick replied. *"A.M.F."* It was one of their favorite sayings: "Adios, motherfucker."

# XV

Steve Chaisson picked up a stack of telephone messages from his secretary. It was Tuesday morning and he had a busy day ahead in court. It was motion day in Criminal District Court, and he was prepared to handle a number of different motions in two dozen different cases. His docket included motions to suppress evidence, statements, and identification procedures, along with a few miscellaneous issues.

As an Assistant D.A. in Orleans Parish, it wasn't unusual for Steve to try three and sometimes four jury trials in a week, and there were days when Steve tried two felony jury trials in the same day. Steve viewed that as a challenge: he'd pick the first jury and send them upstairs to the jury deliberation room to make their telephone calls and use the bathroom while he then picked the second jury. When the second jury was empaneled, they would be sent upstairs and the first jury would be brought down for opening statements in the first trial. When the first trial was finished right down to the rebuttal argument of the prosecution, the first jury would be charged by the judge and sent upstairs to deliberate while the second trial was conducted.

Steve would frequently find himself in the courtroom at eight a.m. picking a jury, conducting an entire trial, giving the case to the jury to decide, and having a verdict as late as midnight or two a.m., then returning to the court room at eight a.m. the following day to repeat the procedure in its entirety for whatever trial was scheduled for that day. He thrived on it, and his conviction record reflected that. He held an average conviction rate of 98%, of which he was justifiably proud.

Steve was skeptical about claims by prosecutors who bragged that they had never lost a case. Those were the prima donnas who picked and chose their cases carefully, and refused to try anything other than a "lock nut" case. *If you haven't lost a case, you haven't tried very many, and you certainly haven't tried any of the dogs lurking in the back of the drawers of the file cabinets in most prosecutors' offices,* Steve thought with scorn.

At the heart of Steve's success, in addition to strong preparation, was his ability to establish credibility with jurors. Many attorneys talk down to jurors, feeling that they don't understand what's going on. Those lawyers forget that, although jurors don't always have a lot of education or high I.Q.s, they have their life experiences and strong instincts about what they like and don't like, and many have more "street sense" than a lot of attorneys. Steve had developed the ability to make the jurors feel that he was talking with them as equals, and it was a talent to which the jurors usually responded favorably.

Steve flipped through his morning messages quickly. One was from Nick Saladino, one from Julie Landry, a couple from victims in cases he was preparing for trial, and a couple from witnesses calling to confirm the necessity of their appearance in court that day. He debated about calling Julie but thought better of it, since he was already late for court.

He was in front of Judge Randolph Hecker today. Hecker pouted whenever anyone was late for court and, rather than sounding the docket to determine which cases were ready and proceeding with those, Hecker would pick a case where he *knew* one of the attorneys was not present, have the first witness sworn and sitting on the stand while everyone in court was left sitting around playing with themselves, waiting on the attorney who had had the misfortune of being late that day. Steve stuffed the messages into his suit coat pocket and hustled across the street to court.

Approximately six hours later, he emerged from court, his business completed. He was already prepared for a trial to be held the following day, so he had the luxury of being able to take a long lunch and return phone calls. He had been looking forward to an oyster loaf all weekend. An eighteen-inch loaf of French bread laden with fried oysters, shredded lettuce, sliced tomatoes and mayonnaise, served up hot at Bozo's Restaurant (one hundred years in operation by the same family). When it arrived, he admired it like a work of art, then tuned it up with raw onions, hot pepper sauce and a little Creole mustard. Topped off with an ice-cold beer, it was one of the finest lunches in New Orleans. Afterward, Steve returned to the office, poured a cup of coffee, put his feet up on the desk, and started on his phone messages.

The first call Steve made was to Julie Landry. He knew this would be a long call. He was constantly amazed at her ability to have an orgasm at any time, in any environment; she could even produce one by mere suggestion. She was capable of virtually unlimited multiple orgasms, which was a great turn-on for Steve.

He dialed the phone, and by the time Julie came on, he had loosened his tie. "What's up, baby?" he asked.

"Well, it's about *time*." Julie sounded peeved. "I wish I had a nice government job like *yours*. It's been almost eight hours since I called."

"*Shit*, baby. You got a *better* job than mine. By far. At least, you make twice as much as this humble public servant. Or in your case, should I say, *pubic* servant?"

"I got tired of fucking around with some of these assholes I have to work with. I was looking to get out for lunch, but you were no goddam help."

Steve chuckled. Julie was always on a rampage about her job as an administrator in one of the city's large, expensive law firms. Her pet gripe was the group that had achieved senior partner status entirely on the basis of being scions of old-line, blue-blood New Orleans families. Most had never tried a case; many had never seen the inside of a court room. Their wives dressed them and packed them off to the office, confident that they would be safe and occupied for the day. She had to deal with squabbles about everything from the color and quality of the carpet in their offices, to the amount of expenses allocated to each on a monthly basis for entertaining clients. She even put up with occasional fumbling attempts at sexual innuendo or outright attempts to touch her ass, although usually those were clumsily disguised as missteps or accidents. She never felt threatened by them because they were so inept as to be laughable.

"So, was it me or was it the one-eyed wonder worm you wanted to see?" Steve knew Julie well enough to know that, had he taken her to lunch, she would have been dessert.

"*Bastard.* Is that *all* you think about?" Julie feigned indignation.

"*Whoa.* Kinda like looking in a mirror, isn't that?" Steve parried. "So you *were* thinking about it, weren't you? I was, too. I had this image during lunch of you naked on a po-boy sandwich."

There was silence on the other end for a few moments, then Julie's voice, low and throaty now. "Is that an invitation?"

"Abso-fucking-lutely." He could feel Julie's heat coming through the phone, and knew she was becoming passionate.

"Oh, shit! *Shit*. Somebody's knocking on the fucking *door*. Gotta go." Julie was gone.

It was a few minutes before Steve could get up and walk around. He got a drink of ice water from the cooler, then returned Nick Saladino's call.

# XVI

"Man, it's about time you returned my call. We need to *talk. Now*. Meet me at Izzy's." Nick sounded concerned, which was unusual for him. Steve had never heard that tone in his voice before.

Steve checked his watch. "Be there in an hour."

Nick hung up with no reply.

*Wow,* Steve thought. He finished up the paperwork generated by his day in court and headed for Izzy's. It was that nasty damp cold outside that only hundred-percent humidity and temperature in the thirties can produce.

Nick was still a little agitated. "What it *is*?" he greeted Steve.

Steve ordered a beer, making a mental note to pace his booze intake the rest of the day. He had a feeling it would be a long one.

"You got anything going tonight, cancel it. I think I'm about to get submerged in a whole pile of shit, and I'm not sure what to do with it."

"Man, I *told* you, I'm not getting involved in your fucking divorce. You got to get another lawyer."

"*Fuck* my fuckin' divorce. This is important. The Collette Prejean case is about to turn into a heater. Somebody from your office is gonna have to be involved from this point on, and you're the only one over there who knows what he's doing and can keep

# BLACK ORCHID

his fuckin' mouth shut. Besides, you're the homicide screener, and this fucker is gonna end up in your lap anyway."

"No problem, mon." Steve used the Jamaican pronunciation of the phrase. "Just another murder case."

"No fuckin' *way*, man. Let me tell you. You're about to find out this is anything but just another murder case. You better have the legal side of your brain with you—at least, what's left of it after all the booze you've sent through the little blood vessels in your gray matter. If anyone has practiced genocide of the brain cells, it's you." Nick smirked. "This thing is gonna be *your* baby eventually, so your ass better be involved now. If this doesn't go down right, my butt will be back walking a beat in the St. Mathias Projects."

The prospect of a "heater case" didn't bother Steve. There were no surprises to those involved in the criminal justice system in New Orleans. Just as areas of the city were built on swamp, causing the city to slowly sink, so was the respectability of some people simply a façade imposed upon a degenerate core of filth, violence, lust and/or greed. Those people eventually sink to their natural level, just as does the city in which they reside. Heater cases usually involved one or more of these elements, occasionally in a setting of politics, wealth, leadership or other quality which made them highly visible to the average citizen.

Steve had been involved in many "heaters," and savored them as a respite from the drone of the more mundane, everyday homicides, of which New Orleans, like most metropolitan areas, had a bountiful, apparently never-ending supply. Only the names changed.

"So what's the deal?" Nick had piqued Steve's curiosity.

Nick looked around and hunched forward, almost conspiratorially. "You remember the alligator case we talked about last week? With the tattooed arm?"

"Sure. Don't tell me you found Cueball? Is he a socialite or something?" Steve didn't see what was so serious about all that, unless Nick was concerned that a jury wouldn't find someone guilty where only a part of a body was available for identification. But that would hardly make the case a heater.

Steve had already tried a case where the defendant had eaten his roommate. The only parts left of the roommate were a few "soup bones' in the freezer. The coroner had testified that the bones were from a human male approximately the age of the roommate, and neighbors testified that the roommate had disappeared. The jury wasted no time convicting the little ghoul. As in most states, circumstantial evidence was acceptable evidence in Louisiana, as long as it met the test that it excluded every other reasonable hypothesis of innocence in order to convict.

"Yeah. Faust found that fuckin' hairbag. We rousted him a little. This is where it gets tricky. And this is where you come in. You gotta help me here. But when you do, you're gonna be mixed up with some of the strongest ruling factions in the city. If the District Attorney gets wind of you being involved in this, your ass might be out on the street instantly." Nick was still hunched forward.

Steve grew a little concerned. How could this case possibly be something of that magnitude, something that could be such a political hot potato?

Nick looked even more serious. "In addition to being a heater, I'm beginning to believe this may involve a serial killer, which is something no one else suspects right now. I'm telling you, this is *big*."

Steve began to sense some trepidation on Nick's part for the first time. What in the hell was he rambling about? "So tell me," he said, with somewhat less enthusiasm than normal.

"Yeah, Faust found the little pimp bastard. His story is that the chick went out one night to meet with her probation officer. He never saw her again."

It seemed a little unusual that she would meet her probation officer at night, but Steve had heard and seen stranger things. "So? Maybe her probation officer couldn't catch her at any other time."

"Naw. Pimp says she was going to his office to report on a monthly basis, and that she made all her interviews. Says last time she went to his office, he told her to meet him at the Slip It Inn, in the Quarter, at eight o'clock at night."

"So maybe he was planning to have her meet some undercover people and pull off some kind of sting?" Steve guessed.

"I thought of that. But there's another piece of the puzzle you need to know. Her probation officer is *Jeremy Claiborne*." Nick had lowered his voice, and looked around for eavesdroppers.

"Jeremy *Claiborne*? Shit." Steve felt a number of warning lights coming on in his brain.

Nick continued, "The pimp said the broad was *afraid* of her probation officer. That, last time she reported in, he was spouting some kinda shit about all women being sluts, that they needed to be punished. Shit like that."

Steve was silent. He knew Jeremy well. The man was decidedly different. Steve had always thought of him as fanatical about some things. He had used Jeremy on the witness stand on occasion, during hearings on rules to revoke probation when some witless asshole had not lived up to the terms of his or her probation. It was his impression that Jeremy didn't devote his full abilities to his job; he wasn't always properly prepared in court. He had considered the possibility that Jeremy was at least a cross-dresser, possibly a full-fledged fag. His mannerisms were definitely effeminate, definitely pedantic. He even had some strange feelings that Jeremy was sociopathic.

Steve thought of Jeremy's father, known by most of the criminal justice system to be the reason that Jeremy held his position as a probation officer. Thomas Claiborne had an aristocratic and arrogant bearing, pompous at times. He had a well-earned reputation for contributing to the consumption of antacids by members of the bar who were unfortunate enough to practice in his division of federal court. Steve, as a state prosecutor, had never had the opportunity to find out first-hand, though.

Jeremy's sister, Charysse, the criminal court judge, had always treated Steve fairly whenever he had business in her court, but he was never able to turn the conversation into a social one. And he had tried on several occasions. Charysse was a looker, and the black robe did little to hide the fact that she sported an hour-glass figure. He could picture her on her knees, those blue eyes framed by that black hair, administering a blow job. A textbook example of perfect aesthetics.

"*Whoa*, cocksucker. If you're trying to take me in the direction of thinking that Claiborne's involved in Collette Prejean's death, we *both* need a stronger drink." Steve ordered a double Crown on the rocks for both of them. "And I'll require a few more of these if you want to talk about serial killings in the same breath.

"*Christ.* If I understand you, you're talking about investigating the son of a senior federal judge, who is also the brother of a criminal court judge before whom I have to appear at least once a week, and someone who is himself a state probation officer? *Fuck.* Why don't we go after the *governor* while we're at it?" Steve took a large sip from his drink. "Plus which, these people are politically aligned with my *boss.* Anything *else* you want to throw in? *Christ.*"

Nick silently enjoyed the effect that his revelations were having on Steve. "Naw, the U.S. Attorney already tried to get the governor. That's *old* shit."

"Claiborne couldn't be *that* stupid. To kill someone who is assigned to him to monitor probation? Is that what you're suggesting? He would know that the police were going to interview him," Steve pondered aloud.

"And I did. And his demeanor was consistent with what the pimp told me. He's got a definite attitude about hookers. Thinks the judges are too lenient with them." The possibilities for such a murder were beginning to sink in on Nick. "Besides, what if the killer is sure that the body would never be *found*? After she's dead, he files a rule to revoke her probation on the grounds that she violated her probation by failing to report in as required. The judge grants the rule and issues an attachment for her. She's never found, and the case officially works its way to the back of the files and is forgotten.

"What could be more perfect? Hookers come and go in the night and leave no trace of themselves, other than an occasional disease for their johns to remember them by. They don't have IRA's, don't contribute to social security, and don't own property. They're disposable, expendable, and in most cases, impossible to identify or trace. No one knows that they're dead until the body has the poor taste to turn up somewhere. Nobody misses them. No body, no murder. No murder, no suspect. Some of these fuckin' killers make it a point to put their handiwork on display, but there are others who devote a great deal of time and effort to make sure that *no one* ever sees their victims. And, looking at this case, what could be a better disposal unit than a fuckin' alligator?"

"Jesus, Mary and fucking Joseph. You're *serious*." Steve shot down the rest of his drink, and ordered another round for both of them. He looked at Nick, his mouth open. "Do you think..."

"Yes." Nick was somber. "Yes, I had the same thought. If this one, why not others? My gut is telling me there are others."

Steve was beginning to understand the agitation in Nick's voice on the phone. He needed time to think about this. They quietly sipped on their drinks.

"Let's get together tomorrow, my office. Ten o'clock," he proposed.

"You got it, bro. Ten o'clock. *Arrivedouche*." Nick got up and left.

# XVII

The next morning, Nick arrived at Steve's office at the scheduled hour. There were no signs of a hangover, no alcohol on his breath. He was actually buoyant that morning. Steve left orders with his secretary that he was taking no calls. He took the coffee pot into his office and closed the door with Nick.

He motioned Nick to silence and took a small electrical meter out of his desk. Nick recognized the probe and waited while Steve checked the office for bugs. "Can't be too careful around here," he said, when the check turned up negative. "I have to do this now and then for my own peace of mind.

"OK, let's start over. You got a dead hooker. We know that. You got her pimp says he didn't do it. Says the last time he saw her, she was going to meet her probation officer at a hard-core gay bar at a weird time. She says she's afraid of the probation officer because he hates women. And that's all you got. Right?"

"A little more." Nick had brought his file and showed Steve the photos.

"*Ick*. I hate gory crap, but it's *great* for making the jurors puke. This tattoo thing is pretty ugly. You've tried to trace it, I assume?"

"Yeah, I've run it by over half of the tattoo parlors in the city, and nobody places her or the tattoo. I've gotta finish running the rest of them. One thing I forgot to tell you. When I went to see Jeremy, he said she didn't have any tattoos last time he saw her. I checked his file, and there was no record of a tattoo."

"*Wow*. So if that's true, the tattoo is fairly fresh. Somebody oughta remember it. I wonder what it's supposed to represent."

"Already got that pinned down, my boy." Nick was smug. "I went to LSU and showed it to a flower doctor. He makes it out as an orchid. Calls it the *Black Orchid*. He came up with one of those long names, Latin. I got it written down. Here's a photo of it." Nick handed Steve the color copy made at LSU.

Steve studied it and compared it with the arm photo. "Looks like it to me. Black orchid, huh? Sounds kind of *sinister*." Steve passed it back to Nick. "So we like Jeremy for the murder? He's got an attitude towards hookers, and the pimp places him as possibly the last person to see her alive. If she actually kept the appointment. She might have used that as an excuse to shake off your pimp, though."

"I just got a feeling that's not what happened. The more I think about Claiborne and the way he reacted when I interviewed him about Collette Prejean, the more I think that he's involved, at least in some manner. I can taste it."

"I'm sure Jeremy would be pleased if you would taste it." Steve ducked as Nick picked up the criminal code book from the desk and threw it at him. "So how do we go about proving Jeremy's guilty? Unfortunately, that's still required by our system. We'll never have more of Collette's body parts than we do now. We don't have any witnesses who actually put the two together. All we've got is a supposed meeting and Jeremy acting hostile towards women, observed by you, and the hearsay that Collette reported to her pimp. Now, *there's* a source of veracity, if ever there was one."

Nick was at a loss for a starting point. "I think I'll go to the Slip It Inn tonight and nose around a little. Maybe somebody can at least put Jeremy *in* the place. In the meantime, I'll finish running down the tattoo parlors." He dug out the list of the parlors he hadn't yet visited.

"Oh, yeah, like you're not going to stand out as a cop in *that* bar. Sure," Steve noted with sarcasm. "What about the idea that this may *not* be an isolated killing? If we've got a serial killer on our hands, there'll likely be more alligator food in the future, and we're not going to be as lucky when it comes to finding their bodies. I don't think anyone has tried testing alligator DNA to see if it contains any DNA from their human meals." He was half-serious. "Worse yet—if in fact this is a serial killer at work, what do we do with the *press*? Those assholes would be all over this like flies. Public panic. The District Attorney up my ass. Multiply that by a hundred if it involves a well-connected family like the Claibornes." The possibilities were stunning to Steve. "*Christ.* I'm not eligible for retirement for *years.*"

Nick looked at Steve with a calming smile. "I think I can get a start on that. I used to ball a little chick in probation. She's on the clerical staff over there. Maybe if I let her get lucky again, she'll provide a copy of Jeremy's case load."

"Gee, to think you would sacrifice the sanctity of your body in the line of duty like that. Brings tears to my eyes." Steve snickered. "Just keep me up on what's happening, in case you get sideways or something. And for now, I don't know nuthin' about what you're doing. You're by yourself out there."

# XVIII

Nick tried a few more tattoo parlors after leaving the D.A.'s office. No luck. He had two left to check out, but decided to save those for tomorrow. It was late afternoon and he planned to swing by the Slip It Inn later to scope out the action, talk to the bartenders, but that wouldn't be until at least ten p.m. He returned to the office, thinking about his conversation with Steve that morning. The black orchid was still eating at him. He felt that he hadn't really accomplished much. Knowing *what* the tattoo was still didn't tell him *if*, or *how*, it fit into Collette's murder.

There was a note to call Sharon on his desk. She sounded almost perky when she answered. *At least she's in a good mood for once*, he thought.

"The kids have been asking about you." Terse.

*Not even a "How are you?"* he thought.

"I'm having my lawyer work out a schedule for you to see them once a month. If that works out without a problem, it'll be increased to provide more frequent visits. The lawyer will call you. In the meantime, you need to send money for the kids. Their school expenses are eating me up!"

"Wonderful," Nick replied sarcastically. "How are y'all making out otherwise?" Too late. The phone was already dead.

By a little after ten p.m, Nick was in the Devil's Den with a nice slow buzz on, talking to a succulent little morsel from South

Carolina who was in town to celebrate her divorce. She was all peaches and cream, the kind you'd give your credit card to if she asked. Well, at least your Exxon or J.C. Penney card. She was talking trash about her life in Charleston, but Nick had tuned out. He had become preoccupied with the Prejean case again, anticipating his visit to the Slip It Inn. He took one last look at her and headed for the door, leaving her still talking about her divorce.

The Slip It Inn was located in the murky part of the Quarter, back on Dumaine Street. It had the dingy facade that the Vieux Carre Commission insisted that *all* Quarter buildings maintain, and the interior matched the exterior. It was dark and dank. As Nick entered, he was able to make out human shapes at the bar, and could tell that there were booths lining the wall to his right. To the left there was a small dance floor, with one couple, both males, moving slowly together, as if they were one human being. The place had been built originally as a bar, and had one of those huge wood back bars, filled in with a mirror that had to be ten-feet by fifteen-feet. Most of the silver backing of the mirror had long ago been eaten out in patches, and now looked as if it had never been cleaned. It gave an eerie, surreal effect to the few reflections that managed to fight their way to the top to be seen.

Nick groped his way to the bar and ordered a Crown on the rocks. The bartender was tall and gaunt with a dew rag tied around his head. He looked at Nick with a sneer.

"Not too many cops come in here."

"Off duty," Nick said. The bartender moved off to the other end of the bar. Nick leaned on his end and let his eyes finish adjusting. Details of the place slowly came into focus. He noted that there were about a dozen people in the place, all male. He caught occasional pieces of conversation from those nearest him.

It was no surprise that many of the voices were in the affected style of voice inflections that many gay males adopt. On the wall near the dance floor were a number of faded, cheaply framed photographs. A few dilapidated trophies were on the shelves. Nick was too far away to make out any detail.

There were a few tall tables scattered around, with some unusual stools. A few of the stools had motorcycle seats on top, one had a western saddle, one an English saddle, and a few had human faces on them. Sitting on the back bar were carved dicks in various sizes and colors, mingled among the liquor bottles.

No one paid any attention to Nick, despite the fact that he was the only one there in a suit.

He ordered another Crown and meandered around the place, looking at the decorations and photographs. When he got to the newest one, his heart stopped momentarily.

"Holy fucking shit," he said slowly and softly to himself.

Staring out of the cheaply framed photograph was the masker he had seen on the Fruit Stand on Mardi Gras Day. The same masker that he thought had stared at him in a sort of malevolent recognition. He realized that he had totally forgotten his original thought to try to follow up and determine the identity of that masker.

Nick continued to stare at the photograph. The masker's eyes seemed to jump out at him, just like they did at Mardi Gras. *Something... something about those eyes*, he thought. His attention was drawn from the masker's eyes to his costume. There was that design in the material Nick had noticed on Mardi Gras Day. He stared for a few more moments and returned to the bar for a fresh Crown.

He had decided not to ask about Jeremy Claiborne that night. He knew any inquiries would get back to Claiborne faster than Western Union, and he definitely didn't want the little bastard on the alert. He decided to build a presence in the joint before asking questions, but the urge to ask about the photo on the wall was chafing to be satisfied. Nick sucked it in. He was close to something. His senses were tingling.

*Fuck. I can smell it, it's intense, and it won't leave me alone. Kinda like the spray of a goddam male cat.* His brain wrestled with it, and he could occasionally almost catch a fuzzy picture of where his brain was going, but it quickly dissolved, leaving him no closer to whatever was trying to surface in his mind. It was like the old principle in Eastern religions, about how the more you try to find something, the more it will elude you. You just have to lay back and let it sneak up on you. Like all those women who try so hard to get pregnant and can't. Then they go and adopt a kid, and *wham,* they're pregnant. Once the pressure's off, your body does what's natural.

*Easier fuckin' said than done,* he thought. He knew he had to let it go for a while, but every time he hit the reject button in his mind, the same goddam thought would creep right back in to haunt him.

Nick had decided to stop in to the joint over the next few days. Maybe Jeremy Claiborne would happen to be in some time. He finished his drink and left, driving straight to the boathouse. He was elated that he would be able to see his kids. He hoped Sharon's lawyer would call soon.

By the third night of stopping at the Slip It Inn, Nick was on more or less friendly terms with Tony, the bartender. He seemed to accept Nick's apparently benign presence. It wasn't unusual to have off-duty cops in bars in the Quarter. Bartenders in the area were generally sophisticated in terms of unusual clientele.

Nick finally couldn't stand it anymore. "Man, I've been trying to place who that is in the photo on the wall over there. I know him from somewhere," Nick ventured, indicating the photo of the masker.

Tony glanced up. "Oh, that's Noogie. He owns the joint."

"Looks like he won first place at the Fruit Stand."

"Yeah. He likes all that shit. Spends a fortune on his outfit every year. Got some little Creole in the ninth ward that sews it up for him, but he designs it himself."

"No shit?"

"Yeah," Tony continued. "He won a trip to Hawaii this time for himself and one other. In fact, that's where he is right now."

"Tough duty. I'd swear I know him from somewhere. What's his real name?"

"I don't really know, but I think I heard somebody call him Jeremy, or something like that."

Nick almost sprayed Tony with the Crown he had just sipped.

"Ho-ly fuck-ing *shit.*" *That's it. That's fucking it. No wonder those black eyes looked familiar Mardi Gras Day. Fucking-A. Jeremy goddam Claiborne. Jesus Christ.* Nick almost couldn't conceal his elation at finally solving the puzzle.

He was almost shaking, and had to force himself to slowly sip the rest of his Crown before asking Tony anything else. He had managed to get that much without putting Tony on the defensive. At least, he hoped that was the case.

# XIX

Nick spent the entire weekend drinking in the Quarter. He couldn't sleep. Fortunately, there was no limit to the number of joints that stayed open twenty-four hours, seven days.

Monday morning found him standing with his back against the wall outside of Reba's, a local hangout on Toulouse Street. He was asleep on his feet, a broken glass on the sidewalk near him. It was starting to rain, and the cold drops on his face revived him. He had no idea where he had left the Crown Vic, and he called Steve to pick him up.

As Steve rolled up to the curb, his right front wheel plopped into one of New Orleans' finest potholes, drenching Nick as he ran for the car. The dirty water only further emphasized Nick's bedraggled appearance.

"Jeez, you smell like *booze*." Steve recoiled at the smell oozing out of Nick's pores.

"*Fuck* you. While you're busy getting laid, *I'm* doing my job. *I'm* an investigator. *You're* a mother fucker." Nick was dour.

"Yeah, well, I guess you got me right that time. I have been known to dabble in a few mothers," Steve chuckled.

"You mean *dribble*, you bastard. Now help me find my car. Then we'll get some coffee and I'll tell you the latest. You'll be proud of me, my man." Nick started to get his bearings again.

Steve drove around the Quarter. They found Nick's car parked in a no parking zone on Decatur, not far from the Devil's Den, with a bright orange parking ticket under the wiper.

"Fuckin' meter maids." Nick ripped the ticket off the windshield. "Meet me at Matanza's. I'm gonna get a quick shower and change clothes."

Steve contemplated his coffee while Nick told him about the Slip It Inn like he was a kid with a new toy.

"So you can link Jeremy Claiborne with the joint. That's interesting. Tends to give a little credence to what your pimp was telling you."

"Is that *all* you can fucking say? *'That's interesting?'* This is fuckin' *dynamite*. This is *hot. I'm* hot. Jesus Christ. It's *Claiborne*. He's a flamin' fag. He *hates* women." Nick was wound.

"Uh-uh," Steve responded.

"Whaddaya mean, uh-uh?"

"It's lawyer talk. It means *no*. No, I don't see. You don't have anything new here. You don't have anything that puts Claiborne with the broad. Your pimp already told you Jeremy told the broad to meet him at that place. All you did was confirm some connection between Jeremy and the joint. You got a part of a puzzle, but you don't got enough of the puzzle to even show it's the right puzzle for this murder. Nice work, though."

Nick refused to let his spirits be dampened. "I'm gonna *get* the little bastard. Watch me."

After a few hot coffees, Nick began to feel human again. He called Nancy Hoffman at probation.

"Well, long time no screw." Her voice dripped sarcasm.

"Sorry 'bout that! How 'bout lunch? Meet me at Matanza's, in the Quarter. 11:30." He hung up. He knew she'd be there, out of curiosity, if nothing else. They had had a torrid relationship for about a year. She knew he was married, and she didn't expect the relationship to be anything other than what it was. Sex. Nick had eventually drifted off when he got interested in a new playmate.

Nick stood up when Nancy entered and gave her a perfunctory kiss on the cheek. She was her usual perky self. Short hair, nondescript style. That was one thing Nick had always disliked about her. It was a boyish haircut, but her body was anything but boyish. She had had a breast reduction at age twenty-one, and still couldn't get close to the table. She purposely hid her feminine charms due to her line of work. She didn't need to attract the clients in her office. Nick remembered those huge tits staring up at him. But she was a screamer, and to him that was a serious turn-off. He remembered one night in particular in her apartment when he was sure the neighbors were going to knock on the door.

"So what's up, Nick? Why so mysterious?"

"I need some help..."

"You've always needed help. I'm glad you finally decided to do something about it," Nancy chortled.

"That's *not* what I fucking mean. Might be true, but it's not what I'm talking about. I need your help in getting some records for me. Quietly."

"Ooh, I'm *needed* now. First time you've ever told me *that*." She looked skeptical.

"Listen, Nancy. I'm serious. I've got an issue going down right now, and I need a list of cases assigned to one of your probation officers. But it's got to be on the *Q.T.*, otherwise it will blow my investigation all to hell".

"*Great.* I don't hear from you for a year, then you pop up one day and want me to risk my job? And who's gonna support me if that happens?" Nancy was serious.

"Listen, baby. No one will ever know where the information came from. The only other way I can get this shit is publicly, and that would set off the next world war, at least as far as this city is concerned." Nick was trying to hold most of his cards for now. "I can't let that happen. If it does, some really scary people will go unpunished for some pretty disgusting murders."

"Not my fucking problem," Nancy replied. "You've obviously mistaken me for someone who really gives a shit. Murders are a dime a fucking dozen in this town, in case you haven't noticed."

"Not like this." He told Nancy some basics about the case.

"I heard a little bit about the alligator thing. I don't see how I can find any information that relates to that."

"Leave that to me. You'll understand if I'm successful in putting this together."

"I'll think about it. What are you offering?"

Nick grinned and stared at her breasts.

"You gotta be kidding!" Nancy feigned indignation. "Well, maybe. Who's the probation officer?"

Nick looked around, then leaned over, and whispered in her ear. "Jeremy Claiborne."

Nancy paled. "You *are* fucking in need of help. Are you *nuts*? Do you have any fucking idea what connections that little piece of shit has in this town? Are you nuts? No fucking *way*. Not even for *you*." She started to get up.

Nick grabbed her arm. "Sit down. Pay attention. There's gonna be a pop quiz! I think Claiborne has been killing hookers assigned to his case load. I think he's responsible for the murder of the hooker whose arm was found. If that's true, he may be a serial killer, and he'll keep going. I need that information. Nobody will be able to trace it to you." Nick rubbed his knee slowly against Nancy's.

"Let me tell you, it wouldn't break my heart any if Claiborne was put away somewhere. He makes my skin crawl when he looks at me. There is nothing good inside those eyes. Let me think about it. I'm afraid of that skank!" Nancy was visibly shaken. "Maybe I can get you a computer print-out... no. Come to think of it, I can't. It'll only generate the office's entire case load, without a breakdown by officer. The only way I can do it is to copy Claiborne's own files, unless he keeps his own list. But I've never seen anything like that in his office. The probation office is still in the dark ages when it comes to automation."

"What about when a case is closed? Where does the file go?"

"We've got a record room where those are kept. When a case is closed for five years, it goes to the warehouse. No way to find it then. Our records are pitiful when it comes to tracking old cases. In the record room, you're talking about thousands of files, only some of which would be Claiborne's. The officers keep their active files in cabinets in their offices," Nancy explained. "Jesus Christ! You really suspect he's involved in something like that? Gives me chills!"

Nick pressed on. "So how would I know what cases he's had which are no longer active?"

"Let's see... I can't think of a way... wait! If you're only interested in hookers, it seems to me we might be able to do it. In fact, it might be possible to use the master computer list for the entire office. It specifies the defendant's name, date of conviction, the offense they were convicted of, and dates that the probation was begun and terminated. With that list, you can pick out the hookers, then go to the closed files to see which probation officer handled the case. What time period are you talking about?"

"I have no idea. How long has Claiborne been a probation officer?" Nick asked.

"I'd say about five years."

"Then we're talking about five years."

"Let me play with it. I'll call you tomorrow after I've had a chance to try it and see if it's a workable system for getting that information."

"Remember, you've got to keep it quiet," Nick reminded her.

"You think I don't know that? I'm scared shitless of even thinking about doing this. I would be terrified if that little maggot found out I was involved."

Nancy left, but not before she had exacted a promise from Nick. "I still live in the same apartment. You got to pay."

"Pleasure," Nick grinned, watching her sashay out. "I can do that."

"You coming out the closet, Nick? Hanging in gay joints?" Clyde Sherman, the assessor for the first district, which includes the French Quarter, had been around for a long time. He knew where a lot of political skeletons were buried, and, no doubt, also had buried some of his own. He also knew where some of the *fresh* political skeletons were hanging out to dry, a talent that inevitably assured his continued re-election as assessor.

Nick had stopped by City Hall to check the tax rolls in an effort to determine who or what really owned the building where the Slip It Inn was located. Tony the bartender was no doubt correct about Jeremy being the owner, but Nick needed proof in some form other than hearsay, which, of course, was not admissible in court. Nick was always meticulous in putting a case together.

Clyde had been the assessor so long that he knew virtually every piece of property in his jurisdiction, and its owner. Of course, each piece of property in the Quarter was distinctive, unlike a modern subdivision, and most had a history. Many of the properties in the Quarter had been in the same family for generations.

"Cute. *Real* cute," Nick growled. He knew that anything he told Clyde might not remain their secret; he also knew that Clyde wouldn't hesitate to divulge a confidence if he thought it might gain him a favor somewhere. For that reason, Nick had to handle the conversation carefully.

"What could a homicide detective possibly want with a joint like that?" Clyde arched his eyebrows and lowered his head to look at Nick over the tops of his mini-sized reading glasses. "I don't recall hearing about any murders there."

Nick hedged. "There have been a few in the area. I've decided to try to check out all the bars in the back part of the Quarter, just to see what's hanging out back there."

Clyde led Nick by the arm into his office, closing the door behind them.

"One of the bad things about City Hall is that you can't trust anybody, even those that you brought in as patronage. People around here find out you're asking about a political family, it's like that fucking commercial for that stock broker. You know the one? Where it says: 'when they speak, everyone listens.' Then they show everybody on the planet stopping what they're doing and leaning forward to hear..." Clyde said, almost in a whisper.

Nick nodded automatically, his thoughts racing to recall what he had said. "I didn't mention any political family."

Clyde laughed softly, removing a well-chewed stogie from his lips.

"Fucking modern ideas. Can't even smoke a cigar in the building nowadays. Goddam pansies around here claim they get cancer from second-hand smoke, whatever that is."

Clyde went on. "Nick, my man. All these old biddies in this office know as much as I do about who owns what property, especially in the Quarter. You mention any particular property, and they instantly know who you're talking about. Especially when a cop comes up here looking for information. Double that when it's a homicide cop."

"Good point," Nick agreed. He was still playing dumb. "But why are you talking about a political family?"

Clyde sighed. "You telling me you don't know who owns that dump? C'mon. You know more than you're telling. You gonna level with me?"

Nick decided to cut a little slack. He could still look innocent about it. "I heard it belongs to one of the Claibornes. Jeremy, I think his name is."

Clyde snorted. "Well, you're partially correct. It's a Claiborne, all right. But it's Thomas, not his dumb kid Jeremy who owns that building."

Nick had experienced a number of surprises in this case, each requiring him to stifle his reaction. This was no exception.

"*Judge* Thomas Claiborne?" he asked.

"None other. That upstanding bastard, I mean *bastion,* of respectability." Clyde was derisive. "Wait here while I pull the records."

Nick got up and looked out the plate glass window at the plaza below. City Hall was an unattractive, 1950s modern steel and glass building with that kind of ugly green façade that was popular then. It had about as much personality and presence as a shoebox, which is particularly sad when you thought about what could have been done to represent a city as culturally rich as New Orleans. Some idiot had even sculpted the plaza next to City Hall with hills. The only fucking hills in south Louisiana! As a crowning *piece de resistance*, apparently the same idiot had filled in the fountains in the plaza with monkey grass. Absolutely *nothing* in the plaza was representative of New Orleans, but some politician's Hershey-highway relative had probably made a fortune off it.

The interior of City Hall wasn't any better. Filthy; stark. Or, stark; filthy. Whichever you preferred. The main hallways of the first floor were filled with crude murals, and the area allotted to the assessors was one giant open area, with antiquated desks butted up to each other behind a long counter. Nick expected to see the clerks still wearing green eye shades and garters on their rolled-up sleeves.

Clyde returned in ten minutes with a couple of letter-sized manila folders. "Like I said, you were asking about a political family. I thought so.

"Let's see. The building with the Slip It Inn is one of three owned by the same person. Thomas Claiborne. Purchased in 1925 from the last descendant of the d'Arensbourg family. Two of the buildings are side-by-side on Dumaine Street, and one is directly behind them on St. Philip. Nine hundred block. Only the one with the bar in it is commercial. The other two are residential, single-family."

Nick could feel his asshole clamp shut at the mention of Thomas Claiborne's name in connection with the buildings. *Just fucking wonderful*, he thought. *This was getting deeper and deeper*. "What about the business?"

"Nothing. For some reason that one slipped through us. The last business I show at that location was another bar of a different name. It was owned by a corporation. But you can check on their liquor license and operating permits with the city. Those would give you the name of the owner. Also, if you're interested, their liquor permit should also include a blueprint of the building in which the bar is located."

"That's true. I hadn't thought of that." Nick thanked Clyde for his time and left, after getting a copy of his records.

Nick's stomach was tight. He had assumed that Jeremy had owned the building, but apparently he only owned the business. He hadn't anticipated the judge's name coming up in such close connection with this investigation, and he didn't like it. The specter of overwhelming political power was looming larger on the horizon. That wasn't good. It raised the stakes higher than he could have imagined.

It was too late to check anything else, since all government offices closed at four p.m., so he headed down Tulane Avenue for the Miracle Mile, a down-and-dirty police bar across a small side street from Criminal District Court, with its walls and ceiling perforated with bullet holes left over from late night binges. He was going to call Steve and update him, but decided to wait until he could confirm whether Thomas Claiborne was the owner of the bar. He reluctantly considered whether the judge himself could be mixed up in murder, but it was more than his mind would deal with for now.

This thing was starting to take on a momentum of its own and he needed to slow it down some before it broke free of his control. He had gone from a point of not knowing where to start to a point where it was like some of that cheap-shit bubble gum: the more you chewed it, the bigger it got until it triggered that uncontrollable gag reflex in your throat and you had to spit it out, instantly, or embarrass yourself by puking it along with everything else you had eaten in the last three hours.

The next day, Nick made short work of rifling through the messages on his desk. No calls from Sharon's lawyer. His last divorce hadn't been such a problem to him. No kids to eat at his guts. He cursed Sharon briefly, then relented. He knew he hadn't been a husband or father for a long time. He knew, deep inside, that his performance was purposeful, hoping it would cause her to seek a divorce.

It was strange about human nature. That unhappiness with a spouse can cause a build-up of walls strong enough for you to retreat inside and not be hurt, even when you see the hearse carrying your marriage careening down the road to divorce.

Those walls can become so impenetrable and all-encompassing that you can tune out everything that goes with divorce, and you think that you can even shut out your kids. At least temporarily. At least until reality sets in. The reality of legal papers being served, for example. Or court appearances where dozens of hopefully anonymous faces sit, waiting to be called, half-tuned to your dirty laundry being aired on the stand, half-tuned to their own.

He spent the rest of the day working on other cases on his desk. He was trying to take a break from the Prejean case, which had occupied him almost full-time for over two weeks.

# XXI

The Catacombs was busy. Besides the usual badges, there was a sprinkling of cop groupies, which were always worth a few grins. Groupies seemed to have basically the same mentality, regardless of whether they followed bands, golf, criminals or cops. They seemed to have no identity of their own, nor any self-validation. Only that identity and admiration bestowed by their peers whenever they compared conquests. Some were more creative than others, with Polaroid photos as trophies which had been known to show up in the wrong places, on occasion, resulting in divorces. Or, if the groupie was too far underage, demotions were known to occur. Of course, if she went in and copped the watch commander's joint, such indiscretions could often be overlooked.

Groupies had occasionally almost made it to the surface, in cases where their hobby became too much of an obsession. Nick remembered one case in particular, where a twenty-one-year-old, who made a living selling cosmetics in a department store, had agreed to give blow jobs to a number of cops in town for a convention, at her apartment. She sat naked in a rattan chair with her legs folded into a yoga position, while she copped the joints of eight cops, some of them coming around for seconds. Unfortunately, she choked on one of them and gagged to death. A few days later, when someone in the next apartment complained of a foul odor, her door was forced open and she was found frozen in the same position. Fortunately for the participants, that was in the days before DNA testing had even been thought of. The death was ruled "unclassified."

Steve was at the back of the bar, watching the action. Nick finally noticed him and walked over.

"Fuck are *you* doing here?" he asked.

Steve shrugged. "Public bar. You paranoid? It's kinda interesting watching the players. And the playees. I just haven't decided which ones are the victims."

"*TFA*." Nick snorted. Typical fucking attorney. "Don't get deep on me."

"Shit, Saladino. You're already deep. In shit, that is. Heard you saw Clyde Sherman today. Asking about Jeremy."

"Jesus *H*. Christ. How in the fucking hell do you know about *that*?" Nick already knew the answer.

"I was sitting in the District Attorney's office. Thomas Claiborne called. I guess you know they're tight. Claiborne told the D.A. you were talking to Clyde. See why I'm concerned about the exposure in this fucking case?"

"Man, all I did was ask who owned the property and business. I didn't bring up the names, Clyde did," Nick said defensively. "Funny. Clyde himself told me the walls have ears."

"Yeah, cocksucker. But he didn't tell you he's in the same exclusive men's club with Thomas Claiborne. He didn't give a crap about trying to maintain your confidence, he just didn't want you spouting any Claiborne names in front of the hired help. Especially considering that buzzard you wear on your lapel. We need to talk. Let's get outta here." Steve maneuvered Nick towards the door.

They headed west on Tulane Avenue and caught the interstate at the parish line. Steve was quiet on the way out. Nick sipped at his double Crown. They exited at West End Boulevard and continued towards the lake. Nick had to concentrate to avoid spilling the Crown as Steve navigated the deep dips of the road where the old navigation canal dug by Irish immigrants had been filled in only a few decades ago.

Nick thought again about the groupie who had died in the line of duty. "Man, do you remember your first blow job?" he asked.

Steve perked up, laughing. "Fuckin-*A*. It took me two weeks to get the taste out of my mouth."

"You dumb fuck." He swatted Steve on the side of the head. They were consumed by laughter for a few minutes, as Steve turned down Lake Marina Drive, heading out to the marina, with its assortment of restaurants and bars, some on stilts in the brackish water of Lake Pontchartrain.

As they got out of the car and headed for Fish Heads, a popular hangout that served boiled seafood with cold beer, they were stung by the cold wind off the lake. The clanging of halyards against sailboat masts was loud and frantic, beating an endless and futile rhythm. Fish Heads was built in more or less the location of the old My-O-My Club, which burned into the water some thirty years earlier. The My-O-My featured some amazingly talented performances by an all-male review, classified simply at that time as "queers." Fish Heads was simply the current name of a joint that had changed hands four or five times in ten years, trying to keep its doors open by attracting kiddies, as Steve termed those under twenty-five; at least those who hadn't achieved the financial status of yuppiedom.

There were no prissy little BMW's in the parking lot, their little chrome vagina-shaped grilles puckered up in contemplation of their next thousand-dollar tune-up. There were only a few beat-up small cars of the type kids favored. Steve also noticed one down-on-its-luck Blazer, and two crotch-rockets, which were tied to the only nearby light post.

The building itself had been nicely laid out, with a raised wooden deck in front where patrons could sit and contemplate the municipal yacht club and the park in front of it. On the water side of the bar was a similar deck overlooking the lake. At the inside bar, Steve watched the lights of the cars speeding over the Lake Pontchartrain Causeway, a twenty-four-mile span that connected the north and south shores.

Crawfish were in high season, and they ordered a rubber tub of boiled crawfish with garlic, corn, potatoes and whole onions along with a pitcher of beer. The crawfish were running small, but the flavor and texture were perfect. Steve and Nick started into the huge pile, effortlessly sucking the heads and eating the tails in an efficient manner that only comes from years of practice.

Steve finally spoke. "Well, Saladino. This one is gonna make or break us. You have definitely opened up a black hole here. This is not gonna be pretty. I've done some checking on my own. Thomas Claiborne owns three properties in the Quarter."

"Yeah, I found that out from Clyde. Two are side-by-side on Dumaine, and the other butts up against the back of those two, facing onto St. Philip."

"That's what you got from Clyde?"

Nick nodded.

"That's all?"

"Uh-huh. So?"

"He didn't do you any favors."

Nick stopped eating bugs, not sure he wanted to hear what was coming.

"Not only have you invoked the name of a senior federal judge, you have also invoked the name of his daughter Charysse

Claiborne, the judge in Criminal District Court. She lives above the bar, in the building owned by her father, Thomas. Thomas Claiborne, the honorable, lives in the building on Dumaine that butts up to the side of the bar. And, last but not least, Jeremy-baby lives in the slave quarters behind the bar, facing onto St. Philip. It's like a compound. All the courtyards interconnect. Clyde didn't tell you about all that, right?"

Nick let that sink in. "Holy crappin' *Christ*. How do you know all that shit?"

"I thought you'd like that little tidbit," Steve smirked. "The D.A. likes to go to parties at Thomas Claiborne's digs. Most of us have been there with him."

"*Crap*." Nick knew that many of the buildings in the Quarter had neat open-air patios that were rarely visible from the street. He also knew that a number of the buildings had slave quarters overlooking the patios, some extending from the main residence in an "L" shape, some forming the rear wall of the patio. He suddenly had a picture of himself and Steve mopping out bars for a living.

"I think I need to think about this for a while," was all he could say.

"I think we both need to think about this for a while. We got no choice but to pursue this thing, but we gotta do it carefully. If the Claibornes find out what we're up to, we're gonna be shut down and shipped to Siberia on the next street car. Same problem with *my* boss," Steve pointed out.

"Where you get 'we', dude?" Nick asked. "This is still *my* investigation."

"*Somebody's* gotta make sure you don't fuck it up. Come on. Let's roll around to a few joints."

"Thought you'd never ask, my boy."

They got back in the car and crossed over into Jefferson Parish at Bucktown on the small road that ran along the Lake Pontchartrain levee, and began a crawl of whichever bars happened to get in their way.

# XXII

Tentacles of daylight were beginning to feel their way through the palpable grogginess of the city when Steve finally dropped Nick off at his car on Tulane Avenue. Nick waved Steve off and staggered to the Crown Vic, which seemed to Nick to have adopted an almost petulant posture at having been left out of the night's action. Nick went home, hoping to catch a cat nap.

It was Wednesday morning. Nick was actually clean-shaven, having slept on the sofa at the boathouse for a couple of hours. On the way in to work, he stopped at one of the two remaining tattoo parlors on his list. It was on North Carrollton Avenue, a couple of blocks north of Canal Street. The man inside was exactly what Nick had always pictured as the stereotypical tattoo artist. Unkempt gray hair, sunken cheeks, snaggle-toothed, with the reek of decaying, cheap whiskey on his breath. The walls and ceiling were a thick yellow from years of nicotine smoke, and an empty bottle of Four Roses was on the desk.

The old man must have sensed Nick's disgust.

"I usedta be the best there was. You know? I done 'em all. When I was in L.A., them little what'cha call it—starlets? Them little starlets usedta come and get, like, little butterflies. Silly shit like that. I seen some a the mos' famous tits and asses in the world. In L.A. Nowadays, these broads ain't the same. Ain't got no class 'tall. These little twats want gang crap tattooed on 'em, and they don't care who watches while they naked. Even offer me a blow job if they don't have ta pay for it. None a' them interested in art no more. Goddam gang symbols, they all look alike. No talent." The old man winked at Nick. "You know, they just ain't got no class no more."

Nick nodded. "Well, they got a lotta class. Trouble is, it's all *low*."

The old man went on. "Then the dumb bitches meet up with some nice guy, and all of a sudden they want the goddam things taken off. Don't care what it takes. They'll fuck my brains out if I tell them I can do it. You wouldn't believe how much young snatch I get. Use clean needles, too. Ain't none of that disease crap around here." The old man pointed to the old sterilizer on the counter. It looked hopelessly outdated, like a 'fifties toaster.

Nick was getting impatient. *Christ, who started* his *Slinky down the stairs?* Nick wondered to himself. He had heard enough, and pulled the photo of Collette from its envelope.

"Naw, she don't look familiar. I'd remember a young twat like that," the old man said, thoughtfully.

"Figures." It was the same answer Nick had come to expect. It was only because he couldn't stand to leave any stone unturned that he was finishing up this tangent with the tattoo parlors. After the first two, he had come to believe that she hadn't obtained the tattoo from a local parlor. He figured this part of the investigation would end up as a circle-jerk. He pulled out the photo of Collette's arm with the tattoo, and passed it to the old man.

He gazed at it for a few moments and started slowly shaking his head in a negative manner.

Nick sighed and retrieved the photo, returning it to the envelope.

"Naw. I h'ain't seen nothing like that in a long time. I was a medic in World War II, you know? Damn good one, too. Got me a purple heart, I do. Got stolen from me, though. Had it hanging right on that wall over there. I was with a unit in the Philippines when we went back in after the Japs. Yessir. Them was some exciting times." The old man's eyes had sparked to life. "I seen lots of body parts like that. Use'ter bother me at first, but you get use'ter anything, after a while." The old man was still shaking his head from side to side.

Nick was heading for the door. "Well, nice try. No cigar," he muttered to himself.

"Been a long time since I seen a tattoo like that, too." The old man was still shaking his head and talking to himself as he busied himself straightening up the area for the day's business.

Nick froze in his tracks. "What the fuck did you say?" He practically jumped on the guy.

The old man was startled. "I didn't say nothin' bad, officer."

"No. No. Relax, old-timer. I mean what did you just say about the tattoo? You did just say something about a tattoo, right?"

"Weren't no big deal. Just said I h'ain't seen a tattoo like that in a long time, that's all." The old man was a little shaken by Nick's aggressiveness.

Nick's heart was pounding hard enough that it made his voice quaver.

"You mean you've seen this tattoo *before*?" Nick had grabbed the old man by his shoulder, and was almost shaking him. "Why didn't you tell me when I showed the photograph?"

The old man was intimidated and lapsed into stuttering. "Y-y-you d-d-didn't ask me nut-nut-nuttin bow-bow-'bout no tattoo."

Nick let him go. He was right.

"Sit down, old man. Talk to me. You're not in any trouble here, so just relax. I need to know what you know about this tattoo." Nick tried to calm him.

The old man was quivering. "I don't know nuttin' about that tattoo."

Nick sat back. He didn't understand. Either this old fart was playing games with him or his elevator had quit making trips to the top floor.

"Let's try again." He pulled the photo of the tattoo out and put it in front of the old man. "Now, tell me. Have you seen this tattoo before?"

I h'ain't seen that one before. I swear it."

"Then what did you mean when you were talking to yourself as I was walking out the door?" Nick insisted.

"I mean... I h'ain't seen that one. I mean it," the old man insisted. "I mean... why you pushing me on this? What's up with all that?"

Nick was losing his patience. "What the fuck did you say? Something about, 'you haven't seen one of these in a long time'?"

"I mean... I mean, like I said. I h'ain't seen one like that in a long time. What's the matter with you, man?"

Nick was silent, the distinction sinking in.

"I seen some like that one, but I h'ain't never seen that particular one. And that one is definitely done by a no-talent. That's the truth!" The old man got up to go back to his chores.

Nick pulled him back down to the chair. "Goddam it! Don't make me drag this out of you! Where the fuck have you seen tattoos like this one?"

"You h'ain't got to treat me like that," the old man whined. "I h'ain't done nothing here. I h'ain't got to talk to you no more. I got me a lawyer, you know. He got a office right down there by the courthouse, right on top of that bail bond office. He'll tell me if I got to talk to you. I'm a respectable businessman here. I'm even a member of the Better Business Bureau." He pointed to a dingy certificate hanging precipitously on the wall.

Nick calmed down again. *If this old fuck goes for his mouthpiece, it's gonna be a while before I get this outta him,* he thought.

"You're right. Like I said, you're not a suspect in this. I just your need your help in a homicide investigation. This woman in this picture was found dead, and we're trying to track her killer. The tattoo may lead us to the killer. It may not. Either way, I gotta follow it as far as it will take me. Now, help me out here."

Silence for a few minutes. Then, "I done one like it. It was back when I was in the Philippines. I was experimenting with tattoos while I was a medic over there. The local witch doctor showed me how to do 'em, in exchange for a couple vials of morphine. He figured he would be more powerful if he could make somebody's pain go away, even if it was only temporary."

"This witch doctor showed you how to do tattoos?" Nick asked.

"Yeah. One of the privates was a Filipino and spoke Tagalog, the native language, real good. He helped translate."

"Where'd you get the supplies?"

"Used the native needles and inks at first. Then I sent for a kit through the quartermaster. Them bastards could get anything you wanted. They were amazing. It didn't have to be nothin' to do with the military." The old man had entered a lost memory channel. "With my medical training, there weren't nothin' to it, and with a little practice, I even got good enough to where you could actually tell what the design was supposed to be. I got the sterile stuff from the hospital supply room."

"So what's with this tattoo?" Nick asked.

"It were some kinda flower the natives prayed to over there. Like a orchid er something. A lot of the natives had tattoos like it."

"So what, you did a native or two?"

The old man's eyes twinkled a little. "You could definitely say I did a native or two, but that h'ain't got nothin' to do with tattooing."

Nick sat back. *Everybody's a fuckin' clown*, he thought. "So tell me about the tattoo."

"Like I said, I got to where I was pretty good at it. Guys on the post started coming to me for tattoos. They'd pay off in cigarettes or rations if they didn't have enough money. That was a big thing in the military."

"You mean cigarettes?"

"Naw. Tattoos. You know, see the world, come back with a tattoo. It were the thing for guys to do back then. One day this captain comes in. Says he's from Louisiana. He heard I was from Louisiana, too, and he wants me to do this flower tattoo on his left forearm. You know, right in the fleshy part." He pointed to the inside of his forearm. "Just like where this tattoo is here. But he don't want it in black, like the natives. He want it in dark red, like goddam dried blood. That's what he said. He want it the color of dried blood. You get what I'm talking about?"

Nick nodded, captivated. He had a brief premonition of what was coming, but his mind shoved it back down instantly. He swallowed hard.

"This captain was from Louisiana?" he asked.

The old man nodded. "Yep. From right 'chere in New Orleans. He a pretty important man, now. Seen his pitcher in the paper right after we come back from the war. Turned out he were some kinda blue-blood society dude—you know the kind? The pitcher in the paper had him in his khakis, and you could see the tattoo on his arm. Yes, sir. Only time any of my art work been published. That were about August 1946, when I got back home."

Nick felt a sickening in his stomach. "You remember his name?"

"Naw. That were fifty years ago. But I remember this here tattoo 'cuz it were the first one I ever did on an officer, and I had a problem trying to get that goddam color to where he said it was OK. This here tattoo in this here pitcher—it's pretty bad," the old man said. "About as bad as some of the first ones I ever did. If this here tattoo man paid for lessons, he oughta get his money back."

#

Nick thanked the old man and hauled ass to the Times-Picayune newspaper's office building. If there was such a picture, it would likely have been in the *Times-Picayune* or the *States-Item*, the two primary newspapers in New Orleans in the forties. The *States-Item* had gone down the tube and been consumed by the *Times-Picayune*, a lackluster rag of a newspaper whose editors fed on bleeding-heart stories, and an extremely liberal agenda. But the paper did keep an amazing library of past editions of both papers, albeit on microfilm.

The microfilm room of the newspaper was dark and dingy, with a row of single lightbulbs hanging along the ceiling down the center of the room. The microfilm files were maintained by a crusty old hag who seemed to consider them her personal property. She was not pleased that he didn't know the dates of the films he was seeking, and made no bones about it. The spools were poorly marked, and in some cases the writing had been worn thin or even obliterated, resulting in a lot of guess work as to what they contained.

After a few spools, Nick came across one that had a marker on the first frame that indicated it covered the dates of June 1 through June 30, 1946. He scanned through it quickly, but, as he figured, that was a little too early for any news of returning G.I.'s. A number of spools later, he came upon one that boasted that it covered August 1 through August 31, 1946. *Bingo*, he thought.

He ran the spool carefully and did in fact find a few stories about some local boys coming home. Some had photos. He kept the film at a steady crawl, stopping to focus on all pictures that appeared. Some were officers, some in khakis. *Flick, flick, flick, flick.* The end of the film flipping around on the spool startled him. That was all there was to August, 1946. No tattoo.

"*Crap.* Dumb old bastard." Nick didn't know now whether to believe the old man.

The prune-faced librarian wasn't pleased when he asked for September and October of 1946. "I don't have the time for you to research the entire history of World War II, young man!" She scowled.

"Yes, ma'am. I'm almost finished," Nick wheedled. "Promise."

She disappeared for a few minutes and reappeared with another pair of the ratty-looking spools. She blew the dust off of them as she handed them over to Nick, causing his suit coat to look like a bad case of dandruff.

He threaded the September spool and sat back, pulsing it until he reached a photo. An hour later, he found himself cursing in frustration.

"C'mon. *C'mon.*" By this time, he was determined to find something. He hated to think he had wasted almost five hours.

He pulled September off and threaded the October spool. Pulsing through, it didn't take long for photos of returning soldiers to pop up. In fact, there seemed to be a flurry of the types of photos he was interested in. He had to spend a good deal of time on each page, examining each photo. The graininess of the microfilm didn't help any.

"*There.*" Something had caught his eye. He clarified the photo as much as the viewer would allow. There was a dark spot on the inside forearm of the person in the photo, who was obviously an officer in a very dashing pose. Nick read the caption beneath the photo. The words burned into his brain, deeply.

*Thomas Claiborne Returns Home* was the caption.

Nick was sweating profusely. He sat back and let the breath ooze out of him slowly. He had never expected that result. Nor was he pleased that that *was* the result. Although the photo was too grainy and dark to determine the exact shape or subject of the tattoo, it appeared to have the same dimensions and shape as the one on Collette's arm. It definitely was *not* a tattoo of a heart or a snake or "mother," as many G.I.'s had. This was something flower-like.

He looked at the photo more closely. Sure enough, it was undoubtedly Thomas Claiborne in his younger days.

*Jesus, Mary and Joseph H.* Christ. *What have I got here?* Nick thought.

Nick made a copy of the photo from the microfilm reader, and the tattoo on Claiborne's arm took on a more positive appearance once it was printed on paper.

He headed for Steve's office, but Steve was in court, wrapping up a one-day murder trial. Nick couldn't wait to talk to Steve, so he walked across the street to Criminal District Court and into Section "J," which was where he'd been told by Steve's secretary that the trial was being conducted. There was always an unusual assortment of society's fringe element hanging around the courthouse, each in one stage or another of his or her descent into the criminal justice system, and, accordingly, into the bowels of the city.

Nick whistled. "*Damn.* I just realized that's Charysse Claiborne's section of court," he said to no one in particular.

It was final arguments, and the defense attorney had just begun his.

Nick got as comfortable as he could on the old wooden bench seat and looked around the courtroom. He always admired the old courtrooms in this court house. Built in the 1920s, no two were alike. The ceilings looked to Nick to be at least twenty-feet-high, with intricate wood and plaster designs. The walls were covered in beautifully carved wood and the judge's benches were set imposingly high to provide a commanding view of the courtroom. The wood had developed a beautiful patina over time; maybe because it had absorbed all of the heartbreak and emotions that had passed before it in the last seventy years, all of which were digested by the wood and returned to its surface in a soft peaceful luster.

And, speaking of beautiful patinas, the image of Charysse Claiborne on the bench before him listening intently to the arguments, her lustrous black hair flowing over her black robe, transfixed him momentarily.

After a while, Nick zoned out. He had come to appreciate the relative efficiency of the criminal justice system in New Orleans, especially after some of the debacles in California called "trials." He was never able to understand how California trials could drag out as long as they did.

*Christ, when Zsa Zsa got a traffic ticket and slapped a cop, it seemed like that trial lasted for weeks*, he thought. *Who are you fucking gonna put on the witness stand? Zsa Zsa and the cop. Thirty minutes max in a New Orleans court. Shit, in New Orleans, it wasn't unusual to pick a jury in a murder case, present the case, give it to the jury, and have a verdict, all in one day.*

Steve was getting up to do his rebuttal argument, and Nick's thoughts returned to the action at hand. Steve started off with one of his favorites.

"Ladies and gentlemen. You know, there's an old saying around this old court house. It goes something like this. If you can't argue the facts, argue the law. If you can't argue the law, argue the facts. If you can't do either one, *blow smoke*. And I'm here to tell you that the defense attorney has done nothing but blow smoke since he got up here to talk to you. He ought to be arrested for *air pollution*," Steve said, in his favorite manner of feigned indignation, turning and pointing at the defense attorney.

The defense attorney jumped to his feet in a rage.

"*Your honor. Your honor.* The prosecutor is attempting to discredit *me*. This is about whether or not my client is guilty, not whether I am doing *my* job."

"Sustained. Mr. Chaisson. I know you know better than that. You have been warned in this court before about such tactics. I don't have to remind you of the court's power to enforce proper conduct. And, as you know, that includes prosecutors." The sultriness of the voice that came from the bench took away some of the sting of the threat, but there was no mistaking that Charysse Claiborne was serious.

"Thank you, your honor," Steve replied.

Nick saw a couple of the jurors snicker with their hands in front of their faces, which didn't make Judge Claiborne any happier. Steve rolled on for about ten minutes more, then sat down. The judge began to charge the jury with the applicable law. Steve swung around in his chair and saw the look on Nick's face. He stared at Nick for a few seconds, then swung back to concentrate on the jury charges. When the jury was sent upstairs to deliberate, he came around the bar rail and sat down beside Nick.

"You look like you just found out you would never have another piece of ass again in your life."

"Don't even say that. That's not funny. This is getting beyond imagination. What if I told you that Judge Claiborne himself may have some ties to this thing?"

"I'd say you got a problem."

"Wait, we've been through this already. You said *you* were supervising this thing so *I* wouldn't make any mistakes. Remember?" Nick was agitated.

"Relax, big boy. Conniption fits aren't gonna help. It is what it is. We just gotta figure out what it is."

"Well, lock your eyeballs onto this photo from the *Times-Picayune* of October 19, 1946." Nick waived the photocopy in front of Steve. "See anybody you know?"

Steve's eyes widened, then narrowed into pensive slits.

"You got something *here*, man. *Yow.* That tattoo is very similar to the one on Collette's arm, and that is definitely Thomas Claiborne. Un-be-fucking-lievable." He looked around the courtroom. "Who else knows about this?"

"Just us kids," Nick replied.

"This is starting to smell like *Twilight Zone* shit. I got to say, though, I don't like Judge Claiborne worth a rat shit, but I'd have a hard time picturing the old bastard as a killer, or involved in a killing. If Jeremy *is* the killer, though, maybe he thinks the orchid looks good on women. Or maybe it's some kinda weird sexual get-off because of some mind-fuck the old man did on him when he was a kid." Steve continued to ramble. "You know, like it's getting back at the old man by putting the old man's tattoo on some poor broad before he kills her. That kind of thing." Little did he know how prophetic that statement would become.

Steve looked worried for a moment. "This tattoo dude. He remembered the judge's name?"

"Naw. Only that he was a New Orleanian, and an officer in the Army. He remembered that because it was the first time he had tattooed an officer. He told me the flower was something worshipped by the natives in the Philippines. He remembered that the officer had demanded that the tattoo be done in dark red because he thought it looked like dried blood. I got the name by going to the *Times-Picayune* archives."

Steve sighed. "God, if this shit hits the media, we are gonna be tattooed, feathered, and hung in Jackson Square for the pigeons to shit on! Can you picture the field day those frontal lobotomies would have? I can see the headline: 'Judge's tattoo found on dead hooker's arm.' *Christ.* We'd end up like fricasseed nutria."

Nick had to agree with that. It was going to be unbelievable if and when he actually arrested Jeremy Claiborne for Collette's murder. *If the old man gets wrapped up in this, too, the heat will be unbearable.*

# XXIV

It was nine p.m. Steve's jury had finally come back with a "GAC." Guilty as charged, of second degree murder. Mandatory life imprisonment. The defendant would soon be enjoying the sights and sounds of scenic Angola.

Steve walked over to the defendant's table and presented him with a travel-sized tube of KY Jelly, a traditional present to all defendants who would be spending life at Angola. "*Here*, asshole. You're gonna *need* this soon."

Steve and Nick left the courthouse for a couple of toasts to the newly-convicted murderer and his future. They started at the Miracle Mile, then proceeded to drink their way back into the Quarter. It was their plan to visit the Slip It Inn, and as they entered the joint and walked to the end of the bar, Tony the bartender recognized Nick and waved at him. They ordered a round, and Steve surveyed the place. He had never been there before.

They watched a couple of men with close-cropped hair swish around the pool table. They were goosing each other with the cue sticks every time one would sink a ball.

"Sweet place. I hope they don't think *we're* fair game," Steve said with a little edge.

Nick smiled at him. "Feel threatened, do you? Don't sweat it. You won't have any problems. I'll just let them know you're *my* boy toy."

"In your fondest *dreams*, cocksucker," Steve growled. "Where's that photo you were talking about?"

Nick pointed and Steve took his drink over to examine the picture. He came back with a smile on his face that was itself almost evil.

"Well, motherfucker, I'm finally starting to think you might have it right. If in fact that *is* Jeremy Claiborne in that costume."

"What 'cha mean?" Nick asked.

"Did you notice the costume? *You're* the fucking detective here."

"Yeah, something about it's been nagging at me worse than a wife, but I can't figure out what it is."

"What it *is*, Sherlock, is that that costume has that fucking orchid design in or on the fabric. Looks like it's made with dark-colored sequins sewed on in a repeating pattern. And, that goofy fucking headpiece also looks like a goddam fucking orchid. It's that black fucking orchid thing. Go take a look," Steve said.

Nick walked over. "I'll be damned. That's fucking *it*. No fucking *wonder* that goddam costume's been eating at me. Jeremy must be fucking *obsessed* with that goddam escapee from a hothouse."

"If Jeremy killed Collette, then your pimp—what's his name? Cueball? He's probably right that Collette met Jeremy right here. Have you asked the bartender anything about Jeremy being with broads in here?"

"Nuh-uh. Been trying not to ask him anything until he thinks I'm just an off-duty cop with a thirst."

"Well, you got part of that right. About the thirst, that is."

"*Whoa*, bro. You got me *wrong*. That's a bum rap. I've been laying off the sauce. You ain't seen me drunk in a long time. At *least* two days," Nick jostled Steve.

"Yeah, you're becoming a regular tee-totaler," Steve snorted.

"*Serious*, man. I'm gonna give up all that hard-drinking shit."

Steve looked up at the ceiling, and moved a few steps away from Nick.

"Hope you're a good shot with that goddam lightning, motherfucker. It's the guy with the *dark* hair. I'll stand back just in case there's a little overspray when you zap him."

Nick cuffed Steve on the arm. "*Stop* that shit. You know God don't like ugly."

"Yeah, well, He sure pulled one off on your *mother*, then."

Steve ducked as Nick feigned a punch towards his head.

Tony the bartender wandered over to see what the ruckus was all about, and he and Nick made small talk for a while.

"Tony, I was just telling my friend here about that kid Jeremy in the photo over there winning a trip to Hawaii for his costume."

"Yeah. Lucky little bastard. Think he'd ask me to go with him? No fucking way. Little shit don't associate with nobody. He don't give a shit about no other human beings. Ain't had one fuckin' social conversation with him yet. Little shit leaves messages on the phone recorder when he wants me to do something. Almost never comes in here."

"No shit? What's his action, then?" Nick felt comfortable pressing for a little new information. "He obviously doesn't mind getting out in front of crowds in drag," he added, hoping Tony would be in a talkative mood.

"Shit. He just don't like people in general. Sometimes when you try to talk to him, he just stares through you like you're some kinda roach droppings. Those goddam little black eyes are never friendly. We get along because I do my job, and I don't try to talk to him much. He don't have no friends."

"What about women," Nick asked.

"Socially? You don't know *him*. Noogie hates women. Says they're *all* sluts. If he's in here and a female wanders in, he gets up and leaves. Goes to his apartment around back. I got to buzz him when they're gone. But I usually wait a while after they're gone before I do. He makes me nervous when he's around. And, he's a pain in the ass, too. A goddam neatness freak. You know what I mean? If I wait thirty seconds after somebody's left the bar to remove the glass and wipe the spot, he's up my ass. If I don't put a bottle of booze back in the exact same spot I got it from when I pour a drink, he gets up, walks around the fuckin' bar, and moves the bottle until he's happy with it. All the fuckin' booze labels have to face just so. He's a real pain in the ass."

"So you never see him talking to anyone, I guess..."

"Every once in a while, he'll meet someone here. Says it's one of his probation cases. That's what he does in the day time. He's a probation officer."

"No shit?" Nick played dumb.

"Yeah. Oddly enough, it's usually a female, which is really weird, considering how much he hates them. Hookers on probation, I guess. Jeremy just calls them sluts. But then, it seems like, to him, every woman on the face of the earth is a slut."

"You mean he just sits and talks with them?" Nick pressed.

"Pretty much. They usually have a drink. He says he's counseling them about their case. They'll talk about an hour, then leave through the back door into the alleyway to the patio. I guess he don't want known hookers seen coming and going through the front door."

"So he does that a lot? Really? It's always *women*?"

"I seen it maybe a half-dozen, maybe ten times. But you can see that Jeremy ain't being friendly with them. He's real stiff, like he is with just about everybody else."

"Wow," Nick said. "When is he coming back from his trip?"

"What's this, Wednesday? He'll be back Tuesday night," Tony answered. "Man, why you so interested in Jeremy? Something going on?"

That was Nick's clue to shut it down for the night. He was pleased with the information he had gotten, and made a mental note to stop by in the next couple of days with a photo of Collette to show to Tony. It was time to start getting down to the short hairs on this case. He was beginning to smell blood. Jeremy's blood.

## XXV

The next morning, Nick called Nancy Hoffman at probation to check on the status of the information he had asked for.

"Well, you better get ready to perform your end of the bargain." She sounded chipper. "I got your information for you."

"*Out*-standing. Meet me at Matanza's for 11:30."

"Matanza's your *ass*. You're buying lunch at *Antoine's* today. I've spent a lot time being scared shitless to get this crap for you."

Nick knew there was no sense arguing. "You got it. See you there."

Antoine's was actually a great place for lunch in New Orleans. Nick normally couldn't afford Antoine's on his cop's salary, but he needed the information that Nancy said she had.

If you knew a waiter, you called him directly for reservations. Similarly, if you knew a waiter, you never looked at the menu. Just told him how hungry you were and whether you wanted fish, poultry or meat, then sat back and let the goodies flow.

Nick called Marko, his favorite waiter, and asked for a table in one of the small side rooms off the main dining room. When he arrived, he was seated in the Rex Room, named after a king of Carnival and decorated with an impressive array of memorabilia from the venerable Carnival krewe. It was located near the restaurant's extensive wine cellar.

Marko came and placed a double Crown on the rocks in front of him. "You trying to hide a chippy? What's up with the private room?"

"What took you so long?" Nick feigned irritation.

"Only the paying customers get *good* service. The cops that order coffee and donuts have to accept a little less," Marko retorted.

The two had been friends for many years, beginning when Marko rode motorcycles in the first district. He had started moonlighting at Antoine's in his second year as a cop, then given up the police to go fulltime as a waiter, making twenty times what he made as a cop, most of it in cash.

"So what's going down, brother? I know she must be fine. Is she married? Is that the issue for the privacy?" Marko wouldn't give it up.

"This motherfucker is *so* fine, you could store your life savings in her cleavage. This chick has tits so big, they need to invent some special kinda jewelry that will float on top of cleavage." Nick wasn't exaggerating, much.

"Don't tell me she's good-looking, too, ya bastard!"

"Fuck. You *had* to ask that, huh? She ain't bad. Definitely doesn't require a bag over her head. As a friend of mine likes to say, 'She's useable.'"

"You must be talking about Steve Chaisson in the D.A.'s office. That bastard is a pervert, if ever there was one. You musta taught him. Most attorneys ain't that smart about chicks." Marko laughed.

"I take a little credit."

"Let me know when you're ready to order. I'll take care of you." Marko winked and walked off.

Nick had finished about half of his drink when another waiter escorted Nancy to his table.

"Don't get up," she joked. "I know you wouldn't, anyway. It just makes me feel good to say it." She smiled at the waiter. "Could you get me a Sazerac? Thanks."

Nick whistled. Nancy had made sure that her outfit displayed her cleavage to maximum effect. He was sure that, if you parted those tits to get to the bottom of their cleavage, you'd probably have to speak Chinese when you arrived. Well, at least it was going to be fun paying this debt.

"Like what you see, hmm? I expect a generous reward for this. I did get you some information, but it wasn't easy, and I was terrified that Jeremy would walk in and catch me in his files. I had to go through damn near every file on the shelves in our office to do it, and you can't imagine the state of some of them. Probation hires so many people who couldn't get a job anywhere else. The political spoils system does at least provide jobs for those who aren't otherwise employable."

Nick was getting excited, but he couldn't tell if it was at the prospect of catching Collette's murderer, or just the view of Nancy's tits that had jump-started him.

"What 'cha got?"

"I found a total of seven hookers who were assigned to Jeremy Claiborne. In each case, they failed to report for an interview at some point during their probation. In each case, Jeremy filed a rule to revoke probation as he is supposed to do, based upon their failure to comply with the terms of their probation. In each case, no one appeared in court on their behalf on the rule to revoke, and the court issued a warrant for their arrest. In each case, that's the end of the file. None of them have been arrested as of this date."

"*Seven* of them. No shit?" Nick was beginning to put stock in the idea that he *was* dealing with a serial killer. He was sure he knew the fate of each of them, and it wasn't a pretty thought.

He swallowed that and started to ask Nancy if she could get a copy of their files.

"I'm way ahead of you, big boy. I'm working on making you a copy of the files on each of them. But I have to do it slowly, when no one else is around the copy machine." She was pleased with herself. "So what's the scoop here? You think Jeremy killed them? You think Jeremy Claiborne is a *serial* killer? Jesus Christ! And I've been working in the room next to the little freak?"

Nick put his finger to his mouth. "You got to keep this *absolutely* quiet. I mean *nobody* can know this shit but you and me. If Jeremy gets wind of this, I may never be able to catch him. I mean *never*."

Nancy looked at him. "No *shit*. If word gets out I gave you this information, that monster may make *me* the next victim. You ain't gotta worry about *me* blowing this thing." She swallowed hard and her eyes slowly started to widen. Listening to Nick and the tone of his voice, she was starting to grasp the true significance of Jeremy's stature as a killer, and the importance of her role in his apprehension, if there was truly to be an apprehension. "Jesus, what about his father? You know who he is?"

Nick nodded.

"I mean, this little bastard has always impressed me as being vicious. He treats me like I'm some kinda street whore, and I mean I've *never* done anything to make him think like that. He's a scary little bastard. He just kinda looks right through you, as if he's evaluated you to be worth nothing more than the dollar's worth of chemicals that make up your body."

"I'm not going to lie to you, baby. I think the guy is extremely dangerous. But he's targeting hookers, and I suspect it's only the hookers who are unlucky enough to land in his case load." Nick tried to reassure Nancy. "It's easy for him to have control of some type over them, and have a reason to meet with them. It's starting to look like it's also easy for him to cover their disappearance."

She sucked on her drink, taking in Nick's reasoning. He hoped she would go for it, because he was about to spring her next assignment on her.

"You know, there *is* one more thing we need to do. As I understand it, you've looked in all the closed case files. What about the *active* files?" He held his breath, awaiting her reaction, and wasn't surprised at the reaction he got.

Nancy gasped, and tried to stand up. "What? *What?* The *active* files?" She was choking on her drink. "You want me to go through the *active* files? *Have you lost it?* Do you know that those files are kept in Claiborne's personal file cabinet in his office? You *are* nuts."

She plopped back down in her chair, and caught her breath. "Have you been smoking left-handed cigarettes? *Jesus Christ.* His door is kept locked. His file cabinet is kept locked. There's not so much as a fucking *dust bunny* in that office. That little toilet-licker is a neatness freak. He would know the minute anyone changed anything in his office. No fucking way."

"Calm down, sweetheart. Nobody's gonna change anything in his office. All I need is the name and address of each of the hookers in his *active* case files, and the next date they are supposed to report to him. I've got someone who can get into the office and the file cabinet, and no one will ever know. You just got to let them into the office after hours. Besides, Claiborne's on vacation right now and won't be back until next Tuesday." Nick was trying to use his best persuasion techniques.

"Why don't you just subpoena the information?"

"No way. This would become instantly public. If I tip him off to this investigation in any way, I may never catch him. Besides which, his family would have me taken off the investigation if they found out about it," Nick explained, calmly. "If he's doing what I think he's doing, he'll just stop doing it, and the investigation is over. I need to catch him in the act of whatever he's doing to these hookers to make it stick. I don't have any evidence that will hold up in court unless I get that. Have another drink."

Nick motioned to Marko, who brought a new round and some of the appetizers for which Antoine's was famous. He mugged to Nick while he was behind Nancy, showing his approval of Nick's lunch companion.

"So what's he doing to these hookers?" Nancy asked. "Although, I'm not sure I want to know."

"I don't know what the fuck he's doing to them," Nick admitted. "All I know is I got an arm from one of them. An arm that an alligator hadn't had time to turn into alligator turds. I don't know if Jeremy dismembered her, or if the alligator did that. I don't know if he is killing them himself or leaving them for the alligator to have that pleasure. The only other thing I know is that one dead hooker was part of Claiborne's case load. That's really all I know at this point."

Nick had decided not to elaborate on the tattoo. He was already sticking his neck out, trusting Nancy to handle sensitive information on a sensational case, but he had nowhere else to go. There was no way he could follow the correct investigation methods in this case without setting off alarms, and, worse, alerting the suspect himself, who was a member of the "law enforcement team" of the city. Worse than all that, *this* suspect was highly politically connected.

Nick had a hunch that Nancy would bear up under the pressure. He knew she had already had a tough life. She was single-handedly raising two young daughters, one of which was autistic, and she hadn't received a penny of child support from her husband, who had run off with a stripper from Bourbon Street five years ago. Her husband had been carrying on an affair with the stripper while he was still living at home, and Nancy had had no idea of what was going on until the stripper called the house one day to advise her of the affair, personally. Worse yet, the stripper had informed Nancy that she had just tested HIV positive. Her husband had come home just long enough to pack his clothes and then disappeared. She had no knowledge of his current whereabouts. On the bright side, she has been tested regularly and, so far, all the tests have been negative.

They finished lunch and Nick walked Nancy to her car.

"I'll call you tomorrow to set up a time to check Jeremy's office. Remember, all I want is a list of name, address, and next reporting date for each hooker in his current case files." He kissed her on the mouth, lightly.

Nancy breathed deeply and got behind the wheel, spreading her legs wide as she did, providing Nick with a delicious flash to remember her by. She wasn't wearing anything under her skirt.

Nick went straight back to his office, eager to sort through the closed file information provided by Nancy. There were seven names: seven women convicted of prostitution and placed on probation by the court. In each case, the file claimed that the defendant had failed to report for a scheduled meeting with Jeremy Claiborne, who had then filed a rule to revoke their probation. In each case, the judge had issued a warrant for them when they didn't appear in court to participate in the scheduled hearing on the rule.

It wasn't difficult for Nick to imagine that each and everyone one of them had become alligator tidbits. Nick also was sure that he had the killer pegged. The only real unknown in his mind was what had happened to them while they were in Jeremy's clutches. He intended to find out.

# XXVI

Steve sat with his chair propped back against the wall on its two rear legs, one of his favorite positions for thinking, as he absorbed Nick's description of Nancy's information to date. Nick sat across from him.

"Wow," he whistled softly. "So we're up to a possible seven victims, using your theory, not counting Collette Prejean. Right?"

Nick nodded.

"What a beautiful scam! A probation officer is the perfect person in society to know who's gonna be missed, and who isn't," Steve mused. "There's no more perfect setup to prey on hookers and cover your tracks. Who's gonna question a probation officer who actually brings it to the court's attention that a hooker has potentially disappeared? It's fucking *genius*. So what've we got?" he asked, rhetorically.

He sat forward and started to make a list on a yellow legal pad, summarizing the evidence to date as he wrote. "We got Jeremy Claiborne, who's known to hate women. His father's got a tattoo similar to the one on the arm of Collette Prejean. At least, he used to have. We assume that Prejean is dead because we got her arm. We don't know that for sure, but it seems a fair bet. But we can't prove that she's dead.

"We got a picture of Jeremy wearing drag with what appears to be the same design on his costume as the tattoo on Collette's arm. We got a pimp says Prejean went to meet Jeremy as a condition of her probation at night at a bar which happens to be owned by Jeremy. Supposedly, she was never seen again, alive or dead, by anyone, until her arm popped up as an interior decoration of an alligator's stomach. And, finally, we know that seven other hookers assigned to Jeremy have supposedly failed to appear as required by the court, and are apparently missing. That's what we got, right?"

Nick agreed again.

"Well, bro, that's a lot of interesting shit, but it doesn't put Jeremy behind bars. It's all circumstantial evidence. If the case wasn't such a heater, we'd have no problem getting a search warrant for Jeremy's building, but in his case, that ain't gonna work. As you well know.

"I mean, *shit,*" Steve snorted. "Can you picture us going to one of the criminal judges around here, all of whom are close to Charysse Claiborne, and telling the judge that we need to search the apartment of the brother of one of their bench-mates, the powerful and comely Charysse Claiborne, her honorable self? No fucking way. We'd be laughed out on our fannies, and the story would be instantly all over the court building, then all over the federal courthouse. Uh-uh. We're going to have to do this in a different way. *Shit.* The minute I tell the D.A. anything, he's gonna have his ass on the phone to Thomas Claiborne, his old fishing buddy, telling him there's a rogue Assistant D.A. after his son, but don't worry, he'll see that it doesn't go any further. I can see it now."

Steve scribbled something more on the page, then drew two red lines beneath it before he continued. "I'll tell you how this is gonna go down. It's gonna be just like constipation. You work with it, but it doesn't seem like it's going anywhere. The pressure becomes unbearable, but you can't tell anybody about it. Then one day, it comes alive solely through its own power and explodes with such force that it drowns everything around it! That's how *this* is gonna go down. You and I are going to have to continue to work this thing on our own, but one day it's gonna hit the fucking fan and anoint everybody close to it. When that day comes, we have to have all the pieces in place and locked away, so they can't be destroyed. At that point, which is Jeremy's arrest, we may have to make sure the newspaper whores are tipped off, so that Claiborne and his cronies will be forced by the tidal wave of publicity not to interfere. That's the only way we're gonna save our butts in the end."

Nick listened to Steve. There was nothing he could disagree with. He had been through heater cases before, but nothing with the lurid sensationalism and variety of personalities mixed up in this one. Add that to the political relationships involved and you were looking at a case that would be sensational in a city already known for such things. They definitely needed to keep the case close until it reached a point where nothing in it could be refuted. Not by political pressure, not by facts, not by any clever defense attorneys.

"Steve, I think we need to determine which people we're gonna need to help us, and out of those, which ones we can *trust*. On my side, there aren't but one or two cops nowadays who I know can be trusted to go to the wall, if that's what it comes to."

Steve thought about that. "Yeah, the problem is even worse here in the D.A.'s office. The D.A. will do what he has to do, once it gets in the press, but if he can stifle it before the press gets it, he will. So I got no one to back me up here. Most of the D.A.s are green kids, just out of law school. They wouldn't know their ass from a hole in the ground when it comes to filing these charges and trying the case to a jury. From my side, I've got to work this thing alone and get it to a grand jury before the D.A. finds out about it. If the grand jury doesn't give me a true bill, the D.A. will disavow any knowledge of my actions, and kick my ass out on the street when it hits the papers. Not that I really mind... I've been thinking about going out to see if there really is life in the legal world after being a D.A."

Nick understood Steve's predicament. His wasn't much better off. He had little trust in the head of the Homicide Division, who had been promoted over a number of better-qualified candidates for the position purely on the basis of his political connections. While there were a few excellent cops in the division, the commander was *not* one of them. The entire police department was suffering from a lack of morale due to the inconsistency with which the force was run. Cops were no longer trained to back one another on sensitive issues, but instead were encouraged to rat on their fellow cops for the slightest transgression, whether it resulted in a breach or not. The result was a sort of mass paranoia on the part of the younger cops, and an indifference that had set in among the seasoned cops.

Although Nick indicated to Steve that he might be able to trust one or two cops on a matter as sensitive as this, he knew deep inside that that wasn't necessarily true, as even *those* individuals could have silently turned into cops who couldn't be trusted, a fact that Nick would only learn after it was too late, should he mistakenly trust them on this matter.

"OK." Steve wanted to organize their next steps. "We need to see if Tony the bartender can place Claiborne with Collette Prejean, but I'm still not ready to tip Claiborne off that we're on to his ass. You got anybody who can go in there with a photo and a story that they're doing a missing persons follow-up?"

Steve perked up for a second. "*Wait.* A stroke of brilliance just hit me. Do we have a female who can go in there posing as a family member trying to find Collette?"

Nick smiled. He did know someone who could be trusted for that. "There's a female patrol cop in the Vieux Carre District who's pretty sharp. Angela DiGiovanni. Super-cute little Sicilian chick. She's handled other things for me in the Quarter. Keeps her mouth shut, got some street sense. Her grandpa ran a grocery store on Elysian Fields for fifty years. Knows her way around the Quarter better than I do." Nick still wanted to keep the number of people involved to an absolute minimum. "You don't think I should take a photo and show it to Tony?"

"No fucking way. With all the talking about Claiborne you two have been doing in the last few days, even that dumb fuck might get suspicious. Just give your chick the photo and a list of ten or twelve bars in the back of the Quarter. Put the Slip It Inn near the bottom of the list, so she can get her story down before she sees Tony. She'll be more realistic that way."

Nick thought about it. "OK, that's probably cool. She can pose as someone in Collette Prejean's family. She'll want to know what's so special about a missing hooker. I'll tell her it's a relative of an out-of-town cop I know. A professional favor."

"You can handle that," Steve replied. "Now, let's see. Your boy's coming back to town on Tuesday night, right? When is Nancy going to get with you on slipping that information out of Jeremy's office?"

"I've set it up for tomorrow night. I got an ex-con who owes me some big favors. *Outstanding* safe-cracker."

"*Cocksucker.* You're not *really* going to break into his fucking office, *are* you? *Christ.* I can see the headlines now. New Orleans detective arrested in break-in of probation officer's office and files. *Probationgate.*" Steve chuckled. "Just remember, we may have to figure out how to get some of that crap admitted into court."

Nick shrugged. "If need be, Nancy will testify that she obtained it because she became suspicious of the little bastard. But at least I'd get my fifteen minutes of fame."

Steve frowned. "I'll have to think about that one. I don't *even* want to know any more about that. So what do you plan to find out?"

"One of the other things Nancy will give me is a computer print-out of Jeremy's active files. He has a current case load of about one hundred probationers, but she thinks only about a half-dozen are hookers. I want to go through their individual files, get their contact information, and see when their next reporting date is scheduled."

"That's got interesting possibilities. Whatta ya figure? Put surveillance on them? We pretty much need to figure a way to catch Jeremy in the act, as I see it, short of letting him kill one."

"Yeah, considering what other evidence we have at this point. A photo of Jeremy in action actually trying to kill one would be nice, but we're not likely to be that lucky. *Fuck.* I don't know yet. Quit asking me all the hard questions. I'll worry about that when I get there."

"What's the deal with the tattoo? What do we do with that?" Steve asked. "Do we have any suspicion that Thomas Claiborne is involved in this personally? I would be greatly surprised if that's true. But we have to nail down the tattoo issue. Seems to me that's the key to whatever is motivating Claiborne to be a serial killer, if that's what he is.

"Do we know anything about Jeremy's mother? Thomas Claiborne is apparently divorced or a widower. I never see him at bar functions with a female—he's always alone. Come to think of it, I never see Charysse Claiborne with a male escort at those functions. And you know, the more that I think of it, Thomas and Charysse don't even seem to mingle with *each other* when they're in public. That's pretty interesting. I think I might do a little research on the family."

"Might give us a new lead."

Steve sat back with a new thought. "You know, I think I'd like to go talk to Jack LaRose. You remember him? He's the forensic shrink I used in the Lambert case. That was the asshole who stabbed a reverend and his wife thirteen times each, then set them on fire and stole the money from the church's collection plates. He claimed he was suffering from post-traumatic stress disorder because he was a Vietnam vet. Had a whore of a shrink trying to sell that shit to the jury, but he had never actually been in *combat* in Vietnam. Jack nailed it down to the jury—that the asshole wasn't suffering from anything except fear of being caught."

# XXVII

The Vieux Carre District station was housed in an old bank building on Royal Street in the three-hundred block, nestled among the antique shops for which Royal Street is famous, even though only the most well-heeled can afford to buy anything in them. Nick parked on Conti Street, and he and Steve entered the station, with its high ceilings and sparse décor. Nick checked with the watch commander to see if Angela DiGiovanni was on duty. No such luck. She had taken a few hours of furlough, and would be in around nine-thirty p.m. He left his beeper number, and they headed for the Devil's Den, just down the street.

Dolly was off. They each ordered a double Crown on the rocks, pouring the drinks into go-cups. Back outside, they strolled down Conti Street to Bourbon and walked slowly toward Esplanade, watching the sights pass by. It was still cold and the neon lights of the strip were already engaged in their nightly battle to ward off the encroaching darkness. The streets were teeming with tourists and the inevitable swarm of vagrants plying their individual and collective scams.

Nick was the first to talk.

"You ever noticed that, whenever you're walking or driving along, when you really *want* to see something, like a fine chick, something always gets in the way at the last, crucial minute? Dwell upon that for a minute, my man. Let's say that there's what looks like a superchick on a street corner, and you're driving by. As you approach her, you start straining to get a good look on her, but you notice that there's someone else walking in her direction. You keep trying to scope her out but just when you're in a perfect position to see her face, the other person walks right fuckin' in front of her, like a goddam eclipse, and you never really get to see her face or other attributes?"

Nick was getting into his subject. "Or, as you approach, she's got her face turned just to one side so you can't see it. The closer you get to her, the more she continues to turn her face away from you, almost to the point where you'd swear she's capable of turning her head more than 360 degrees, like in *The Exorcist*. You never *do* get to see her face. It's what I call 'Saladino's Law.' If something can happen to prevent you getting a good look at a fine chick, it will."

He was on a roll. "And you know, there's a corollary to that. You know what it is? If you actually *do* finally get to see her face, it turns out to be one that you wished you hadn't wasted so much effort on. I mean, as you would say, it's not fit for human consumption. Or, even worse yet, it turns out to be some *dude* with long hair."

Steve laughed. "You've noticed that, too? *Shit.* I thought it was some personal affliction I was suffering from. Usually in my case, though, I'll be driving along and spot what looks like a *superfox* on the street, and just as I'm almost alongside of her and staring hard to see what she looks like, some fucking truck or van drives between us and I'm halfway down the street before I can see her again, in my rear-view mirror. It must be one of the natural laws of physics or some shit like that. Some kind of bad karma."

They turned down St. Peter Street and into Anthony's, near Pat O'Brien's, a joint frequented mainly by locals. It was a throwback to the way joints in the Quarter operated in the fifties and sixties, and it was still owned by one of the old-time minor hoods. Anthony Conducci sat at the cash register at the far end of the bar every night, seven nights a week. He looked the part: curly gray hair, shirt open halfway down the front revealing an equal amount of curly gray hair on his chest—enough hair that the gold chains around his neck had to fight for space.

"Nick, my friend. What *is* this?" Anthony stood up and hugged Nick, never moving from behind the register. He motioned to the barmaid, who looked like a retread from a drug rehab program. "For Nick and his friend."

"Tony, meet Steve Chaisson. D.A.'s office." Nick swung around to the barmaid. "Crown on the rocks, double. Same for my friend here."

"What? What is this, my friend?" Anthony rasped, his vocal chords long eroded by booze and cigarettes. "I know you not here on business. Tell me that's so."

"Uh-uh, Anthony. Just out enjoying the sights," Nick replied.

"Sights? You want *sights*? Sights I got." Anthony waived his hand around.

Nick looked around slowly. It had been a while since he had been here. Anthony always had a few hookers stashed around the bar, b-drinking. Some of them were Tulane, Loyola or UNO students, trying to pick up a little cash. Some were bored housewives, looking for a little spending cash or entertainment when their husbands were out of town. They were usually succulent. Some of them dressed up, some came casual. They rarely went away empty-handed. Nick admired the three or four who were sitting around.

Anthony never got busted, and it was rare for one of his hookers to get busted. "Yeah, Anthony, you always got enough sights in here. The tour busses oughta stop here on their route."

Anthony slapped Nick on the back, heartily. "Business is good, my friend. Go. Walk around the bar a little. Talk to the birds. Relax. Let me know if you see something special."

Nick and Steve walked back mid-bar and leaned on the counter, surveying the chicks and watching the action. Almost as one, the chicks around the bar surveyed the pair like fresh meat, wondering if some money could be made.

"What's up, guys?"

Steve and Nick looked around behind them. A tight-lipped blonde was standing in front of them with a challenging expression on her face, one foot propped up on the bar rail, one hand on her hip, and a tight sweater ironed on to her braless tits.

"Why the sour look, boys? Y'all not gay, are you? God, I hope not. You wouldn't fucking *believe* how many homos have been in here today. *Christ.* Is it *that* difficult to figure out this is *not* a gay joint?" The lips were pouty. She moved in between them with her back to the bar. "Wouldn't you guys like to buy me a drink? It's tiresome having to sit here talking to the competition."

Nick noticed the fine features of her face. Her skin was perfect, with little make-up, and what was there was expensive. Her face was classic, with high cheek bones, and he could tell that she lived the good life somewhere in one of the more expensive areas of the city.

Nick nodded to the barmaid who produced some dark-colored drink, probably iced tea. The blonde ignored it and started rubbing her leg against Nick's, while pouting at Steve.

"Are you guys *always* this talkative, or did I just catch you on a special occasion?"

Nick felt his beeper go off and looked at the number. It was the Vieux Carre District station number. It had to be Angela. He headed for the house phone, leaving Steve to fend off the blonde.

"Meet us at Anthony's." It was hard for Nick to hear over the music in the joint.

"No shit," Angela scoffed with skepticism. "You're really doing the *hot* spots tonight. Who's 'us'?"

"Worry about that when you get here."

Nick returned to Steve, relieved to see that the blonde had moved on. They ordered a second round and watched a tourist being fleeced out of a croaker, a hundred dollar bill, in return for which he bought a pitcher of iced tea for the hooker and got his thigh rubbed.

Angela showed up a half-hour later. Even in her undercover sweats, she was a knock-out. Five feet four, jet-black hair and black eyes with perfect Sicilian skin and an oval face, she drew looks, even in those drab clothes. She walked by Nick and Steve to talk with Anthony for a few minutes before returning to the bar. Nick had ordered a soft drink for her when he saw her enter, and handed it to her.

"Meet Steve Chaisson. D.A.'s office. He'll be able to talk when he's finished stepping on his tongue."

"*Hi.* Angela." She reached out her hand.

Steve felt a strange throw-back to that airline commercial that used to feature women saying, "*Hi.* I'm *Susie.* Fly *me.*"

*Gladly,* Steve thought to himself.

Angela looked back to Nick, all business.

"What's up?"

"We need a little help," Nick replied.

"*Shit.* You've always needed help—a *lot* of it," Angela said, getting off the first shot.

"*Ouch.* You got me right." Nick laughed.

"Yeah, well, if the foo shits..." Angela's laugh had the pure sound of crystal when struck.

"We need you to hit a few joints in the back Quarter with this photo." Nick took out the picture of Collette Prejean he had retrieved from the file in his car. "Just check with the bartenders and anybody else in the joints to see if they've seen her."

Angela looked at Nick skeptically, knowing that he could do this as easily as she could.

"You don't *even* want to know, sweetheart. Just do it for me. Her name is Collette Prejean. Tell them that she's the daughter of an out-of-town cop, and you're doing him a favor because he and his wife are grieving and don't know where she is. If somebody recognizes her, get the information as to where and when—you know the routine."

"Great timing, Nick. We just rousted every fucking joint in the Quarter last week, checking licenses. Three of them were closed down until they got their licenses updated. Their owners went to the pokey overnight. We're not real popular right now, all because the district chief got a bug up his ass to do something after the city council started bitching about businesses in the Quarter not paying their taxes." Angela sighed. "Let me see your list." She reviewed it and said, "Well, you're definitely equal opportunity here. You got a black joint, a gay joint, a punk joint, and the rest are nondescript, other than character hangouts. No tourist joints?"

"Nuh-uh. This is strictly a local deal. I need it done in the next day. Can do?"

"Maybe. I'll let you know. I'll call you." Angela headed for the door.

"Angela! *One* day. That's *all* I got."

"Nice to meet you," she flung back over her shoulder at Steve as she hit the door.

He raised his drink in salute, and turned to Nick. "Where the fuck have you been hiding *her*? I haven't *ever* seen a cop that fine."

They finished their drinks, and Nick thanked Anthony on their way out.

"Why don't you stay a little longer, Nick? If you like something, take it upstairs. Use my office. There's a small cot in there. It's clean."

"Anthony, that's generous. Very generous. But we've got a few things to do yet tonight," Nick said. The last thing he wanted was to let Anthony get some grease on him, with the cameras that were probably mounted in the ceiling in that office. If not Anthony, Nick suspected that the feds had the office wired, which would almost be worse. He wasn't indebted to anyone, and he planned to keep it that way.

"Nick, you know I remember your papa. He was a good man, not afraid of anything." Anthony tapped the inside of his left wrist with his right fingers, indicating that the person he was describing had balls. "From the same village in the old country. You know, me and him useta talk about the old country. He would be proud of his boy." With that, Anthony reminded Nick not to forget where he came from, and none too subtly.

They continued walking down Bourbon, and went into one of the bars where they could sit close to the open doors and watch the crowd go by out on the street. The crowd was always the best show on the street. It was like taking a six-pack to the Greyhound station and watching the travelers, but the Quarter held a much larger volume of people.

"You gonna walk in the St. Pat's parade this year?" Steve asked, noting the green shamrocks and other decorations on the walls of the bar. "Don't forget, it's next week."

"Kinda depends. I haven't had time to get a set of tails. I guess I still could. I need to help a friend with a St. Joseph Altar about the same time."

Steve knew that Nick had for many years helped a friend with his St. Joseph's Altar, an undertaking the friend had promised St. Joseph when his little girl recovered from a serious illness. St. Joseph's Day was only a short period after St. Patrick's Day, and a number of parades were also held in honor of the Italians. Many New Orleanians celebrated both St. Patrick's and St. Joseph's, not from a heritage standpoint, but because the holidays were simply another reason to celebrate life in New Orleans.

There were at least four different St. Patrick's parades in various neighborhoods around the city and its suburbs, not to mention the Italian parades. The altars, however, were another story. Some were huge, publicized affairs, while a large number of others were smaller altars limited to family and a few close friends.

The altars were a serious undertaking in New Orleans, and were made by those who had prayed to St. Joseph and had had their favors, such as the healing of a family member, granted. In many cases, friends volunteered to work on the altars, and some of the altars grew to immense proportions, requiring that food preparation begin weeks and even, in some cases, months in advance.

Altars consisted of an elaborate display of food offerings, including stuffed artichokes, fish, vegetables, pasta, cookies, cakes, breads, lucky fava beans blessed on the altar, and St. Joseph candles. When the altar was opened, it was blessed by a priest, and a small pageant was usually held to tell the story of St. Joseph. After the pageant, visitors were fed, and the remainder was donated to charities.

Steve and Nick had noticed that the number of females in the bar had grown while they were talking, and it appeared that the males were outnumbered at least three to one.

"Ladies' night," Steve said, nudging Nick. "The women drink free. This joint's starting to look like feeding time at the zoo."

"You are absolutely correct, my boy. See anything?"

"Not a thing. Almost blinded me."

"Not to change the subject, dickhead, but I'm just realizing that tomorrow makes two weeks since this case got dumped in my goddam lap," Nick said. What's really bugging me is that Claiborne will be back in town in a few days, and he still has an inventory of hookers in his current case files. If he's actually killed any or all of the seven hookers in his closed cases, we still don't have a clue as to how he's doing it. We don't know if there is some special day or month he celebrates by killing. If there is such a thing, it could be coming up soon, especially with him having been away for a while, and we got no way to anticipate it."

"You think he might be operating on some kinda schedule, maybe a theme?" Steve asked. "If he's actually a serial killer, it would make sense, since he seems to confine his victims to hookers under his control, at least as far as we know. I haven't dealt with serial killers before, but the literature seems to indicate that they usually have a hard-on for something, and act it out in their murders. If it's tied to a date, it could be an anniversary or something, or it could just be that the compulsion becomes too strong to control—not regulated by any specific time period. Either way, with Claiborne having access to a guaranteed supply of victims within easy grasp, we need to be ready to act when he gets back."

# XXVIII

Dr. Jack LaRose, a *cum laude* graduate of Harvard University School of Medicine, was a New Orleans native who had displayed brilliance in his early academic career and throughout his first decade of practice as a psychiatrist. His practice had flourished and he was sought out by the rich and famous of the Deep South. His office in the Quarter had a private rear entrance for select patients; the rest used the front door off of Pirate's Alley. Dr. LaRose served on all the correct civic boards and, in his forties, was at the peak of his career. Unfortunately, that peak was short-lived.

He had married one of the city's most luscious debutantes, or, as he was fond of putting it, a debutramp. It was Dr. Jack's misfortune that this in fact turned out to be an accurate description of his bride, who was afflicted with a raging case of nymphomania, spreading her wares throughout all levels of New Orleans society. She had become infamous for giving blow jobs to coworkers in the supply rooms of the various law firms by which she had been employed over the years. By the time their daughter had reached mid-teens, Dr. Jack's wife, whose beauty had eventually faded through natural aging and twenty years of having her furrows constantly plowed, had begun using their daughter as a lure to attract lovers.

Dr. Jack had been aware of his wife's obsessions and simply tolerated them. It was like the old story that the leaky faucets in the plumber's house are never fixed; he's too busy taking care of other people's problems. Dr. Jack was not aware, however, that his wife was pimping their daughter, until he came home early one afternoon and found them both in bed with a family friend. Dr. Jack divorced his wife, and his daughter ran off. The last he had heard of her was that she was in California, living on the streets.

Dr. Jack immediately devoted himself to self-punishment. His private practice fell apart, and so did he. He started binge drinking in the Quarter, in some cases for weeks at a time. His home on Coliseum Place, once a showpiece, was allowed to deteriorate. He lost his office in the Quarter.

After about five years of reeling out of control, he started to pull himself together. He cleaned up his house and hung a shingle on Tulane Avenue, upstairs above a bar that used to be a strip joint. Thanks to his political contacts, he was able to get contracts from the judges at Criminal District Court to examine defendants and inmates. From that time forward, he practiced forensic psychiatry almost exclusively, in a small dingy office up a narrow flight of creaky stairs.

Dr. Jack still binged on rare occasions and was a relentless chain smoker, his nicotine-stained fingers always lighting a Camel from the remains of its predecessor. He looked like a cross between the Marlboro Man and John Lennon, his gray beard and curly gray hair occasionally allowed to grow to shaggy lengths. His rugged, dimpled chin was strangely offset by the octagonal spectacles he wore, and he took great care in handling them, whether unwrapping the ear pieces from around his ears one at a time or simply posing with them while talking.

The man gave off great charisma, and was a genius on the witness stand, charming each juror, male or female, black or white. When he spoke, people had the impression that whatever this man said or was about to say, it was something you could take to the bank.

Steve was selective about using Dr. Jack in his cases, as some defense attorneys took great joy in making him rehash the pain in his past, hoping to destroy his credibility with the jury. But Steve always sought out Dr. Jack's advice in any case involving psychiatric testimony. Besides being a friend, Dr. Jack had the ability to slice to the heart of a situation quickly and concisely without the usual superfluous observations and ramblings that others in his profession seemed to relish.

Even more importantly, in a city as given to lurid crimes as New Orleans was, the sheer volume of Dr. Jack's experience with the flotsam and jetsam of humankind was virtually unsurpassed. The feds had nothing on him when it came to evaluating the criminal human mind; in fact, he had many times contradicted F.B.I. profilers and, on all of those occasions, he was correct and the profilers had made mistakes.

Steve had decided to discuss Jeremy with Dr. Jack, and was at Dr. Jack's office at 9:00 the next morning. It was cold again that morning, and the dirty windows of the office seemed to make a dismal day even more depressing. Steve was waiting for Dr. Jack to come to work, and the heavy rasping of his long-suffering secretary, Olivia Figueroa, an overweight, asthmatic Guatemalan in her late fifties, provided a rhythmic background to his thoughts of Jeremy Claiborne. Olivia had been with Dr. Jack in his original practice and had stuck with him through the hard times. She had offered Steve a cup of coffee, which he gratefully accepted.

Steve walked around the waiting room area and looked at the unpainted walls with the lone pair of bedraggled Vasarely prints. The pictures' once-brilliant colors had faded from the relentless glare of the overhead fluorescent fixtures. In Dr. Jack's office, a large black-and-white print of Picasso's version of Don Quixote hung lazily atilt behind the desk, which itself was a disaster, with jumbled papers and files spread hopelessly across it. The sofa and chairs in front of the desk were fifties modern: stark and garish, the only real color in the room.

Steve heard the stairs creak, and the door opened. Dr. Jack was wearing a camel-colored sport coat with a maroon corduroy shirt and a very thin navy tie that had some sort of diagonal club design on it.

"Mr. Chaisson's waiting for you," Olivia wheezed, handing Dr. Jack a few notes and a cup of coffee. "Judge Rafferty called. He needs you on a sanity commission today."

Dr. Jack barely acknowledged the information, throwing his well-worn, tooled-leather briefcase onto the desk and flopping down into the chair. He had a Camel dangling from one side of his mouth.

"Well, Steve, it's a little early, isn't it? What've you got on your mind?" Dr. Jack leaned back in his chair and propped his boots on the desk.

"Doc, I'm afraid I got Pandora by the short hairs. I'm working on a case that could easily be the end of my career as a prosecutor, win or lose. And once I ignite this little powder keg, there'll be no going back, no sweeping it under the rug. No amount of singing by the fat lady will stop it." Steve, aware of Dr. Jack's constant evaluation of anyone with whom he spoke, made a special effort to appear cool and in control.

Dr. Jack sipped his coffee. "So?"

"Doc, I may have a serial killer who is a member of a very prominent local family."

"That's not necessarily unusual. We already know of some society members who have gone astray, don't we?" Dr. Jack raised his eyebrows.

*Oops,* Steve thought. *I hope he's not getting his back up at this.* Steve didn't really know how sensitive Dr. Jack was about his past. It was something the man never talked about. Understandably so.

Dr. Jack saw the look on Steve's face. "It's a *joke,* son. Relax. Now, who are we talking about?"

Steve saw a momentary twinkle in Dr. Jack's eyes and knew he had been had. He relaxed.

"Doc, you got to promise me this stays between us. I'm goddam serious here." Although Steve trusted Dr. Jack implicitly, he was still reluctant to have the Claiborne name drift out into the open air. His paranoia over the case made him doubt the sanctity of any office, or of any friend, for that matter. Still, he had no choice if he was going to assist in apprehending Claiborne and preventing further murders.

When the words came, he was almost whispering, causing Dr. Jack to take his feet off the desk and lean forward to hear.

"I'm talking about Thomas Claiborne. *Judge* Thomas Claiborne."

*Damn*, he thought. *That wasn't exactly the way I wanted that to come out.*

Dr. Jack was silent for a moment, sipping on his coffee and inhaling the Camel slowly, holding the smoke in for maximum effect. He finally swung around in his chair to look out of the window at the dark gray sky then swung back around and put his boots back up on the desk.

"You really mean you're talking about *Jeremy* Claiborne, don't you?" Dr. Jack lit a fresh Camel from the ember of the old one. Steve noticed the heavily nicotine-stained fingers.

"How...?" Steve didn't get to finish his question.

"I've had concerns about Jeremy for a long time."

"How...?"

"Let me finish." Dr. Jack had raised his hand, motioning for Steve to be silent. "I've watched Jeremy for years. Most courts hold motion days on which the courts hear and decide motions connected with the criminal cases before them. You're familiar with that, I know."

Steve nodded. He was quite familiar with motion days. Take a number and stand in line, because some courts may have as many as twenty or thirty motion hearings on motion days.

"As you know, it's common to have probation revocation hearings and sanity commission hearings on regular motion days, so Jeremy is frequently in the same court as I am. I've had the opportunity to observe him in court and on the witness stand on many occasions over a long period of time, and a man in my trade spends his life observing and listening to people."

Steve nodded again.

"To my observation, Jeremy exhibits aberrational behavior, especially in his testimony concerning hookers who have violated the conditions of their probation. The man appears to me to have a problem with women in general, and hookers in particular," Dr. Jack explained.

"Funny," Steve muttered. "Nick Saladino said much the same thing after an interview he had with Claiborne."

"Saladino is the detective on this? *Excellent*. He'll see it through, regardless of the pressure. Good man." Dr. Jack lit up his next Camel.

Steve ran the story to Dr. Jack in detail, including the tattoo of the black orchid, showing Dr. Jack the photo of the arm and a copy of the *Times-Picayune* photo of Thomas Claiborne with the tattoo.

"You know, I used to run in much the same circles as Thomas Claiborne, in the fifties. He entered law school at Tulane and was quite the sport about town. Always had the best cars, a membership in the Southern Yacht Club, use of his daddy's sailboat, and a bevy of willing debutantes. After he returned from the war, he married and settled down. Didn't really run with the pack anymore. He married a beautiful woman, quiet and submissive. They had a daughter, Charysse, whom you know, but you probably don't know that she was named after her mother, also named Charysse. Tom, of course, worked for the most prestigious law firm in town and quickly made partner, mainly on the basis that he would handle his family's legal business for the firm. A guaranteed position.

"Tom was able to secure his spot on the federal bench thanks to some generous donations to the Democratic Party, and to a Democratic senator who was very powerful at the time. He's actually been a pretty decent judge, although his personality hasn't won him any friends since he's been on the bench."

Steve nodded. "I'll say."

"Now that I think of it," Dr. Jack continued, "I believe his wife died not long after the time Jeremy was born, apparently from complications that developed from the childbirth. She and Charysse had been traveling for a number of months up east, and she died somewhere out of town—I want to say Boston. There was a lot of gossip about why she didn't return to New Orleans to give birth to Jeremy, but it kind of died off after a while.

"Something else is coming back to me now," Dr. Jack continued, looking immersed in his memories. "I recall that Charysse, the daughter, was in her mid or late teens at the time, and she pretty much raised Jeremy through her college and law school years. Old Tom wasn't much help. He kind of withdrew into himself after his wife's death and developed the charm for which he is now known."

Steve snorted, still listening intently. He hadn't considered the possibility that Dr. Jack had close ties to the Claiborne family in any manner. With anyone else, he might be concerned about a leak, but Steve was still certain that Dr. Jack would never betray his confidence.

"I really don't remember Tom having a tattoo. I'll have to think about that."

Steve returned him to the present. "Doc, if this killer is actually putting tattoos on his victims, you got any ideas about what that means?"

"Well, if Jeremy *is* the killer and is in fact putting tattoos on his victims, particularly some kind of tattoo worn by his father, I would say he is a schizophrenic, and suffering from delusions connected with some form of hatred for his father and/or his mother. The tattoo could represent a transference of his father's identity onto his victims, and, by killing the victim, he thereby kills his father. What we don't know—the missing link—is why he chooses hookers to be his victims, if in fact those are his *only* victims. He could just as easily choose anyone else assigned to his case load, male or female. The hookers bear some special significance for him. He may be selecting the hookers as some reference to his mother or to some other woman in his life, in which case his killings would accomplish a dual purpose, eliminating both his father and that woman at the same time."

"I see," Steve said. "But I can't imagine what he would hate about his father so much that he would act out in such a violent manner."

"Could be a reaction to stern discipline or perverted discipline on the part of his father, possibly combined with a starvation for love. But I suspect that's not the case, given his predilection for hookers as victims. I believe, if you figure out the female connection, it will lead to clues about his hatred for his father." Dr. Jack paused for a minute. "If you don't have a problem with it, I've got a couple of ideas I'd like to check into myself."

"I don't have a problem, doc. What are they?"

"I'd rather not say right now. They seem a little preposterous at this point, even to me. But some of the things you've told me this morning have brought back some memories I had long since buried."

"Just don't let it leak out right now, doc, if you don't mind. I really don't want any shit from anybody right now. I want this thing glued together first."

"You don't have to worry, Steve. No one will know."

Steve returned to his office and put his thoughts together about what Dr. Jack had told him. At least he had a plausible scenario of why Jeremy would kill, but it still didn't seem like enough to act on. He was thinking about what would happen if and when Jeremy was arrested and charged with murder. Any decent defense attorney would automatically, and rightfully so, enter a plea of not guilty by reason of insanity, at the time of the arraignment, or "arrangement," as Steve liked to call it. In Louisiana, an insanity plea must be lodged at the time of the arraignment, or the defense would not later be able to use an insanity defense at trial.

Steve reviewed the system in his mind. Once Jeremy pled "not guilty by reason of insanity," the matter would be virtually out of the prosecutor's hands almost immediately. The court would have no choice but to convene a "lunacy commission," at which time the court would appoint a team of at least two forensic psychiatrists to examine Jeremy to determine whether he was sane at the time of the offense, and whether he was mentally capable of standing trial.

The District Attorney would have no input into the court's choice of psychiatrists, but then, neither would the defense, although either side could also retain their own psychiatrists. Dr. Jack would likely be chosen, but would likely decline due to his familiarity with the Claiborne family. If Jeremy were to be found insane at the time of the offense, he could be committed to Feliciana Forensic Facility, the state's hospital for the criminally insane, located in Jackson, Louisiana. That would at least get him off the streets, but there would be no guarantee he would remain there. If, during later examinations, he was found to be no longer a danger to himself or anyone else, he could be released into society again.

Steve was willing to bet Jeremy would be found insane, which, under Louisiana law, was simple. Louisiana had long ago adopted the M'Naghten Rule, which essentially held that a person would be ruled insane where there was sufficient evidence that they were unable to distinguish between right and wrong at the time of the offense. Many other states also adhered to M'Naghten, which dated back to England in 1843.

Daniel M'Naghten shot and killed one Edward Drummond, the private secretary of Sir Robert Peel. M'Naghten had actually intended to kill Peel himself, thinking that Peel spearheaded a conspiracy to have M'Naghten killed. M'Naghten mistakenly shot Drummond, thinking him to be Peel. M'Naghten claimed that he had acted out of delusion and could not be held responsible. The jury agreed and found him not guilty by reason of insanity. The case caused an uproar in Britain at the time, and was even debated in Parliament.

Steve had perked up when Dr. Jack mentioned that Jeremy could be suffering from delusions, and for the first time Steve gave serious thought to the possibility that Jeremy might never actually be *convicted* of murder, regardless of the strength of the case that Steve and Nick might be able to put together against him. Considering the status of the Claiborne family, it would be a perfect face-saver for the family and everyone else involved in the criminal justice system, to put Jeremy in an institution rather than face a messy trial, especially a trial with the specter of the death penalty looming over it.

It was something that Steve would just have to deal with, and the possibilities were unsettling. All he could do for now was to get sufficient evidence to get the case in front of a grand jury and get an indictment before anyone else found out about it. As a Senior Assistant D.A., he could take any case to the grand jury without approval, but there were a lot of pitfalls ahead before he could do that.

# XXIX

It was 3:00 p.m. The buzzer on his intercom brought Steve back to reality.

"Detective Saladino." Melanie, his secretary, had a very soft voice, and Steve often referred to her as "mellifluous Melanie." The first time he called her that, she stormed off in a huff, thinking it was some type of devious insult that Steve had come up with. After consulting Webster, she calmed down, and even started to brag about it.

Steve remembered that Nick had been planning to break into Jeremy's office using some ex-con, and he felt a sickening in the pit of his stomach. A large part of him hoped that Nick hadn't been successful.

"Steve. Bad news," Saladino grunted into the phone.

Steve's stomach tightened into a full Windsor knot.

"My fuckin' day has gone 10-7," Nick said.

"Let me guess. You didn't get laid last night."

"*Ixnay*, cocksucker. We gotta talk, and it ain't gonna be over these fuckin' phones. Meet me at the Mile." Nick hung up.

"Oh, well. What the fuck, over?" he asked rhetorically, then slammed his door shut and walked across Tulane Avenue to the Miracle Mile.

Nick was clinking the ice in his rocks glass. The cubes were still slightly bronzed from the Crown Royal that had once surrounded them.

"At least you're prompt."

"One of the things that I've come to know and admire about myself, buck. If you can't be on time for a drink, you'll never be anywhere on time." Steve ordered a double Crown and stood quietly, waiting for Nick to talk.

Nick leaned on the bar and faced Steve.

"Uh-oh. If this is gonna be a long story, I'm gonna get comfortable," Steve said, sitting on a bar stool.

"*Q*," Nick barked. It was short for "fuck you," commonly pronounced by the two as "fuck que," and was used when the person didn't care enough to send the very best by taking time to fully pronounce the entire phrase. Nick had also raised his middle finger in salute to Steve. Nick still used the old, more formal version of the middle finger salute, with his two surrounding fingers parallel to the middle finger up to the first joint from the palm, then bent at the first joint, at right angles perpendicular to the upright middle finger. Younger people don't bother with such elegance, preferring to simply raise the middle finger by itself, with all other fingers held down equally towards the palm.

"Ain't *that* nice," Steve replied. "When was the last you *wore* a Crown Royal?"

"Been a long time, buckaroo! Just remember, catch-back is a mother fucker!"

They both relaxed, some of the tension relieved.

Steve couldn't stand it any longer.

"What? *What?* What the fuck you gotta tell me? You're worse than a fuckin' *chick*."

"*OK. OK.* Remember Angela? Checking out the bartender with the picture of Collette Prejean?"

"Of fucking *course* I fucking remember. That was only last night. I didn't have *that* goddam much to drink. *Christ*."

"Fuckin' *nuthin.* Can you believe it? She goes to Jeremy's joint, no pun intended, and talks to Tony, the bartender. Tony tells her the girl looks familiar. He's probably seen her around. Then he tells Angela she may have been in by herself a time or two... Dwell on *that.* She may have been in *by herself.* Right. Angela never asked him that. He's a lying goddam yeast infection *asshole.* I guarantee you that dildo-sucking piece of shit can put Collette with Jeremy, and I'm gonna pin his fucking balls to a board with straight pins until that jockstrap-chewing wart tells me about it! As *if.*"

Steve had a 3-D picture in his mind of Nick extracting the information from Tony.

"You may want to come up with some method of obtaining information from Tony that would be somewhat more palatable to a grand jury. That's all you wanted to tell me? What about getting to Jeremy's current case records?"

"I already *told* you my day went 10-7. Don't you *ever* pay attention? Did I tell you I had a safe man that owed me a favor? A few years ago, I had caught him right on a job uptown, and I let him go, to be an informant. Jeremy's office and file cabinets would be child's play for him. So I try to find him today, and where do you think the bastard is? In the House of fucking Detention, on a domestic abuse rap, along with a charge of molestation of a juvenile. Him and his old lady both. They got into some kinda beef because he's hittin' on his old lady's teenage daughter, and out comes the cutlery. *Both* of 'em get cut. *Both* of 'em go to Charity. *Both* of 'em go to jail. Inconsiderate little bastard," Nick fumed.

"Yeah, I hate when that happens." Steve breathed a sigh of relief. He felt the knot in his stomach loosen slightly. "So what's the next plan, dude?"

"No problem. I'm gonna furlough my safe man from the House of D tonight for a few hours. Let him do what he's gotta do, and return him to his cell. He'll be happy to be out for a little while, engaging in some recreational breaking and entering. The Special Operations Division at the Criminal Sheriff's Office will help out a little." Nick looked pleased with himself.

Steve's knot came back with a vengeance. "*Jesus.* So when is this happening?"

"Tonight, my boy. Tonight," Nick replied with a smirk.

*God protects children and idiots*, Steve thought to himself, hoping that in fact would turn out to be true in this case.

It was as if Nick had read Steve's mind.

"Speaking of children—*good news.* I get to see mine for the first time in three weeks. My old lady doesn't want me to be alone with them yet, so she's sending her older sister along with them. I'm supposed to meet them at Monkey Hill in Audubon Park. Fine with me. I don't mind Sharon's sister. She's kinda aesthetically-challenged, but she's always liked me. I got to tell you, though, I'm actually feeling a little nervous about seeing them. I hope Sharon hasn't been putting a lot of shit in their minds about me."

"Man, that's *great.* Hope it works out well for all of you. Like I told you, though, stay cool no matter what happens. Every little snit you and Sharon get into will only put money in the pockets of the lawyers and drive you further from the children. There aren't many lawyers in domestic practice who view their role as anything other than to make like fuckin' Evinrude, and stir shit! The more they stir the shit, the more they can bill the file. That's one of the reasons mediation is becoming popular in domestic cases. That and the fact that judges are becoming afraid of courtroom violence in domestic cases. Losers in domestic cases have absolutely no fucking sense of humor, and the mortality rate among the judiciary and members of the bar involved in domestic cases is becoming a problem."

Steve continued, "Personally, I've never understood the hassle. Somebody picks out their version of the ideal mate, then later wants to tear their fingernails out when they break up. Go figure. It's still the same two people who thought they had found the ideal relationship. People nowadays don't look any further than the pubic triangle in selecting a mate, then they wonder why the other parts of their ideal mate aren't worth a damn."

"I'm beginning to believe that. I'd like to keep a friendship with Sharon when this is over, and continue to be a father to the kids. I'm thinking I can be a friend more easily to her, now that I don't have the pressure of having to report home to her every day of my life. I'm starting to feel free again, and I don't ever want to lose that feeling again."

"You're learning. It just takes time," Steve said. "I've got Julie coming over tonight. Says she wants to talk. That's not a real good omen. Usually she wants just one thing and it isn't talk, so this can't be good."

"I don't know *what* that broad sees in you, man," Nick said. "I used to think she had a lotta class until I found out *you* were porking her. Destroyed my picture of *her.*"

"Eat your heart out, cocksucker. She knows talent when she sees it," Steve retorted.

Next morning, Steve woke up around 7:30 with Julie's naked butt pressed up against his. He wiggled his ass and Julie slowly came to.

"I'm hungry. Get your butt up and let's go get some breakfast."

Julie moaned again, muttering some crap about how early it was.

"It's goddam near eight o'clock. It's goddam *Saturday*. Now get goddam *up*." Steve's stomach was growling as he headed for the coffee pot. Julie rolled over, and Steve stopped and admired the sight for a moment.

"Christ, I *must* be hungry if that's all I can think of when I look at you." He laughed and stepped into the shower. When he was finished, the coffee maker was making its weird orgasmic sounds as it turned water into the thick black ooze that Steve called coffee.

"Steve, we still haven't talked, and I want to talk," Julie said with a pout.

Steve felt his asshole clamp shut and his stomach twinged. *Oh, well, nothing lasts forever,* he thought. He could tell by the tone in Julie's voice that this was going to be a conversation he wasn't ready to deal with.

"Sure, baby. After I've got some food in my stomach." He went to the kitchen, pinching Julie on the ass as she passed him en route to the shower.

When she was dressed, they headed to Mama's Café, a small grungy operation that made the best breakfast in town, washed down by chicory coffee that was always steaming hot.

"I'm going ahead with my divorce," Julie said, a strong resolve in her voice. "I'm going to be free."

"I think that's a great move. What about your community property settlement?" Steve asked, dreading the conversation.

"I don't really give a shit. The bastard's got to give me something. He's making megabucks now, and I put him through med school. Whatever deal my lawyer makes, that's it. I'm not interested in dicking around with it anymore."

Steve just nodded and devoured his breakfast. He only wanted to relax and enjoy his food.

Julie started rambling about how she wanted to travel. Places like Italy, Greece—anyplace.

"And I want to have a couple of children before I'm too old for it to be safe," she added, her tone getting more intense.

Steve shuddered inside as they got up and left the restaurant.

"Steve," she said, staring at him almost forlornly. "I'd like to do all that with you."

Steve had just slammed the door of the car and started the engine.

"I would love to travel with you occasionally, but I've got financial and time restraints," he said. "I don't have the jack, and I don't have much vacation time as a state employee, baby."

He was heading for the lakefront so they could sit on the seawall and finish this with some privacy.

"Steve, I'd think I'd like to go to Italy on a honeymoon," Julie added, relentless.

Steve had just pulled into a parking space and his foot involuntarily hit the brake, throwing them both forward. He feigned surprise.

He had always had a concern about whether Julie's clock was starting to run out. It wasn't that he, too, hadn't considered the possibility. She was a great source of pride and satisfaction to him. She was conversant in things Steve had never had the time or money to experience, and she represented the kind of woman he thought he would never be able to attract. She had looks, class and intelligence. Tragically, that made for a two-edged sword upon which Steve had impaled himself. Now that he had such a woman, he knew he could never provide permanent satisfaction to her; that she would outgrow his world quickly, and that their relationship would not survive her attempts to alter her world in order to accommodate the drabness of his. As if that wasn't a big enough problem, he knew he didn't want children, and he had no right to deprive her of her natural instincts. The two obstacles together virtually insured that the relationship would eventually crumble.

"You want to get married?" he asked.

"To *you*, Steve. I love you." Julie looked at him expectantly.

Steve was silent for a moment, looking out at the lake and choosing his words carefully.

"I've thought of that possibility. In fact, frequently so. But there are a few things we need to think about. You are the most sensual woman I have ever known. You are absolutely the most sexually exciting woman I have ever been with, or ever dreamed of being with, for that matter. And we're very compatible, in *most* respects."

Julie started to tear up and looked away.

"There are a couple of basic problems that you need to consider," Steve continued. "In the long run, I don't think I am, or even could be, everything you need to be happy. In many ways, you are a much larger person than I am, especially in terms of worldly sophistication. You float around easily in the circles of wealthy, worldly people. Educated people. You are accepted in those circles, actually invited into them. You are A-list all the way. Those people desire your company and seek you out." He took his time, enunciating each word carefully after he'd chosen it.

"Baby, I just don't fit there and never will. My parents never had money or social status. They never had access to those circles, and never had a dream of attaining that kind of access. I don't walk your walk. I don't talk your talk. I'm just a coarse fucking criminal lawyer. I'm the best at what I do, but my world is the bleak, vicious underbelly of society. I'm cynical and opinionated, and I am not good at generating the small talk that's required at cocktail parties. I have no patience with left-leaning liberals who are more concerned with criminals' rights than they are with the suffering imposed by those criminals.

"Probably worse yet," he continued, "I don't have experience with summers at Cape Cod, or the weekend's menu at the Southern Yacht Club. The majority of those people who do operate behind shallow facades; those people have an acute instinct for recognizing that someone like me sees them for the vacuous life forms that they are. They treat people like me like lepers. It's hard to make small talk when vibes like that are flowing between you at a party."

Julie started to say something, but Steve put his finger to his lips to quiet her.

"You are precisely the type of woman I've always dreamed of. But to marry you would be like putting a butterfly in a colorless glass jar and watching it fade. I couldn't do that to you. I *do* love you, and because it is a true love, I couldn't put you into a world that would suffocate you, even if it means giving you up. You need someone who can share your world with you. I'll never be that person."

Steve watched Julie's eyes darken. He knew what was coming.

"That's not *true*," Julie protested. "I don't need that life. I want to be with you."

"I hear what you're saying, baby, but I think you also know that what I've told you is true. We're not going to resolve this in one session. I don't want to lose you, but I will not do something I know is wrong for you. Don't forget—I've told you in the past that I don't have a strong interest in having children, which is another problem."

"But, I don't *need* to have children. We can be happy together," Julie whimpered.

"Listen to what you're saying, baby. How many times have you told me in the past how important it was to you to have a child? You said it again a few minutes ago. We can keep talking about it, but I know that what I've said is what I truly feel. It's not likely to change."

Steve knew this was the end, that there would be no more talk. His heart hurt at what he was giving up, but he knew there was no other way. He knew Julie would eventually hate him for depriving her of children, even if not for taking her from her world.

Back at the apartment, Julie went straight to her car and took off. A bitter emptiness enveloped Steve, but he knew it was not a new one. It was only a deeper version of the one that he had nurtured deep inside him for most of his life.

# XXXI

Monday morning. Steve made it to the office by seven-thirty a.m. He was normally there early. Being an Assistant D.A. was the most enjoyable thing he had ever done for a living. He had never, since becoming a prosecutor, experienced a day when he had hated to go to work. To the contrary, he usually rushed to work each day to see what was going on in the city. It was like being tuned to the city's heartbeat. The D.A.'s office was in the middle of most of the events that made headlines each day, at least those involving crime. In his line of work, people were busy creating work for him twenty-four hours a day, seven days a week, fifty-two weeks a year, and each day brought new challenges. Steve was only subconsciously aware that the satisfaction derived from helping crime victims was virtually the *only* thing that kept his spiritual cup from running completely dry.

He reviewed the list of first appearances for the ten a.m. magistrate court session, which was always worth a chuckle. On any given day, the names on that list were the same ones that were named in the morning news for having committed the previous night's criminal atrocities. It was like a "Who's Who" of the city's scum.

At seven forty-five, he was surprised to see Nick Saladino walk in, looking buoyant.

"What 'cha say, buckaroo?" Steve offered, looking up reluctantly from the list.

"Good weekend, Steve. Saw my kids. They climbed all over me for a couple of hours. They seem to be OK in the head. Looks like Sharon isn't poisoning them about me."

Steve nodded. "That *is* good news. I think Sharon has more class than that. I don't think that'll happen."

Nick was all smiles. "Kids were all upset. Fucking dog ran away. Sharon put an ad in the newspaper's lost-and-found. Don't see what fucking good that does. Fucking dog can't read!"

"*Dipshit.*" Steve threw a legal pad at him. "Let's get some coffee."

They went to the coffee shop at the corner. Steve was starved. He hadn't eaten much since the showdown with Julie on Saturday. He started breakfast with a double Bloody Mary and coffee, then started to tell Nick about the break-up.

"No shit? You and Julie really crashed and burned this weekend? I've been telling you all along that that broad's Timex was ticking. You wouldn't believe me."

"*Fuckhead.* When I need a fucking shrink..."

"*Fucking-A.* Just call *me* when you need one. *I'll* set your ass straight."

"That's *not* what I was going to say. I'll fucking call *anybody* but *you*." Steve started to warm up inside, the liquids hitting all the right places.

Nick started to flip back a retort, but Steve waved him to silence.

"Pay attention, sucker. I'm gonna give you the scoop, so make like you're at Bastard and Robbins. I talked to Jack LaRose Friday. We spent a couple of hours in that pigsty he calls an office," Steve began. "Get *this*. Would you believe he personally knows old man Claiborne. I mean knows him well. They went to school together."

Nick's eyes widened.

"Now, get *this*. He told me he's watched Jeremy Claiborne in court on several occasions over the years, and that he had long ago formed an opinion that Jeremy is some kind of *psycho*. Dr. Jack gave me a sort of a personality profile of the type of disorder that he thinks Jeremy has." Steve smiled.

"I'm not real surprised that he knows Claiborne," Nick said. "This is New Orleans, the smallest big city on the fucking planet. Everybody here knows everybody. Ever try to hide in this town when you were out with a chippy? *Christ*. That's when you run into everybody you know."

"Dr. Jack thinks the black orchid tattoo thing may be Jeremy's way of getting back at his father. Putting the tattoo on his victim, then killing the victim, is Jeremy's way of killing his father. Jack's just not sure why Jeremy has selected hookers as his chosen class of victims, unless it combines some additional hatred for, or obsession with, his mother, or some *other* fucking broad who caused some deep traumatic blow to his little psyche. Also, he doesn't know why Jeremy would want to kill his father."

"Sounds logical to me. *If* you can *ever* say that shit like that sounds logical, that is. It's kind of an old song nowadays. Sounds like something recorded on the Insanity label, right?" Nick shook his head.

"That's the bad part. *If* Dr. Jack's right, Jeremy can end up in Jackson, for Christ's sake. And it sounds like Dr. Jack is right on point with Jeremy. He says people like Jeremy are loners, suspicious, distant, aloof, cold and unfeeling, and they masturbate frequently. They always think other people are talking about them, and they feel inadequate or inferior."

"Christ, that's Jeremy. *Dead ringer*. And to think I shook his *hand*." Nick chuckled.

"Yeah, I think so, too. Dr. Jack said he had an idea about why Jeremy is using hookers to act out on, and that he would get back to me after he checked it out."

Nick looked at him. "Are you sure can trust that old shrink?"

"So far, I've got no bad feelings from talking to him. At this point, I can only pray."

Nick frowned. "What else?"

"I got a bad feeling about this one, buck. I just got a bad feeling about this one. With Jeremy's connections, we've got to keep this thing absolutely between the legal lines. No funny shit. We can't afford to fuck up anything. I just somehow got a feeling that we haven't heard the worst yet."

Nick was only momentarily subdued by Steve's pessimism.

"Well, while you were hanging around this weekend feeling sorry for yourself over the loss of some exquisite pussy, I at least was out earning what little money the taxpayers pay me as a public servant." Nick was buoyant.

"Doing fucking what? Escorting a city councilman around to socials?"

"*Cute*, cocksucker! Keep that shit up, and I'll believe what other people say about you—that nothing ever grew on the north end of your fucking brainstem. You'll be pleased to know that my little escapade at the probation office worked out beautifully."

Steve groaned. He had forgotten about Nick's planned break-in of Jeremy's office.

"Don't tell me. I *don't* wanna know," he moaned, cupping his face in his hands.

Nick pulled out a folder, which Steve thought was disappointingly thin, if they were going to go to jail for it.

"We got everything we need for now. We have the name, address and telephone of each hooker in Jeremy's current files.

We got the next reporting date for each one, and the files indicate that none of them have any tattoos resembling this black orchid thing. And, dude, guess what?"

Steve didn't want to guess.

"We even got a copy of each hooker's photograph from the file."

Steve asked, "How many are there?"

Nick's smile dimmed somewhat. "We found six of them. More than I hoped, but it should be a manageable number."

Steve leaned back in his chair. "So we've got six hookers to check out before Jeremy comes in tomorrow, to make sure that they haven't already been turned into alligator snacks. How the fuck are we gonna cover all of them without blowing the lid off this deal?"

Nick was nodding his head up and down.

"*I'm* the detective here, remember? Everything is *lovely*. Don't worry 'bout nuttin'."

"Don't worry 'bout nuttin'? *Fuck*." Steve was almost apoplectic. "We're getting down to the wire on this thing. That fucking *lunatic* is coming back *tomorrow*. He's probably spent the last two weeks in Hawaii sitting at some cabana bar in shorts and a flowered shirt, drinking some fucking rum drink and planning his next victim. And you don't want me to worry about nuttin'? *Goddam*. If we mess this up and there's another victim, the press *and* our superiors will skin us alive. Damned if we do and damned if we don't! *Fuck*."

Steve looked around and saw that a couple of other patrons in the coffee shop were staring at him. He calmed down and waited for Nick to speak. Nick looked like the proverbial Cheshire cat.

"I've already started working on it yesterday. Here's the score. We got six hookers: four white, two black. I got a feeling he's not into chocolate candy, so I'm working them last. One of the white hookers got permission from the court to have her probation modified so she could return to her parents' place in Pensacola, Florida and be handled out of the probation office over there. I called the Pensacola office and they confirmed that she's registered and has been complying with the terms over there, so no problem. They last saw her in person five days ago, which is after Jeremy went on his little trip. So she's not a priority for now."

"So that leaves us three to check out," Steve tallied.

"It's wonderful the way you're able to slice through a difficult math equation and come up with the answers. Would you believe I came up with the same goddam number?"

"Q," Steve retorted. "So who are the three other candidates?"

"Candidate number one is Bridgette Griffin. Local girl. Alias is 'Hoover', wouldn't you know it? Only address is on Perdido Street. It's a flophouse, naturally. The telephone there is the lobby pay phone. She doesn't bring her johns there. Front desk clerk cooperated after a small private chat. Says she does most of her tricks in cars. She usually hangs out in one or two of the bars on North Broad Street, no pun intended. The johns pick her up and they go for a ride. Clerk says they haven't seen her in a couple of days.

"Her next reporting date with Jeremy is this Wednesday, two p.m.," Nick added, consulting his notepad. "At least, that's the information from Jeremy's files. I'll be out front watching for her. Shouldn't be hard to pick her out with this photo."

Nick held a black-and-white copy of a photo of a girl with dark hair, a thin face, and stone-cold eyes. She might have been pretty at one time, but life on the streets had exacted its toll.

Steve sighed, more from sadness than weariness. "Who's next?" he asked.

"Candidate number two is Eileen Edwards. From Monroe. Little country girl. Well, not exactly *little*." Nick held up a photo of a girl in her mid-twenties who had obviously reaped the full benefits of a steady caloric intake for a number of years. Country life had been good to her.

"A.k.a. 'Suzy'. Works days as a waitress at Denny's. Makes a little extra money on the streets at night and on weekends. I've already talked to her. She's not due to see Jeremy until Friday. Somehow I'd be surprised if Jeremy selects this one as his first victim after his vacation. Sure would feed a few gators, though." Nick chuckled.

"What'd you tell her?"

"Not a fucking thing. If I give them any idea that we're looking at Jeremy for anything, they'll either be nervous as a cat when they talk to him again or, typical probationers, they'll tip him off in return for a break on their probation. Either way, that little bastard will be on the alert."

"Cool. Who else we got?"

"For our final candidate, we got Karen Higgins. She's a call girl. This is one super-fine bitch. We'd *both* give her our Shell credit cards for the weekend. College graduate, married to a lawyer. She works the tourist and convention trade by call only. Even had her own business cards printed on pink paper. Got caught because she worked a party of cops in town on a fraternal convention, and one of them, a rank, got pissed because she wouldn't take on three of them at one time in his room. So he puts some pressure on some nimrod of a lieutenant from the First District to get her busted. Her husband's law partner worked a deal for her to plead to some misdemeanor bullshit charge, with only six months' probation. She's supposed to see Jeremy on Thursday."

Steve let out a soft whistle when Nick held up the photo of Karen Higgins. Classy. Intelligent. Blonde hair swept back fashionably at her temples. It was a face of a woman who would look right at home at a Junior League cake sale, but who would stand out like a beacon next to the frumpy competition. Probably had one of those obligatory nicknames like "Bitsy" or "Muffin."

"Jeez, nice stuff. I might even consider paying for some of that myself." Steve was impressed.

"I thought you might like that," Nick said, handing Steve the photo.

Steve stared at it for a few moments, then handed it back, shaking his head.

"So where're we at?" Steve asked. "You've talked to her?"

"Naw. Not that easy with this one. She's got a maid who screens her calls. But I'll get to her before her next appointment with Jeremy, which is also on Friday."

"So that makes three you've got to cover this week. That number one, what's her name?" Steve looked at the notes he had written on his legal pad. "Oh, yeah. Bridgette Griffin. How're you gonna find her?"

"I may not be able to. It's gonna be tough because I can't use the normal cop-on-the-street system, having the district cops talk to their informants—not without tipping Jeremy off. Best I can do for now is wait outside of probation for her to show up for her two o'clock appointment. When she comes out afterward, I'll tail her for a while and do an information stop on her. That'll give me an opportunity to ask her about her probation visits."

"I don't know, buck. Seems to me like you're putting a lot of confidence in the idea she'll actually show up like she's supposed to. What if she doesn't?"

"Actually, that would probably be the smartest thing she ever did. But if she doesn't, that'll give me a little more time to find her. That is, of course, if she's still alive," Nick said.

"What time does Jeremy come in from Hawaii?"

"Five-thirty p.m. Continental. I'm gonna be there, mainly because I want to see who the little psycho took with him on his trip. If there's another fruitcake close to him, I'd like to know who or what it is."

# XXXII

It was Tuesday. Nick had that earthy scent in his nostrils. That scent that always came when he was hot on a target and closing on his prey. He could smell blood, and it was Jeremy's. Without realizing it consciously, he ached to respond to the base killer instinct that dwelled deep inside of him, although he could not have put into words the feelings he was experiencing. He sensed it rather than understood it with his conscious intellect. He could feel the adrenaline starting to seep slowly into his system, making even the hairs on the back of his neck tingle. Nick knew that rush that a predator feels just before it terminates the life force of whatever victim it has relentlessly stalked. He savored the feeling, reveling in its thrill and anticipation, momentarily lost to his surroundings.

But he knew that Steve was right. In this case more than any other in his career, Nick knew that the very thing that made Jeremy such a delicious target was one and the same thing that made him insidiously dangerous. Dangerous to his prey; dangerous to his would-be captors.

Jeremy was a psycho, and the worst kind. He was imbedded in society, much like a tick imbeds itself in the flesh of its victim. And, like any other bloodsucker, Jeremy would continue to take blood until he was stopped. And stopping him wasn't that easy, for Jeremy wasn't your garden-variety bloodsucker. Son of a respected (or feared) federal judge with one of the oldest names in New Orleans' blue-blood history... this was going to go down in a big way.

Nick swore he would control his instincts. He resolved to continue stalking Jeremy silently and to make no moves by knee-jerk reaction, even though, in his guts, he ached to pounce.

He drove the Crown Vic into the automatic car wash at police headquarters then up the ramp of the incorporated high-rise garage into his favorite spot on the third floor between two posts, where no one else could park too close. Even though the Crown Vic was a 1984 model, four years old, Nick kept the black finish lustrous and, like a number of other cops, had even applied pin-striping to the sides himself, when he first got the unit. Before he and Sharon had split, he had spent some of his own money to replace the plastic grille after it was backed into in the Quarter by one of the city's finest garbage trucks. Naturally, that caused a major argument between them, since money was always a concern.

Back at his desk, he reviewed his files on the three hookers he had discussed with Steve. He spread their photos on his desk. Karen Higgins would be his first choice for a victim, based upon her beauty, but Nick guessed that female pulchritude did not interest Jeremy. Nick also had a feeling that she had too many strong ties to the community for Jeremy to mess with her. She would be missed too quickly by too many people—people with the assets and contacts necessary to pursue looking into her disappearance.

That left Bridgette Griffin and Eileen Edwards as the prime choices, because they had backgrounds similar to Collette Prejean's. It would be a while before they were missed, *if* they were missed at all. They had no close family ties. They represented the fungible people of the planet, who collectively take up space but individually are never noticed, despite what Andy Warhol said. Between the remaining hookers, Bridgette Griffin and Eileen Edwards, Nick was putting his money on Bridgette Griffin, although he couldn't give a rational reason for it. Just a hunch.

Bridgette's appointment was at two on Wednesday. Jeremy came in at five-thirty tomorrow. Nick felt that Wednesday would be the day that this pimple of a case was going to pop open and reveal its messy contents.

Nick leaned back and gazed at the picture of Collette, still on his bulletin board. He wondered how many other victims there had been. He wondered how many anonymous people like Collette had been born into the world and had their light snuffed out at an early age, never to be missed, never to be mourned. Considering how many Jeremys there were in the world, he imagined that the figure was considerable.

It was all just kind of a pathetic joke, and the joke was on the human race. Fucked if you do; fucked if you don't. The few quality people in the world struggle to bring meaning to their lives and those of their children, paying a large portion of their income in taxes so that a bunch of untalented, shallow, arrogant, self-aggrandizing fools called senators and representatives could have expensive mistresses on their payroll and gilt-lettered stationery on which to communicate their babble, while actors, ball-players and others of little value to society reaped unimaginable rewards for their portrayals of themselves as themselves: trash, illiterates, and others who would either be on skid row or food stamps in a more rational society.

Collette never had a chance to join any of those groups. She never got a fucking ticket to the dance. She was born to a life of deprivation and shame, without ever having earned or deserved it. Nick couldn't decide whether she should be pitied or envied for having her admittance to this life terminated so quickly.

Nick was going into a black mood. He began his standard bitch, that anybody who believed that God was real and all-powerful never had to have this job. He snorted derisively at the thought that there were some fools walking the planet who would tell you that it was because of *"original sin."* If that was true, then this God must be one mean, vindictive bastard, to have generations stacked upon generations of descendants suffering in this way. Babies being raped, people being tortured and killed. Nick had always thought that if he ever got the opportunity, he and God were gonna sit down and have a talk about God's bullshit attitude, even if Nick had to go to hell afterward.

*Fuck,* he thought. *Maybe it's because people are just breeding indiscriminately, like cockroaches. Maybe God only had just so many souls available to inhabit bodies, and now that there's so many goddamned bodies in the world, He's running short on souls and is having to continuously split the available souls into fractions of themselves just to keep up with the demand and ensure that there was at least a portion of a soul in every body. Maybe He just flat runs out sometimes, and some bodies are born without souls. That would explain a lot.* Either way, it seemed to Nick to be one of God's major fuck-ups. Not the *only* one, but certainly one of the *major* ones. *If the bastard is really in control, we have a problem. If He's not, we've got a problem.* Whatever. *I need a drink.*

Nick closed his files and slammed his chair against the desk as he left the office. He was down, and down bad. He knew that it was going to be a long night; he could feel the depression starting its cold grip on him. He had been there before—too many times to count. Enough that the thought of past depressions drove him even deeper. He could feel the tension in the back of his head and at the base of his neck, along with the overwhelming tired feeling, the listlessness.

He burned rubber as he pulled off the parking lot ramp, turned right onto South White Street, and headed for Tulane Avenue with his blue grille lights flashing. It was another fugly, drizzly night, which perfectly fit the mood that had gripped him.

*Beautiful. Just fucking* beautiful, he thought sarcastically, as he headed for the Quarter. There was nothing aesthetic about Tulane Avenue, except, ironically, the Art Deco Criminal Courts Building. He knew that he would spend most of the rest of that night trying to drown the demons that were rioting inside of him, and he was in a hurry for the first installment of a double Crown on the rocks—something, anything, to soothe his inner turmoil.

As he drove through the city, he seemed to notice only the depressing things. A bag lady on the corner of Basin and Iberville on the outskirts of the Quarter, rooting through somebody's garbage across from the Iberville Projects, in search of an evening meal, scratching herself with one hand while digging with the other. As he parked the car in a law enforcement zone on Royal near the Devil's Den, he noted the stench of stale vomit in the gutters, a souvenir of some tourist from the midwest who couldn't hold his liquor. "*Yeah, yeah,*" he muttered. "Some dumb fuck will go back to Kansas bragging about all the things he did in New Orleans, but he won't tell his friends he couldn't handle it."

Dolly had seen the Crown Vic pull up, and by the time Nick made it through the door, she had placed a drink on the bar for him. It didn't last ten seconds.

"M*other-*fucking *goose*. You look like you just escaped from the psycho ward on the third floor of Charity. Fuck is wrong with *you*?" Dolly poured another double and stood by with the bottle, not unlike an EMT holding an IV.

"Don't know. Don't *even* know. Just felt like something was about to get me, but I can't tell you what it was. Just knew it was coming and I didn't want to be around to see it." Nick was exhausted.

After a few minutes Nick started to calm down a little. The heat from the Crown was starting to penetrate his guts, or his brain. It didn't matter which. It felt good, steadying.

"You're lucky. I can't shake it off that easily anymore," Dolly said wearily. "Even the booze won't chase it off anymore. It's like, I can't tell what causes it or where it comes from, but it starts off as a sort of sadness and it kind of mushrooms, until I feel like my poor ass is about to be turned into some kind of fucking Tinker Toy hung on Satan's fucking Christmas tree for everyone to see. I won't even have to die to get there. In fact, I won't be *allowed* to die. I'll just be hanging there, with the ornament hook up my ass and some type of flashing sign on my tits, surrounded by those stupid bubbling lights. If I come back from *there*, I'll probably find that I'm in one of those silly suits in a padded room, drooling on myself and contemplating the boogers on the upholstered walls, to see if what they say really is true, that boogers *are* like snowflakes—no two are alike."

Nick had been leaning on the bar on both elbows. He cocked his head up to one side to look at Dolly, then raised one eyebrow and grunted agreement. He hadn't come in there to listen to somebody else dump.

*God, guess that's* one *way to put it*, he thought to himself.

Dolly wandered off and Nick thought about what she had said. To him, the feeling was more one of waste: waste of life, waste of space, waste of breath, waste of effort. Like, "Why am I here for this?" His kids came into his thoughts, and Nick was struck with the cold reality that even they could do without him.

He had once thought that his immortality was grounded in the hearts and minds of people whom he had helped in his line of work, but that neat little illusion had long ago been trampled, leaving him with the same cynicism shared by most people who worked within the intestinal tract of society. Life had come to consist of waking moments, where Nick subconsciously spent most of his time hiding from the corrosion eating at his soul, and sleeping moments, where he had no choice but to confront them in dreams, usually in an inane and inescapable sort of way.

He shook himself, trying to clear his head, and silently held up his glass for Dolly to see.

"*Somebody* drank my fuckin' drink."

New Orleans International Airport is actually not located in New Orleans, but in another town which is in another parish. Nick lazily guided the Crown Vic out I-10 westbound, savoring the twenty-five-minute drive. Fortunately, there were no accidents or stranded motorists to tempt the rubber-neckers to slow traffic to a crawl, which was often the case.

On the service road to the airport, he noticed the huge sign welcoming visitors to New Orleans on behalf of the mayor, but which made no mention of the citizens of New Orleans, who were likely footing the bill for the free political advertisement.

*Typical fucking politicians*, Nick thought, still grumpy from the night before.

He parked his car on the passenger ramp and, after a minor verbal scuffle with the local traffic cop, headed for the Continental ticket counter. He noted with satisfaction that Jeremy's plane was listed as being on time and due to land in fifteen minutes.

Although the airport was singularly unattractive inside, it was no different than any other airport in that respect. He walked down the concourse and motioned to one of the security guards at the metal detectors, discreetly displaying his badge and I.D. to the guard as he approached. With a cursory glance at the I.D. folder, the guard waved him through, signaling the other guards so they wouldn't be alarmed when the alarms sounded as he passed through the security station with his Smith & Wesson in its shoulder holster.

Nick chose an area some fifty feet down the concourse from the gate at which Jeremy was due to arrive and blended with the crowd. After what seemed like an eternity to Nick, the arrival of the flight was announced, and within a few minutes Jeremy appeared, carrying a folded garment bag.

Nick dropped in behind at a good distance, taking great care to be sure that Jeremy wouldn't burn him. It was only after they had traveled a distance of almost fifty yards that Nick realized he had been holding his breath, and let out a great sigh.

"Little bastard goes to fucking Hawaii and doesn't even get a fucking *suntan*," Nick sneered. "Probably never saw the light of day while he was there."

Jeremy appeared to be alone, and Nick stayed with him until he disappeared down the escalator to the baggage claims area, at which point Nick went outside and sat in the car. It was at least twenty minutes before Jeremy finally emerged, loaded with luggage, and got into a cab. Nick followed the cab back into New Orleans as far as West End Boulevard, where Nick exited and returned to the boathouse he was still occupying.

He had seen what he had come to see. The first move of the final chapter of this case had been made. The little skank was back in town.

It was seven-thirty p.m. Nick was starved, and rooted through the kitchen to see what was edible, finally deciding to whip up some "scud," as he called it. Actually, scud was a name used generically by Nick for any concoction he was able to force together in a pot. He did have *some* vestige of cooking ability, as did most New Orleanians.

On this particular night, scud was going to consist of potatoes and onions sautéed down in olive oil and fresh garlic with bell pepper, zucchini and black olives thrown in, for no reason other than they happened to be in the wrong place at the wrong time.

After an hour or so, he sat out on the balcony of the boathouse, washing the food down with a couple of Abita beers and watching the boats move in and out of the harbor around the breakwater. He made a mental note to find out if he could somehow afford to buy the boathouse in the future.

He fell asleep with his feet propped on the railing, a dead Abita beer bottle on the floor at his feet.

# XXXIV

Steve wasn't so lucky. Or, from a different viewpoint, maybe he was luckier.

It was about 2:30 a.m. The phone was ringing. Steve had only been home for a little over an hour, following a brutal Tuesday night bar crawl.

His phone number was unlisted, and he let the phone ring a few times while he mentally ran through the list of people who had the number, trying to figure out who might be calling. Only Julie, his secretary, Nick Saladino, and the D.A. himself had the number, or so he thought. Steve decided to let the answering machine earn its keep and rolled over, trying to go back to sleep.

It wasn't going to work. "*Steve. Goddam it,*" the machine barked. "Pick up the goddam *phone.* I know you're *there.*"

The voice was familiar, but Steve couldn't place it.

"God *damn* it, Steve. Wake *up.* Pick up the fucking *phone.* This is Jack, Jack LaRose. You have *got* to come meet me." The voice on the phone was insistent, not typical of LaRose.

Steve reluctantly picked up the phone and dropped it on the pillow near the spot he thought his ear might be located.

"Doc, are you OK?" he groaned. "What in the name of shit are you doing up at *this* time of night?"

"Don't ask dipshit questions, Steve." Dr. Jack was irritated, and obviously excited. "You wanna crack this case? Meet me *now.* Rockery Inn. Thirty minutes."

Steve had never heard Jack LaRose display this kind of mood before. He had obviously been drinking for a while, and Steve could barely believe it was LaRose.

"What's wrong, doc? Can't it wait...?"

"*No*. It goddam *can't* wait." LaRose cut Steve off mid-sentence. "Thirty minutes."

"But..."

The line was dead.

"*Wow*. What the fuck was *that* all about?" Steve sat slowly up in bed, then got up and threw cold water in his face, his eyes stinging.

He threw on some jeans and a flannel shirt, along with an old Air Force leather flight jacket, tattered at the cuffs. On the way to the car, he paused for a second, then returned to the apartment and put on his shoulder holster with his Model 37 airweight.

It was gross outside. Gross as only winter can be. The dew point and the humidity had come together with a vengeance, and the fog was thick enough to mix with scotch. Steve briefly wondered what fog would taste like if you could make it into ice cubes. Maybe that's where the idea for the "Fogcutter" drink came from.

As a Senior Assistant D.A., Steve was fortunate enough to have a company car. It was an old hand-me-down, ragged-out police car, but it was free. Steve put on the small flashing red-and-blue strobe lights in the grille and got onto Interstate 10 headed towards New Orleans. The neon signs on the buildings were blurred by the fog, reminding Steve of grainy images in photographs that have been over-enlarged. Traffic was scarce, and what few cars were out were difficult to see in the fog.

Steve spotted the Canal Boulevard exit with some difficulty, and navigated the steep curve of the exit ramp carefully, turning towards the lake onto the boulevard. The Rockery was only a few blocks down and the parking lot was crowded, no great surprise for any bar in this city at this time of morning; many of the bars didn't even have locks on the doors. Guess you don't need them if you never close.

The Rockery was definitely an after-hours joint catering to the "trade": those people who worked as bartenders and barmaids, waiters and cocktail waitresses, together with those known as the "night people."

Steve spotted Dr. Jack's old MGB in the parking lot. It stood out among the anonymous sedans patiently waiting for their owners to reappear in one stage of intoxication or another. It was one of the older MGBs, and had steel bumpers. Steve noted with amusement that some of the dents in the hood were deep enough to hold the dew in small ponds of water, giving it an odd sort of moonscape effect when matched with the various textures created on the hood's surface by uncounted cheap repaint jobs over the years.

Steve entered the bar. The cigarette smoke inside was about as thick as the fog was outside. The joint had a respectable crowd, but not nearly as many people as Steve expected based upon the number of cars in the parking lot. *Typical fuckin' chippy joint*, Steve thought. People meeting each other at the bar, leaving one car and heading for some trysting place to return later and retrieve the other car.

The music was loud—loud enough that the center nipples in the base speakers on the walls were visibly rising and falling with the base beat.

"....*believe half of what you see, some or none of what you hear*...."

Steve chuckled. One of his favorite songs. Somehow seemed appropriate for the moment.

The circular bar stood in the center of the room. One side of the room was lined with booths that were curtained for privacy—a popular feature in some of the bars from the fifties era. Steve began to make his way slowly, picking carefully through the groups that were clotted together near the bar. Half-way around the bar he spotted Jack LaRose, leaning on the counter and watching him approach. LaRose looked out of place in the crowd, like an aged hippie submerged in a crowd of yuppies and left-overs from the gold-chain era.

He raised his glass as Steve nudged in alongside of him.

"Here's to the fuckin' *orchid*."

Steve stared at LaRose but his face was inscrutable.

Steve was about to ask the obvious question, like, "Are you *OK*?" or, "What could be so important to make you wake me up at this time of morning?" or even, "What the *fuck* are you doing out drunk at *this* time of morning?" He got cut off before he could get the first word out.

"Steve my boy, you have gone and done it *this* time."

Steve couldn't decide whether LaRose was morose or ecstatic. Seemed either the man'd been fooling with those left-handed cigarettes again or he was simply drunk. Steve looked more closely, then decided it was booze.

LaRose steered Steve to a table off to one side of the bar, near a booth in which the curtains had been pulled shut.

"To think that after all these years, I had *never* thought to question it!" LaRose was ebullient.

Steve picked up LaRose's glass and smelled it. Straight Scotch. Good stuff.

The cocktail waitress came up as Steve was putting the glass back on the table and looked at Steve, raising her eyebrows slightly.

"Two of whatever he's drinking," Steve ordered.

The drinks appeared quickly and Steve took a long, slow pull on his, then turned back to LaRose. The man was muttering to himself; his lips were moving, but no sound was coming out, at least not that Steve could hear over the music. He put his hand on LaRose's shoulder and the old man seemed startled.

"Doc, not to interrupt you, but what the hell is this all about? Are you OK?"

Steve regretted the last question the minute he heard it leave his mouth. He knew he was going to catch flak from LaRose.

"Am I *OK? Am* I OK? Am *I* OK?" LaRose repeated the question three times, putting the emphasis on a different word each time and savoring the effect, then turned to face Steve. "You're asking *me* if *I'm* OK? *Jesus*, son. I'm a shrink. A fuckin' forensic *pee*-sychiatrist. *I'm* the one that asks everybody *else* if *they're* OK. I'm the guy that gets to sit back and judge other people and get paid for it. Not paid *enough*, mind you... The *question*, my boy, is whether *you're* going to be OK." LaRose had a disdainful sneer on his face.

Steve played along with the mood, not quite knowing what else to do. Something was going on and he had to assume it was something to do with the Prejean case.

"OK, then. Am *I* OK?"

LaRose looked down his nose at Steve.

"Whaddaya think I look like? Jean Dixon? I told you, I'm a shrink, not a *pee*-sychic. Besides, she couldn't have been much of a psychic. Woman died and didn't even predict her own death." LaRose snickered at his own joke.

Steve sighed heavily and took another long pull on his drink, becoming slightly miffed at being pulled to a bar at this time of morning only to face some sort of exercise in mental masturbation. He leaned on the table. It seemed that he would just have to wait for LaRose to play out his mood.

LaRose turned to the fresh Scotch that Steve had ordered and held the glass up, looking at it as if it were mystical.

"I just can't believe I accepted it so blindly. *Everybody* did. Un-be-fucking-lievable!" LaRose was shaking his head side to side with a lopsided grin.

Finally, he leaned over conspiratorially and began talking in a voice that Steve had to strain to hear.

"It's the *orchid*. It's the fucking *black orchid*. It's like I told you, I knew the Claiborne family fairly well when we were all younger. Tom Claiborne and I were in the same fraternity at Tulane. I had never seen anyone light a fart before, much less thought of the possibility of it, until myself and fifty others watched Tom do it at the Alpha house on Broadway one night after a rush party."

He paused and lit a Camel while Steve sipped his drink and tried to figure out the relevance of lighting a fart. Evidently, LaRose hadn't finished his mood yet.

"It's an impressive sight with the lights turned off," the doctor reminisced.

Steve had to chuckle despite his impatience. The thought of fifty young men sitting around in various stages of inebriation watching Tom Claiborne pull his pants down and put on such a floor show would make an interesting anecdote for the *Louisiana Bar Journal*.

"I told you I thought Tom's wife had died shortly after giving birth to Jeremy, while on an extended trip up East with their daughter Charysse." LaRose had resumed his story, finally. "Turns out, that's not true. It seemed to me those events occurred in Boston, so after you left my office, I contacted the Massachusetts Bureau of Vital Statistics for a copy of Jeremy's birth certificate. Turned out my suspicions were correct." LaRose was digging in his shirt pocket as he talked, the exhausted Camel dropping a substantial amount of ash inside when he pulled the pocket open.

"Look at *this*." LaRose handed Steve the paper he had finally removed. It was obviously a telefax copy, and had been folded many times, making it even more difficult to read in the dark bar. "The mother on that birth certificate is listed as 'Charysse Claiborne,' just as you'd expect. Right?" LaRose was still leaning forward.

Steve peered closely at the paper and was barely able to make out the names on the certificate. He nodded in assent.

"Looks like it to me," he agreed.

LaRose's face was getting brighter.

"*Wrong*. I mean *right*." LaRose's nostrils were flared like a bloodhound's on a scent. "That thing confirms that Tom Claiborne and Charysse Claiborne *are* Jeremy Claiborne's parents. *You're* the goddamned attorney. What's wrong with it?"

Steve still wasn't in the mood to play games.

"I'm a little slow this morning, Doc. What's wrong with it?" Steve was puzzled and growing more annoyed as LaRose played his little game. He wished the man would get to the fucking point.

"*Goddamn* it. You don't fucking *see* it?" LaRose grabbed the paper out of Steve's hands. "*Look*. Look right *here*, goddam it. Look at the fucking *age* of the goddam mother." LaRose's hand was shaking as he pointed out the proper box on the certificate to Steve. "What does that fucking say? Right *here*."

The number was on a crease in the paper, of course. Steve peered intently but couldn't truly make out what was on the paper.

"Looks like 'sixteen' to me," Steve volunteered, hesitantly.

"Fuck-ing *bingo*."

Steve's eyes widened slowly. He looked at LaRose, mouthing the figure to himself again, the circuits in his brain starting to glow like a burner on an electric range.

LaRose was sitting back now, watching Steve with a sly grin, nodding, Scotch in one hand.

"*Sixteen*." Steve repeated the word out loud. "And you said the mother and the daughter had the same name?"

LaRose nodded.

"And you said the daughter was a teenager when she and her mother went on this trip?"

LaRose nodded again.

"Oh, *fuck*. Oh, *Christ on a crutch*. Are you telling me that..." his voice trailed off.

LaRose nodded again.

"I am." LaRose was grinning ear to ear, obviously pleased with himself and enjoying Steve's reaction.

Steve's caution finally returned.

"But this is only a fax of some obscure record from a thousand miles away..."

LaRose looked at him with that disdainful sneer, of which he was a master.

"You couldn't have said that better. Obscure, and a thousand miles away. Away from the local noses. In a place where Tom Claiborne is unknown. A place where no local would think to look to find dirt on Tom Claiborne."

He went on, producing a couple more folded pages which he handed to Steve.

Steve looked at the documents. They at least were a little clearer than the certificate.

"Wow, this is the admit page for Charysse Claiborne at Massachusetts General Hospital for a live childbirth." He looked at LaRose.

"I already got the complete medical chart. Contacts are wonderful, aren't they? Do you want to venture a guess as to the information in those records?"

Steve was quiet. He motioned to the waitress to bring another double for both of them.

LaRose went on. "That admit sheet *also* has the age of the Charysse Claiborne who gave birth to Jeremy Claiborne. *Sixteen.*"

"*Motherfucker.*" Steve whistled. "Je-sus *Gawd.* So..."

"You *got* it," LaRose interrupted. "Charysse Claiborne, judge of division "R" of the Criminal District Court, is Jeremy's *mother.*"

"Ho-ly shit." Steve was starting to revolt at the picture he was developing of someone as lovely as Charysse Claiborne giving birth to something as revolting as Jeremy Claiborne. "And you believe..." He spoke very slowly, not wanting to believe that such a tender morsel had given birth to a salamander like Jeremy. He didn't want to believe that there was something else very dark about her besides that mop of radiant black hair.

"You *got* it." LaRose was almost radiant.

Steve was still wading through the implications of what he had just been told.

"Then..."

LaRose cut him off again. "*Right.* Charysse Claiborne is *also* Jeremy's *sister.*"

Steve literally threw down the rest of his double. He hadn't wanted to hear *that*, inevitable as it was.

As he slammed the empty glass down on the table, the remaining rocks flew out onto the floor. He had a bad taste in his mouth.

"*Fuck.* Awww, shi-it." He let it drag out for a few syllables, and slumped down in his chair.

"Well, what about Claiborne's wife, then? Didn't you say she died shortly after Jeremy was born?"

"That's true." LaRose was still acting smug. "Also in Boston. But she didn't die of complications from *childbirth*. She was never goddam *pregnant*, for God's sake. She died of a broken heart. I also got her records already."

"Fuck have I gotten *into*?" Steve looked at LaRose as if to say, "You're full of shit," but he could tell that the man had done his research, and knew LaRose wasn't the type of person to joke about something like this.

The two sat in silence for a while, ordering another round of doubles and finishing them silently.

Steve was the first to speak.

"So federal judge Thomas Claiborne had been porking his own *daughter* and got her pregnant." He thought about that, revulsed. He had always known that she was generally unfriendly to men, in spite of her beauty and hour-glass figure. Something like that in her past would certainly explain her attitude towards men. "*Wow.*" His tone was hushed, almost reverent. "Wow."

LaRose's mood had changed. The man seemed almost consoling in his manner towards Steve.

"*Now* I understand what's up with your killer. It all falls into the classic pattern." He patted Steve's forearm, which lay on the table in a pool of melted ice cubes. Steve was oblivious to the moisture.

#  XXXV

The next day, Wednesday, Nick tried unsuccessfully to locate Sharon and left a message with her lawyer's secretary that he wanted to set up a visitation schedule with the kids. The lawyer called back a few hours later and told Nick he would discuss it with Sharon, but that Nick was going to have to start paying child support if he wanted to establish visitation. That conversation didn't go well, and ended with Nick calling the lawyer a sack of "motherfuckers" before slamming the phone down.

At one p.m. he headed over to probation and set up surveillance outside the grimy building, waiting for Bridgette Griffin to appear for her appointment with Jeremy. There was only one public entrance to the office, so it was easy to keep track of the people who came and went. There weren't many that day, thankfully, and Nick scrutinized each female carefully, occasionally checking the photo of Bridgette in his file to be certain. He had no idea whether Jeremy was even at work that day, but relied on the information from Jeremy's files.

When two o'clock arrived, there was still no sign of Bridgette Griffin and Nick started to get edgy, checking his watch constantly.

When it was two-thirty, Nick had to confront the sick feeling in his gut; it wouldn't be ignored any longer.

"Maybe she forgot, maybe she's out of town," he told himself, not believing a word of it. He knew better, deep inside;

his instincts told him something was wrong. He just hoped it wasn't deadly wrong.

He hurriedly called the probation office to ask Nancy Hoffman to check on Bridgette's appointment.

"She's not in today," an expressionless voice told him.

It hit him then. Nancy had probably taken the day off just so she wouldn't have to be around if anything happened involving Jeremy. She was totally spooked by the sick little bastard.

"Aw, *shit*." Nick felt his asshole clamp shut.

Without Nancy there, he had no way to find out what had happened to Bridgette's appointment with Jeremy, and he didn't have enough evidence to play his hand yet.

The rear tires of the Crown Vic screamed in agony as Nick tore out into traffic and sped toward the flophouse on the seamy end of Perdido Street that was the only address he had for Bridgette Griffin. As he drove furiously, he cursed himself continuously for not having acted sooner to protect her from Jeremy. He had nothing to expect but the worst.

# XXXVI

The inside of the place was dark and the smell was foul, like a combination of old carpet that had been wet too many times for all the wrong reasons, and human body odor that had accumulated in the pores of the dilapidated sheet rock walls, marinated with decades of cigarette smoke and spilled booze.

The furniture in the lobby was tattered and grimy, clammy from years of sweat and excess that had dripped off of unwashed inhabitants and kept moist by the year-round hundred-percent humidity, along with the lack of air conditioning.

The walls were fuzzy, furry with growth from the incessant dampness. The sheet rock was swollen in many places from unprotected exposure to moisture, looking much like malignant skin tumors on an acne-pocked surface. Wherever hands could touch, such as doors and windows, the surfaces were black with built-up grease thick enough to lodge under an unsuspecting fingernail.

Nick shuddered. He wondered how drastically he was shortening his lifespan by breathing all this shit.

He found the clerk sprawled on one of the sofas, an empty bottle of Cuba Libre-flavored grape wine on the floor next to him. His head had rolled to one side and was hanging down on his shoulder, his mouth gaping open and a coagulated stream of drool hanging from one of the two teeth left in his head. Nick kicked his foot to wake him up. Normally, he would have thrown him up against the wall immediately, but this scrounge was too disgusting to touch.

"Bridgette Griffin!" he yelled.

No response.

Nick kicked him again, harder. He heard a faint crack in the man's ankle.

*Action* this time.

"*Yow.* You *broke* my fuckin' *leg*," the man wheezed, bending forward slowly in an attempt to grasp his leg over the giant expanse of stomach.

"Bridgette Griffin!" Nick yelled again.

"Who da fuck are you talking about?" Then the old man started to moan from the pain in his leg.

Nick kicked the foot again.

*Screams,* that time. The old man managed to actually reach his leg with his left hand, breathing hard from the effort.

"You talkin' 'bout that fuckin' hooker? That's a *crazy* bitch. *Crazy.* She's fucked up in the head." The old man howled between gasps. "You crazy *bastard.* You broke my fucking leg."

Nick had no patience, and poised himself to kick the leg again.

The old man held up his right hand, left still holding the leg. "Don't kick me again. I ain't done nothin'. Nothin'. If this is about that crazy bitch, I ain't done *nothin'* to her. I ain't raped her. I swear it. She wanted to work a deal, didn't have no money. She gave me a blow job every other day to pay for her room. It were *her* idea. I swear it. That were a crazy bitch.

Nick was sickened at the thought of any living thing going down on this encrusted escapee from a cesspool. He started to kick the foot again, but the old man started talking more.

"I ain't seen her for a week or two. Ain't left nothin' in her room—it's already rented out. I don't know nothin' else. I mean, these street people, they come and go like a bad cold. Ya' don't know when they're comin' and ya' don't know when they gone. Most a' the time, ya' don't even know their name. Ya' get what I'm talkin' about, don't you?" The old man was almost pleading.

Nick was having a hard time fighting a wave of nausea that wanted to engulf him. There wasn't anything else to be kicked out of this old asthmatic hulk of a being. He bolted out of the place, feeling suffocated and dirty. His entire body felt the same way the flophouse smelled. All he could think of was a shower and, back at headquarters, he went straight to the locker room and soaked himself under the hottest water he could stand, making a mental note to spray the seat and steering wheel of the Crown Vic with some kind of disinfectant.

When he came out it was 7:30 p.m. and dark. He headed down Tulane Avenue towards the business district, intent on finding a stiff drink. As he approached Claiborne Avenue, he noticed activity at St. Joseph's Catholic Church, a huge building standing alone in an otherwise barren block in a worn and threadbare area of the city. The area was home to Louis Armstrong when he was a young boy. Nick hadn't been to church in years, but some impulse made him pull over and enter the church.

There were maybe fifty people scattered around, apparently for some sort of special Mass. Nick sat in a pew near the entrance to the church and zoned out while the priest droned on in Latin.

*"In nomine de Patris, et Filii, et Spiritus Sancti. Amen."*

Nick couldn't get Bridgette Griffin out of his mind. He knew he was letting her down somehow, but the pieces just wouldn't quite come together. There was precious little he did know, and an enormous amount he didn't.

*"Judica me, Deus, et discerne causam meam de gente non sancta: ab homine iniquo et doloso erue me."*

Nick began a mental review of his information on Bridgette. He knew that she was to meet with Jeremy at the probation office at two o'clock. He knew she didn't show up at that time.

*What were the alternatives?* he thought to himself, the organ music in the background.

The first and most optimistic, but most unlikely, was that she forgot the appointment or had skipped town. The second was that she and Jeremy had agreed on a different time or location.

Nick snapped to and cursed out loud, startling those around him and causing them to look at him apprehensively. He had forgotten to note whether Jeremy's car was in its parking space at the probation office. In fact, he didn't know if Jeremy had showed up for work at all today.

The third possibility, and most sickening, was that Jeremy already had Bridgette—possibly since before he went to Hawaii. Nick blanched. The thought was even more sickening because he might have been able to rule it out if he had tailed Jeremy since his return to the city.

"*Shit*. Shouldn't have been so goddam cocky. *Shit*."

Nick was still unaware that he was disturbing the service, and that people were telling him to be quiet. He knew in his heart that Bridgette hadn't forgotten her appointment. It would be nice to think that the appointment had simply been changed to another time and/or place. But Nick dreaded the other possibilities.

# XXXVII

It was misty and dark as Nick raced down the church steps to the car.

His car radio was blinking red, indicating a message waiting for him. He picked up the mike and checked in.

"1251."

"*1251.*" There was that voice again. Did this chick ever take a day off? "Mr. Chaisson from the D.A.'s office wants you to call him at this number. He's called a few times. Said it was urgent."

"See if you can get him and patch him through to me."

"*10-4.*"

Nick was heading for the Quarter.

"1251. Mr. Chaisson is on."

"Nick, where the hell *are* you? I've been trying to reach you all afternoon."

"I'm heading for the Quarter. Usual joint."

"Got it. Be there in thirty minutes." Steve hung up.

Nick pulled up in front of the Devil's Den and had finished his first double Crown before Steve arrived looking harried. Nick had a double Crown waiting for him.

He watched Steve practically scurry across the room, eyes dead serious.

*Fuck*, he thought to himself. *He couldn't have had a worse day than* me.

# XXXVIII

"*Jee-zuz.* You are *never* gonna believe *this*," Steve began, pacing his words by pronouncing each syllable with distinction.

"Look, douchebag. If it's bad news, I've had *enough* for today." Nick turned back to his drink. "Goddam broad didn't show for her probation appointment. I went to her flophouse, which may be the most disgusting one in the city, and she hadn't been seen there for a couple of weeks. She might be out of town, but I got a bad feeling about this. I hope she ain't already been made into alligator Twinkies."

"Man, that's *nothing* compared to what I'm gonna tell you. You ready for this?" Steve had finished his Crown and was signaling for another. "You know how we were always worried that the Honorable Thomas Claiborne might somehow show up in this thing?"

Nick nodded, not wanting to hear what was coming.

"Well, my boy, I hate to tell you that he *is* somehow involved in this thing," Steve continued, still measuring his words. "But not the way we were concerned about. I don't believe he's got anything to do with killing hookers.

"Get this. I get a call from Jack LaRose at two-thirty this morning, insisting that I meet him immediately at the Rockery. I get out there and he's crocked. *All* pissed up. Turns out he's been doing some investigating on his own. He pulls out Jeremy's birth certificate. No question that he's Tom Claiborne's kid, but guess who the mother is?" Steve was starting to develop a leer on his face, and couldn't control it. "Jeremy's *mother* is Charysse Claiborne."

Nick looked up. "*So?* Seems to me that I remember that was his wife's name. They named their daughter after her." Nick paused for a minute, then straightened up. "*Wait* a minute, cocksucker! You're not telling me what I *think* you're telling me? No fucking way! You and LaRose are both fuckin' nuts! I ain't believing *that*. No fucking way!"

Steve pulled out the paper LaRose had given him.

"Look at *this*, peckerhead." Steve threw it down in front of Nick, fortunately missing the wet rings left by Nick's glass.

Nick picked the paper up, holding it near the only available light, a beer sign.

"What the hell are you talking about? It shows Thomas Claiborne as the father and Charysse Claiborne as the mother... *Holy shit.* Charysse Claiborne was *sixteen* at the time of Jeremy's birth? No *way* that was Thomas Claiborne's *wife*."

"*Goddam.* You are sharp tonight." Steve was enjoying Nick's reaction.

"Thomas Claiborne was screwing his *daughter*. Thomas Claiborne was *screwing* his daughter," Nick said slowly, letting it sink in. "So the mother and the daughter went on an extended trip, and Jeremy was born in Massachusetts so nobody would realize which Charysse Claiborne was Jeremy's mother."

Steve chimed in. "And Claiborne's wife died shortly after that of mysterious causes. LaRose says it was a goddam broken heart. Which left young Charysse to raise her own son and brother without grandma's help. Claiborne probably hired nannies to help out.

"In the meantime," he continued, "can't you just see all the uptown tea crowd making a big deal over how sweet and good it was for little Charysse to raise Jeremy like he was her own?

*Christ.* Wouldn't those hens croak if they knew Jeremy really *was* Charysse's *own?*"

# XXXIX

"*1251*." Nick's radio crackled into life, startling the two. "You have a call from a Nancy Hoffman. You want it patched through?"

Nick started to blow it off, given the advanced stage of alcohol funk he was in.

"No. Get a telephone number and I'll call her back." He scribbled the number on a napkin and pulled the phone from behind the bar.

"*Nick*." Nancy's voice was stressed. "I've been looking for you."

"Yeah, I've been looking for you, too. You didn't go to work today?"

"Couldn't. My mother has been sick. I had to take her to the hospital."

Nick felt a little guilty that he had assumed she stayed away from work to avoid any confrontations.

"I wanted to tell you that Jeremy called in and cancelled all appointments for today. Didn't say why, but they were rescheduled for tomorrow. *Nick*. Are you there?"

Nick was stunned. The raw emotions he had felt earlier raced through him again at a speed that must have been at least Mach 2. He held the phone away from his ear for a minute, staring at Steve.

"*Christ*, man. What is it?" Steve asked, putting a hand on Nick's shoulder. He could hear Nancy's voice over the phone.

"*Nick.* I *know* you're there. I can hear bar noise." Nancy was still talking.

Nick put the phone back to his ear. "What did you say?" He was only able to croak the words. "Tell me again. What did you say?"

"I was telling you that Jeremy called me late Tuesday and told me to move all his Wednesday appointments to Thursday."

"Are you *shitting* me?" was the best that Nick could manage. "Are you fucking *serious*?" He stood up straight, a huge smile on his face. "You *are* serious, aren't you? I *love* it." Nick was ecstatic. "So, tell me about Bridgette Griffin. Did you talk to her? Did you reschedule her? Where did you find her?"

"*Whoa*, big boy. One at a time." Nancy was nonplussed at Nick's demeanor. "Yeah, I got hold of all of them. Bridgette Griffin had left a number of some kinda distant cousin that she had been staying with for the last week or so. She's been pretty good about obeying the rule that we have to have current contact information on defendants at all times. Actually, she seems kinda like a nice... What the fuck are you *laughing* at?"

Nick had broken out into a howl and started to dance a little jig in place. Very uncharacteristic, and Steve made a point of saying so. Dolly walked over to their end of the bar, too.

"Silly bastard. Too much Crown in the last few years. I oughta cut him off." She shook her head, poured fresh ones for Nick and Steve, and returned to the other end of the bar, still shaking her head.

"So tell me," Nick said, calming down. "When and where is Bridgette Griffin's appointment with Jeremy?"

"Tomorrow. Two o'clock."

"That's *outstanding. Out*-fucking-standing." He was still grinning.

"You still owe me," Nancy said and hung up.

*She's right, and I will have to deliver this time*, Nick thought, a small part of his brain making a mental notation while another small part offered up a small taste of the memory of past times with Nancy.

"So, what *is* it? Don't keep me here being embarrassed about being seen with you acting like a moron. What? What is it?" Steve tapped his glass impatiently.

"Turns out I didn't miss Bridgette Griffin today, after all. Nancy said that Jeremy had called on Tuesday and had her change all his Wednesday appointments to Thursday. She had a phone number for Bridgette and was able to reach her. Bridgette's appointment is two o'clock *tomorrow*. Thank Christ!"

"*Wow*. That *is* good news." Steve raised his glass in salute.

# XL

Thursday, 1:45 p.m.

Nick pulled up across the street from the probation office to await Bridgette Griffin.

*OK, a little déjà vu here*, he thought to himself, as much to relieve the tension as anything else.

It was cold, drizzly. The area was virtually deserted of foot traffic. Nick had the Crown Vic idling to take advantage of the heater. The wipers were on intermittent, at the slowest speed. He thought about the events of the previous day, pondering how bad things must be at home for a girl like Bridgette Griffin to think that what she had here was a better deal.

He checked his watch, 2:10 p.m., and shifted his position in the car, a little anxious.

2:15 p.m. The radio was playing Willie Nelson's *Blue Eyes Crying in the Rain*. Nick had started to hum along when he spotted a figure get off the Tulane Avenue bus and walk towards the probation office. He could tell that it was a white female dressed against the cold and rain, the right height but he couldn't see her face due to the hood on her jacket. It had to be her. He watched as she entered the building and then sat back to wait for her to exit, drumming his fingers on the steering wheel.

3:00 p.m. No sign of Bridgette Griffin exiting.

*Oh, well*, Nick thought. *She probably had to wait to get in to see Claiborne. That little skank probably makes them all wait.*

3:30 p.m. Nick was getting fidgety. *All they have to do,* he thought to himself, *"is say 'Hi, I'm here. I haven't been arrested this week. My urine sample came back clean. Can I go now?' What in the name of Jesus could she still be doing in there?*

He started to call Nancy Hoffman to make sure that Bridgette hadn't gone out the back of the building. Just to be sure, he put the car in gear and nosed around the back of the building.

Nothing.

As he headed back to Tulane Avenue, he spotted her, headed for the bus stop across the street. She *had* gone out the back door.

Nick whipped the car out and into a sharp u-turn, then pulled up at the bus stop, rolling down the passenger side window and holding his I.D. up for the figure to see.

"Get in. I'll take you where you're going."

The girl peered in and stepped back.

"Why? I haven't done anything. I just left my probation officer, and I'm clean." It was a whimper, but made as forcefully as someone accustomed to being a victim could muster.

"You *need* to get in. And get in *now*. Believe me, it's for your own good." Nick was trying not to alarm the girl any more than necessary. He reached over and opened the door, pushing it outward and motioning for her to get in.

She stood there for a moment, defiantly, her blue eyes as misty as the weather that engulfed them.

Finally she moved reluctantly toward the car and sat down, letting out a sigh of resignation to her fate; the type of sigh that was likely a frequent expression of hers.

"I'm Nick Saladino. I'm a homicide detective. You're *not* in any trouble. Just the opposite. We're going to get a cup of coffee and sit and talk, and then I'll take you wherever you're staying."

"You can't do that. I'm staying with a cousin who doesn't know anything about the way I've been living in New Orleans. If you brought me home in a police car, they'd throw me out. What do you want with me?" Bridgette obviously had some education beyond elementary grades. She spoke well, and her voice was free of drawls or accents. "Could I get something to eat instead of coffee?"

Nick nodded and pulled into the parking lot of the Allgood Diner on Carrollton Avenue. Bridgette shivered as they walked to the building and sat in a booth near the window.

Nick ordered coffee and a cheeseburger with grilled onions. Bridgette ordered the special of the day, fried chicken with mashed potatoes and gravy.

"So? What's up with all this? Why do you need to talk to me?"

"You just met with your probation officer?"

"I told you I did. You can call there. His name is Jeremy Claiborne."

"I know who he is. How did the meeting go?"

"What's it to *you*? You a friend of that creep?" Bridgette shrank away from Nick.

"Hardly. And he's worse than a creep. Are you supposed to meet him again?"

"You still haven't told me why you want to know." She stood her ground quietly, but some fear crept into her eyes.

"Just tell me. Has he told you to meet him at a bar?" Nick was pushing gently.

A look of alarm crept over Bridgette's face. "*How* do you know that? You *are* a friend of his. I got to go." She attempted to stand up but got tangled in her coat.

Nick put out his hand to stop her but she had already fallen back into the booth.

"Darlin', you gotta trust me on this one. I am most definitely *not* a friend of his. You need to work with me here. It really *is* for your own good."

Bridgette's body went limp as the fight went out of her.

"Yeah, he told me to meet him at a bar. Told me if I did he could probably find a way to set me free from the rest of my probation requirements. I still got almost six months left, you know?"

Their food arrived and Bridgette attacked it, licking her fingers as she went.

"Did he say *how* he could get you out of your probation?"

Bridgette was still holding the chicken in her fingers, pulling at the skin. "Naw. I figure the little bastard just wants sex. That's fine with me. I've done worse than him. *Much* worse." Her face formed a sarcastic sneer.

Nick winced, remembering the scum who was running the flophouse.

"But I can't figure it," Bridgette went on. "That little asswipe creeps me out. The way he looks at me, like I'm some kind of monster. I wouldn't have figured him for the kind of dude looking for a free piece of ass. I mean, he doesn't look and act like he's into *girls*. Know what I mean?"

Nick nodded. "Yeah, well, I've been assigned to check on whether or not he's molesting the women assigned to him. That's why I stopped you." No sense in scaring her with the real reason he was talking to her.

Bridgette looked at Nick, searching his face for any hint of guile that might be there. She seemed satisfied with what she saw. Being on the streets had taught her something about people.

"Oh. No, I got to say the creep's never touched me or said anything, until now. I figure he wants something when I meet him, but it's worth it to me to get off probation and get the hell out of here."

She went on. "I came here to get away from my family. I was tired of my uncles feeling me up all the time. My parents knew it but they acted like it was *my* fault. My mother told me to just avoid them. Unfortunately, it didn't stop there. I was sixteen, and both of them had their way with me two weeks apart. When the second uncle did me, he kept telling me that my other uncle was talking about what a great piece I was. I told my mother again, but she still refused to believe it.

"I stole some money I knew they had hidden in the house and took a Greyhound to New Orleans. When I got off the bus, the terminal was full of pimps looking for kids like me. They knew just what to do and say. They tried to get me on crack, but I wouldn't take it. Didn't need it. Booze kept me drunk enough that I could stay away from my feelings. But I've had enough of all this shit. I'm going back to a small town and get a job."

Nick had heard her story many times before; only the faces changed. He was impressed that she was apparently getting a handle on her life, and became even more determined to catch Jeremy before there were any more victims. Unfortunately, he would have to put Bridgette in harm's way to make a case against Jeremy that would stick. He reached out and touched her wrist.

"So, tell me when and where you're supposed to meet Jeremy," he said softly.

"Tomorrow afternoon at two o'clock. Some weird place called the Slip It Inn, in the Quarter."

Nick nodded. "I know where it is."

"He told me to wear a dress and look nice. No jeans. That's why I figure he wants some kinda sex." She looked at Nick. "Do you think he's going to try to hurt me? What should I do?"

"Just go there like you were told. I'll have someone in the bar to watch what's going on. You won't know who it is, but if anything happens, they'll step in. I promise you'll be OK." He tried to reassure her, and gave her a business card.

"If you need anything in the meantime, call. C'mon. I'll drive you home."

He slipped her a twenty as they walked to the car, and dropped her a block away from her cousin's home on an upscale street in uptown New Orleans, as she requested.

# XLI

Nick considered having Angela DiGiovanni stake out the inside of the Slip It Inn, but thought better about it when he remembered the bartender saying that Jeremy would make it a point to leave the bar if some unknown female walked in. That might mess up any chance of watching Bridgette hook up with Jeremy and maintaining control of the situation.

He swung the Crown Vic out St. Claude Avenue, having decided that Mike Faust would be the best bet to go inside the place, plus Mike could keep his mouth shut. He picked up the radio and requested the dispatcher to notify fifth district station to have Mike Faust available at the station.

Mike was amused. "You want *me* ta' go hang in 'dis gay jernt?"

"Man, it's got to be you. I don't have anybody else that would go to the wall if this turns to shit."

"I un'nerstand dat'. I'm just afraid dat' I'll stand out like an undercover cop in a gay jernt. Ya know dey're gonna boin me da' minute I walk in."

"Do your best. Make like a tourist. I just need some ears and eyes inside the bar when this chick is there. I'll be sitting right outside. If anything happens, I may need some back-up to take the situation down."

Nick had already explained the whole story to Mike, including the involvement of the other members of the Claiborne family. Mike was always stoic on the outside. It was no surprise to Nick that the only response from him when Nick finished the story was a low whistle. Mike understood the risks to his career in law enforcement.

"Whatever you need, Nick, m'boy," Mike said. "I already got my twenty in fer full retirement and I been bored out here fer a long time, fighting wit' dis terlet trash. If I got to go down, why not do it on a big case? What's it dey say? In a blaze a' *glory*."

Nick nodded. That was one way to look at it. He reminded Mike to get there at 1:30 p.m. and to look for Nick's car before going into the bar.

Nick headed for Steve's office. Steve was just getting into his car in the parking lot with his back towards Nick. Nick hit a low growl on the Crown Vic's siren. Steve was startled and looked around to see if anyone saw him jump, slightly embarrassed.

"*Goddam it. Motherfucker.* Can't you just pull up and honk the horn like normal people?"

"You forget. We are *not* normal people. Normal people go home after work, kiss their wives, throw sticks for their inbred dogs and spoiled brats to chase around the yard. Normal people decidedly do *not* view dead bodies and parts, nor deal with victims and criminals, nor do they have any idea of the real heart beat of the city around them while they are in their cocoons."

"Yeah, yeah. You ain't nuttin' but *right* about that. So what's up?"

"We're back on track. If *you'll* be kind enough to get into my *Crown Vic*, I'll transport you to an establishment where *I'll* be kind enough to buy you a *Crown on the rocks*." Nick was in good spirits, which didn't happen often these days.

"*Wow.*" Steve was pleased. "So it's a go for tomorrow night. I might come sit it out with you."

Nick thought about that. "Naw. Probably not a good idea. You need to maintain some distance from this professionally, in the event you get dealt this case."

"Actually, the D.A. is thinking about starting a new system of having a 'Duty Assistant D.A.' on call twenty-four hours, seven days, to be called out to advise the police on the scene, to cut down on some of the legal mistakes they're making, which are jeopardizing prosecutions." Steve went on. "At any rate, if I do get caught up in this and it turns sour, what better way to go out than on a wave of negative press and abuse?"

Nick shuddered as the Crown bit at the back of his throat. Mike Faust had just said something similar to that not an hour before.

# XLII

The next day passed slowly for Nick. Try as he might to concentrate on the rest of his cases, he could only think about Bridgette Griffin, and wonder what she might face in the hands of Jeremy Claiborne.

Although totally unnecessary, he called Mike Faust around ten a.m. to assure himself that Mike would be on time at the proper location.

Mike laughed. "Man, I ain't seen you dis' noivous in a long time. Calm down. Everyt'ing is *lovely*."

Nick knew Mike was totally dependable, but he couldn't help himself. It was similar to the first time Sharon had given birth to one of their children. His mind was focused on concerns about the baby's health, to the exclusion of all other thoughts. During the few moments he was able to focus on something else now, intrusive thoughts about Bridgette forced their way back in.

About eleven a.m., he couldn't stand being in the office any longer. He got the Crown Vic and swung out to the lakefront, stopping at the Empress Lounge on the way for a quick snort. Feeling steadier with a couple of ounces of Crown warming his stomach, he stopped for a po-boy sandwich at one of the joints looking out over the lake, but found he had no appetite. He walked out to one of the benches and stared out at the lake for an hour, absent-mindedly reviewing his dismal family life.

Nick knew subconsciously that he was wrong for the break-up of his family, but he would never be able to verbalize his feelings about it. His macho bravado would never let him admit that he was capable of giving to his family at home some of the tenderness he displayed towards crime victims in his work. The persona he had developed as a street cop, like that of most street cops, would never, in this lifetime, allow him to drop the barriers he had erected inside in order to cope with the demands of this job in this city. He couldn't be a person sensitive to the needs of his family *and* still be an effective cop. Once he had been assimilated into the culture of "cowboys and crooks," there was no sharing it, and no going back.

He finally headed back to the car, not realizing that he had let out a heavy sigh. All he could think of was the idea that he would never let his kids go into law enforcement. There is no personal happiness there. There is only a silent culture shared exclusively among the players, each of whom lives on a constant adrenalin high; one which is far beyond an addiction, and one which results in total, irreversible self-encapsulation, resulting in an iron wall that even families can't penetrate.

He looked at his watch. It was almost one p.m. He steered the Crown Vic towards the Quarter, arriving in fifteen minutes. He parked virtually outside the front door of the Slip It Inn and radioed Mike Faust.

"Faust, what's your twenty," Nick gave the code for location.

"I'm 10-97, right behind ya."

Nick looked in his rear view mirror and saw Faust grinning and waving.

"10-4," Nick replied. "You might as well go on in."

"On my way. I'll have one fer ya. I'm leavin' da radio in da car." Mike got out of his car and crossed the street, entering the bar. He was dressed in jeans, a worn plaid shirt, and an old Panama hat, his white hair sticking out under it.

Nick relaxed and turned the radio on, listening to the oldies as he watched tourists gawk along the street.

At 1:45 p.m., Nick sat up somewhat from his slouched position and began to stare intently up and down Dumaine Street for signs for Bridgette Griffin. A couple of times, young females with approximately the same build as Bridgette approached and passed him up. He eyed each one expectantly, hoping it was Bridgette. His shoulders tensed as he anticipated each one who might be her, and then slouched back down when it wasn't. He fought back the impulse to enter the bar and sit with Mike, but he knew Jeremy would recognize him instantly and change his plans.

Two o'clock. No sign of Bridgette. Nick was again feeling a very sharp *déjà vu*, and it was unpleasant. He could sense his stomach acid flowing.

He was startled by a banging on the passenger window of the unit. It was Steve Chaisson. Nick let out a mild curse under his breath, and leaned over to open the door.

"Chick show up?" Steve asked, but he knew the answer when he looked at Nick's face.

"Not fucking yet. I thought I told you not to come here."

"Yeah. Yeah. Yeah. Like I'm gonna let *you* have all the goddam glory. Who you got inside? I know you're not sitting out here without someone inside. Did you use that fine little Sicilian chick? Angela what's-her-name?"

"*DiGiovanni*, you feeble-brained bastard. No, I was afraid that sending a female in there would affect the way Jeremy has this thing set up. I sent in Mike Faust. He's the only one that knows the whole story."

"Faust is cool. Good choice."

"Glad you approve, cocksucker."

Nick looked at his watch. Two-fifteen. Something was wrong. He hadn't picked up any hints from Bridgette during their talk that she might not show up for this meeting with Jeremy. She seemed to be resigned to it. His instincts were telling him she wouldn't have been late, either, in the fear that it would piss off somebody as psychotic as Jeremy Claiborne. He resolved to wait until two-thirty, and had to force himself to sit in the car for another fifteen minutes.

"Calm down, bro. She just might be running late. She is a female, after all." Steve tried to make light of it.

"Something's wrong. I can feel it." Nick's neck veins were standing out from the tension. He got out of the car and started pacing the sidewalk.

Finally he couldn't stand it any more and headed for the bar, with Steve on his heels. He threw the door open and walked in, navigating from his memory of earlier visits. His eyes couldn't see anything at first, due to the darkness of the bar.

"Nick, m'boy. Nice ta see ya." He recognized Faust's voice. Mike grabbed Nick's sleeve as Nick stormed past him, not seeing him in the dark. "Have a seat."

Nick slowed his momentum and let Faust reel him in and onto a bar stool. Steve sat on the opposite side of Faust.

"Nice ta' see ya' too, counselor." Faust stuck out his ham of a hand and squeezed Steve's hand mercilessly.

"Y'all decided ta' come in fer a col' one, did ya?" Mike looked surprised at the invasion.

"*Christ.* It's after two-thirty. Did you see Bridgette come in?" Nick asked.

"Naw. In fact, dere wasn't *nobody* come in after me." Mike took a chug out of his beer. "But the beer's cold. Have one." He waved at Tony, the bartender.

"Sit tight. I gotta find out what's going on." Nick walked back outside onto the street with his radio and called the dispatcher.

"*No calls for you, 1251.*" Even in his anxiety, the voice on the radio was mesmerizing. He added an additional mental note next to the last one, swearing he was going to visit the dispatch room and check out the chick connected to the voice.

He re-entered the bar, cursing. He felt that he had built enough rapport with Bridgette that she would let him know if there was a problem. He grabbed the telephone off the bar and called his office.

His secretary answered. "Where the hell have you been? You got half the goddam city looking for you. I got at least twenty messages here for you. You think you're on a goddam leave day? Pay attention, there's gonna be a pop quiz. You got three from the watch commander—wants to know where you are and what case you're working on. You got two from your ex-old lady—didn't leave a message. You got one from the motor pool—it's time for your unit to get an oil change. You got..."

"*Can* all that shit," Nick interrupted. "Anybody named Bridgette Griffin call me?"

"I'm getting there. I'm getting there. Keep your pants on. But of course, we all know that would be a difficult thing for you to do." She laughed.

Nick cursed.

"Yeah. She called about eight thirty this morning. She wanted to tell you something about some appointment today that had been changed."

Nick didn't know whether to be elated or upset. Then he found out the news wasn't good.

"She said something about a two o'clock appointment that got moved up to ten o'clock in the morning."

Nick slammed the telephone down, his face turning bright red.

"*Mother goddam fucker.*" He slammed his fist down on the bar. Mike and Steve looked at each other. This wasn't gonna be good news.

"Somehow this goddam meeting got moved up to ten o'clock this morning! *Goddam it. Shit.* Jeremy already *has* Bridgette. *Fuck.* One of the last things I told her was that I'd keep her safe."

Nick looked around and spotted Tony the bartender at the back of the bar. He looked perplexed as Nick approached with a dangerous expression on his face, and cowered back and away from the bar as Nick neared him.

"Man, what's up with *you*?" Tony said, just as Nick grabbed him by the collar.

"You need to *talk* to me right now, and you need to tell me *only* the truth," Nick said slowly and deliberately. "Someone's life depends on it, and that may include *you*, if you lie to me."

"Man, are you loco?" Tony howled from the pressure of his collar being pulled tightly. "I haven't done anything."

Mike and Steve walked up. Nick pulled the collar tighter. "Just tell me. Today. This morning. Jeremy was in the bar, right?"

Tony nodded.

"Good answer."

"Now. Next question. Jeremy met a female here, right?"

"Man, I don't know. I've been busy all morning. I didn't see..." Tony let out a squeal as Nick picked him up by his collar and threw him up against the wall.

"*Wrong* answer. I know you watch those things. You've told me before that Jeremy occasionally meets defendants on probation here, and they're usually female. Now, I know you didn't just happen to stop noticing those things today. *Right*?" He slammed Tony against the wall again for emphasis. Tony nodded.

"Man, you don't understand. I'm *afraid* of that little bastard. He's fucking dangerous," Tony whined.

"Goddam, I'm getting tired of telling people to stop *whining*. You are really pissing me off. You think Jeremy's dangerous? Keep lying to me and you'll see what dangerous *really* is. Now, Jeremy met a female here this morning, right?"

Tony whimpered.

Nick applied pressure to his ribs. "Right?"

Tony nodded.

"Good boy! Now tell me what happened."

"Nuthin' happened. Chick came in and sat at a table. Jeremy came in and sat with her. No big deal."

"How long were they here?" Nick asked.

"I dunno. Maybe thirty, maybe forty minutes."

"What did they do? Did they have any drinks? Did you hear them talking? What did they say?"

"Man, slow down. They didn't do nuthin. *Nuthin*. I *swear* it."

Nick slammed Tony up against the wall a third time, eliciting more howls.

"Did they drink anything? Did you hear what they were talking about?"

"Yeah, they had one. Jeremy has a special drink he likes me to make for them when they come in."

Nick relaxed his hold on Tony slightly. "What are you talking about, a special drink?"

"You know. It's like one of those drinks that females like, the sweet shit. A White Russian."

"What's so fucking special about a White Russian?" Nick was harboring a suspicion that it wasn't just a drink.

"Nuttin, man. It's just something the little creep likes to give the chicks when they come in. It's his way of having fun with them. I make the drink and put it on the end of the bar. The little creep comes over to pick it up and puts some kinda chemical in it, winks at me, and takes it back to the table."

"What 'cha mean, a *chemical*? What *kind* of fucking chemical?"

"Man, I don't know. I ain't a goddam *pharmacist*. Just a chemical is all I know."

"So what happens after that?"

"The chick passes out, and Jeremy takes her through the back door there to his place."

Nick tightened his grip on Tony. "I *know* that little bastard isn't big enough to carry a chick somewhere. So you *help* him, right?"

Tony was silent. Nick spun him around and up against the bar, and pulled the .357 Magnum out, sticking the barrel against Tony's cheek.

"Right? *Right ?*"

Tony nodded.

"Then what?"

Tony was silent.

Nick fired a shot into the floor of the bar. The sound was deafening.

"I didn't do it voluntarily. The little creep *made* me do it. I didn't have a choice."

"You didn't do *what* voluntarily? What did you do to the chick?"

"That's what I'm talking about. He made me do it."

"Do what?" Nick put the gun barrel back on Tony's cheek.

"The little fucker made me take her clothes off and put her in his bed. He stood there and watched me."

"He watched you take her clothes off?"

Tony nodded. "And he made me fuck her while she was knocked out. He'd watch, and sometimes he'd tell me how to do it. *Kinky* stuff. *Weird* stuff."

"*He* didn't fuck her?"

"No. He just sat there watching and kinda playing with himself, with no sound at all other than an occasional instruction on what he wanted done."

Nick, Steve and Mike were quiet. They had never anticipated this angle.

"What else?"

"That's all. That's it. When he was finished with me, he walked me back to the bar and locked the door to his place."

"What happened to the chick?"

"I don't know. I've never seen any of them again after that. That's all I know. That's the truth!"

Nick thought about that. "Is that what happened to other women? Where are they?"

Tony nodded. "I don't know where any of them are."

"Where's the key to the door to Jeremy's place?" he asked Tony.

"I don't have one. He'd never trust anybody with one."

Nick walked over and examined the door.

Steve placed a hand on his shoulder. "Well, we need to talk about this for a second. We don't have a warrant, and nobody's gonna give us a welcome reception when we walk in with an application to search the premises of the son of Thomas Claiborne."

"My thoughts exactly. I got no choice *but* to go in there. Bridgette could be alive in there. The ends justify the means, my boy. Now, if you'll kindly step back..."

Nick pulled out his Magnum and blew the door lock to kingdom come. He was able to force the heavy wooden door open, and he went through with Mike and Steve at his heels.

# XLIII

They found themselves in a lush patio paved with dark green slate, and stopped to get their bearings. They were under a Greek-style pergola, thickly interlaced with honeysuckle. To their left was a two-story slave quarter of crumbling brick, its mortar crusted in places with thick algae. Directly ahead was the main residence, three stories, with a dark carriageway tunnel under the right side of the house leading to heavy black iron gates that opened out onto St. Philip Street. It was obvious that the carriageway doubled as a parking area for Jeremy; although no cars were present, typical automobile oil stains dotted the concrete. There was one rear entrance to the house, an imposing eight-foot-high door painted black, with no windows. The door hardware appeared to be as old as the house.

"Go get the bartender. I want him to show us around," Nick said.

Mike retreated back into the bar and reappeared with Tony, just as Nick shot out the lock on the back door of the house, startling both of them.

"Man, I'm as good as fired," Tony whined.

"That's far from your *worst* problem, *asshole*," Nick said as he opened the door and peered in. "Get up here and show us where you took the girls."

Mike pushed Tony forward, and he and Tony entered first. Tony was cringing.

"Turn on the goddam lights." Nick growled.

Tony found the switch and a number of halogen track lights announced themselves, temporarily blinding them. They were in the kitchen. A totally white kitchen. It was a kitchen that was obviously perfectly designed by a professional for a client with a perfectly sterile personality. It was designed to be a functional room, with absolutely *no* décor. It had the appearance of a room that had been placed into a museum, with everything perfectly placed, then never again touched. It was spotless, but it had no warmth or personality whatsoever. None. Just the cold, bland efficiency of a pathology lab.

Nick pushed Tony along. "Keep going."

Tony reluctantly led the group through the door at the opposite end of the kitchen into a formal chandeliered dining room, which itself opened up into a formal living room. The dining room walls were a dark blackish purple, with gold linings and ties on royal purple velvet floor-length drapes. The floors of both rooms were heart pine, lustrous with a patina that only comes with a century of use. The living room was wall-papered in a pouting deep orchid color with gilt swirls in a random pattern, and the same drapes as the dining area. A huge crystal chandelier hung from the fourteen foot ceiling in the living room. The windows were shuttered. All of the furniture was authentic Louis XVI, enameled in white. There was no other color in the room, except for a few vases of blood-red roses scattered around the room.

The group stopped in their tracks momentarily, taking in the sight. After a moment, Nick pushed Tony again. "Take us where you did the girls, goddam it."

Tony moved slowly into the living room and veered left towards a doorway on one side of the room. In the next room, he turned on the light and pointed toward a large four-posted bed that had mirrors installed in the ceiling above it. Nick's stomach recoiled when he noticed that there were dark red silk rope restraints tied to each bed post, their loose ends trailing towards the center of the bed.

The dominant color in the entire bedroom was black cherry, but the comforter on the bed was black. All of the room's furniture was the same white Louis XVI style as in the other rooms. Nick looked around, shaking his head at the various leather restraints attached to the walls and ceiling. There was a large cabinet on the wall alongside the bed. He opened it and found a stock of virtually every type of bondage equipment known. Mike and Steve walked over to the cabinet and whistled, rifling through its contents.

"You used this stuff?" Nick asked Tony.

"Naw, man. I wouldn't know what to do with all that shit."

"What about the ropes on the bed?" Nick asked.

"Jeremy made me use them. I had to tie the chick's hands and legs with the ropes before I could do her. He'd sit right there the whole time." Tony pointed to a tall director's chair at the foot of the bed. "When he was finished with me, he'd walk me back out the way we came in and into the bar. Then he'd lock the door to the bar and go back to the broad."

"How many women did you and Jeremy do this to?" Steve asked.

"Not that many. Maybe ten, maybe twelve."

Steve shook his head. "I was afraid of that."

Nick walked over to Tony and put cuffs on him. "Sit on the floor there. You're going to be a major exhibit in what is promising to be a major freak show."

Nick looked around the rest of the room. There was a sterile white bathroom off of the bedroom. Given the rest of the furnishings, the bathroom was amazingly out of place, identical to the small nondescript bathrooms found in cookie-cutter subdivision houses. He noted a door on the other side of it.

"What's on the other side of the bathroom?" he asked.

"Man, I don't know. I wasn't even allowed to use the bathroom when he was finished with me. It was strictly 'put your clothes on and get back to work.' The little fucker wouldn't even look at me. It was like I was doin' something for him he couldn't do for himself and he was disgusted with the whole thing. Really weird."

Nick tried the door, but it was locked. He tapped on it, noting that it was heavy, possibly iron. Odd for a bathroom. The sill around it was metal also, so he eliminated the idea of kicking it in.

Steve and Mike, still rooting through the bondage collection, jumped when Nick shot out the lock in the door.

"*Shit*. Let us know when you're gonna do that." Steve yelled.

Nick never heard him. He had already entered the room, which was pitch-black with a curious odor and mustiness. He stumbled into something, striking his shin on a hard object, and cursed. He hadn't brought his flashlight. He backed up to the door and started to grope the walls, looking for a light switch. Although there didn't seem to be one, he noted that the walls were surprisingly damp and rough to the touch. He backed out into the bathroom and turned on the light, which threw some faint illumination into the room behind the metal door. He could make out shapes, but needed more light.

"Look for some kinda goddam light I can bring in here," he yelled out to Steve and Mike.

Mike found a small flashlight in a bedside drawer, and brought it over, peering into the room with Nick. "*Wow*. Dat is some kinda *dark* in dere. I'm'a go back in da kitchen and see if I can find a' extension cord."

Nick nodded.

Mike came back a few minutes later, carrying an extension cord and a floor lamp from the living room.

"Dis oughta do it." Mike grinned, pleased that he had found something, then plugged the cord into the bathroom mirror outlet and handed the floor lamp to Nick.

When Nick turned the lamp on and walked through the door with it, he didn't get far.

"*Ho*-ly *Je*-sus," he muttered, as Steve and Mike walked up behind him.

There was silence for a moment as they stared into the room. It was obviously a crude homemade add-on to the house, constructed of concrete block. The entire room was painted black: the walls, the ceiling and the smooth concrete floor. It was small, maybe fifteen feet square, and the ceiling was not more than eight feet high. It reminded Nick of a dungeon.

Their attention was drawn to the center of the room, which contained a horizontal medieval torture rack approximately ten feet long, complete with leather restraining straps, and hand and foot screws at each end.

"What da' fuck is *dat* t'ing?" Mike's voice sounded hollow in the room.

Nick walked over and examined it by holding the floor lamp down to it.

"It's some kinda goddam torture device," he said, turning the wheel and noting that, the more he turned, the further the hand and toe clamps moved away from each other. "It's designed to pull your ass apart."

Steve approached the rack slowly. "*No way.*" Then he saw the clamps moving as Nick turned the wheel. "*No shit.* I never had any reason to believe I'd ever see one of these, except maybe in a wax museum or something." He reached out to touch it and recoiled, then leaned in to examine it closely. "*Gag* me. There's some kinda shit crusted on it. I got to tell you, I think that's blood on it." He reached in his pocket and took out his handkerchief, wiping his hand furiously. "*Ick.*"

Nick moved the lamp around to illuminate the rest of the room and noted a small typewriter table next to the rack. As he approached it with the lamp, he recognized a tattoo gun on it, along with a few bottles of ink. Although it was caked with dried ink, he was able to make out the inscription "*Paul Walters*" on it, which he surmised was the manufacturer of the machine. Despite what he now knew about Jeremy, he was nonetheless somewhat startled when he picked up the bottle and found it to be tattoo ink, "Mom" brand, in black cherry color. His mind vaulted back to the old black tattoo artist who had told him the story about Tom Claiborne wanting his tattoo done in dark red. His stomach began to knot in disgust.

"Here's the source of our black orchid tattoo," Nick said calmly, holding up a tattoo stencil that appeared to be stained and well-used. As he looked back toward Steve and Mike, he noted Tony hanging in the doorway, trying to see what was going on.

"Get that asshole *outta* here." he yelled.

Mike turned and pushed Tony back into the bedroom, and down onto the floor.

"*Stay put.*"

Nick backed out of the room, shaking his head, and picked Tony up by the collar.

"You, my boy, are now a principal in what looks like multiple homicides. Now, think hard, before I make you give blood without the benefit of getting a donut and a fucking souvenir t-shirt."

"I'll tell you anything I know. I had no idea what that morphodyte little bastard was doing. I *swear*."

"You need to tell us *where* Jeremy takes the chicks when he's through with them."

"Man, I'll tell you anything I *know*. But I don't know *that*. I swear."

Tony saw Nick's eyes turn black.

"I *swear*."

Nick held him for a minute, then let him go. Tony crumpled to the floor and into fetal position.

Nick motioned to Steve and Mike and they returned to the kitchen, out of earshot of Tony.

The brightness of the kitchen was a sharp contrast to the dungeon. They squinted for a while before being able to fully open their eyes again.

Nick was thoughtful. "*Where?* Where the fuck is Jeremy taking them when he's through with them? How the fuck are we gonna find Bridgette?"

"Yeah. And how does he get dem from here inta a' alligator?" Mike asked.

"Well, we know that the alligator that had Collette Prejean's arm in it was shot out in eastern New Orleans. So that narrows it down to only a few thousand acres of swamp."

"But why would he pick *that* area?" Steve asked. "There's swamp on virtually every side of New Orleans. Many killers simply dump bodies off the side of the elevated Interstate-10 bridges on the west side of the city, out past the airport."

"Dat's true. 'N summa' dem take da bodies across da river and dump 'em in da swamps around Barataria."

"So why pick *eastern* New Orleans?" Nick mused. "Closer? Not really."

"And it's not any less populated. If anything, there are more people out there," Steve added.

"True," Nick agreed. "So what's the connection to the swamps in the east?"

There was silence for a minute while they all absorbed the concepts.

"*Connection?*" Steve spurted suddenly. "Maybe that's *it*. Maybe there actually *is* a connection."

"What the hell are you talking about?" Nick asked.

"Come *on*, man. It was *your* word. *Connection*. Get it? What if maybe the Claibornes have *property* out east?" Steve chirped, slapping Nick on the arm. He could see the lights start to come on in Nick's eyes.

"Makes sense," Nick nodded. "That would give Jeremy a way to handle a body without being seen in public."

"But it's after hours. The property records won't be available until tomorrow morning. How do we find out if the Claibornes own property out there? I can't go back to Clyde Sherman with a question like that at this time of day. He'll be on the telephone instantly to the wrong people. Come to think of it, he didn't mention any other Claiborne properties when I was talking to him."

"Of course he didn't. You were only talking about the French Quarter. There was no reason for him to volunteer information about every piece of property the Claibornes might have," Steve said. "I don't think that omission by itself is enough to suspect Sherman of any complicity in this, if that's what you're thinking."

"Maybe so, maybe no." Nick was reluctant to let Sherman go that easily. He really didn't like the guy. "But, either way, how do we find out what's out in the east? If anything?" He couldn't stop thinking about Bridgette Griffin and wondering if she was still alive. His guilt at letting her fall into Jeremy's dirty little hands was suffocating him.

"There *is* a possibility," Steve offered. "You might be glad I came along, after all."

"Cut the crap. What the fuck are you grinning about?"

"If you recall, I was very surprised when LaRose told me he was an old friend of Thomas Claiborne's. Remember? LaRose knew virtually everything there was to know about the Claibornes because he had socialized with them in their college years. He's the one that figured out the reason for Jeremy being some kinda demented freak."

"So you think LaRose might know if they have a place out east?"

"Worth a shot."

"But…" Nick didn't get to finish.

"Don't tell me. I know. You still got reservations about bringing somebody else in on this. But it's too fucking late. LaRose already knows everything, except for what we found tonight. I told you that. *Now…* Do you or do you not want to find your girl, and catch Jeremy?"

"You're right. Call him," Nick conceded.

"He's not gonna be at work this late, and I know his home number is unlisted. But that doesn't make much difference, cuz' he's not gonna be at home this early on a Thursday night. We gotta go look for him."

Nick looked at Mike and motioned toward the bedroom. "Stay here with that asshole, in case the creep comes back."

"Ya got it."

Nick and Steve went back out through the bar, closing the door behind them. There was a pair of cross-dressers leaning on the bar.

"*Hey.* Can we get a drink?"

"Beat it. The joint's closed."

"But it's *never* closed. Where's Tony?"

The high falsetto was just not the right voice for Nick, given the mood he was in.

He went for them, but Steve grabbed him. Nick settled for walking them backwards out the front door.

Once on the sidewalk, one of them yelled: "Ooh, you are *such* a *bitch.*"

It was wasted, though, as Nick and Steve didn't hear it. They were already in the Crown Vic and headed down the street.

"OK, bright guy. Where to?" Nick asked.

"Gonna have to be a process of elimination. I think I know a couple of possible joints he might be in."

"I'm with you. Name one."

"Well, we're already in the Quarter. Head up Royal Street towards Canal Street. We'll check out some of the tourist joints. He likes to watch the tourists, like us."

Nick nosed the Crown Vic up Royal, parking partially on the sidewalk in the two hundred block. They got out and walked the one block over to Bourbon Street, then walked the street, weaving among the college kids from up north and retired couples from the midwest who all stopped to gape into dark, dank bars, encouraged by barkers to enter and build some memories into their lives that they could tell the folks back home about. Many of the barkers closed their doors when they recognized Nick, waiting until he and Steve passed before returning to their attempts to separate the tourists from their money.

Fortunately there weren't too many bars on Bourbon frequented by locals, and Nick and Steve were able to satisfy themselves that LaRose had not set his sights on Bourbon Street that night. They returned to the car and drove to the back of the Quarter to survey the local joints.

As they turned onto Esplanade Avenue, Steve grabbed Nick's arm.

"*Stop*, goddam it. There's his car." Steve had spotted the old MG parked on Frenchmen Street, mostly hidden from view behind the firehouse.

Nick pulled up in the neutral ground, (called a median in other cities) irritating a couple of locals who were out walking their mutts in the neutral ground. Years of such practice by the locals had built up an impressive array of canine intestinal products in the narrow grassy area. Not the best place to walk in the dark.

"*Goddam it.* Why you gotta stop in the goddam neutral ground?" Steve bitched. "You know all these sadistic bastards make it a point not to clean up their dog shit."

Nick laughed. "Just watch your step, my boy. No place else to park."

"*Jesus Christ.*" Steve was not pleased. "They got goddam dogshit as thick as oatmeal on the ground, *and* they got the goddam birds up in the trees overhead with *no* goddam sphincter control. Are you a fucking masochist?"

Steve was talking to himself. Nick had already made it to the sidewalk and was standing there glaring at him, waiting impatiently for him to move.

"Come on, you sissy bastard."

Steve finally popped out of the car and stepped gingerly around a few fresh piles.

"*Shit.*"

"Well, yeah; that would be correct," Nick replied. "All right. Where do you think LaRose is?"

"All we can do is check the joints on Frenchmen."

As they walked by the MG, Steve reached down and felt the hood. It was cold. LaRose must have started fairly early that afternoon.

Five bars later, they scored partial pay dirt at Ruby's.

"Yeah, the Doc was here." The voice was coming through one of the most shapely pairs of lips Nick and Steve had ever seen. Framed by strawberry blonde hair, her two lips were surpassed only by the two creampuffs that flowed gently up and almost over the top of her white tank top, every time she bent over to fix a drink. Where had *this* fox been all their lives? Nick and Steve swapped glances of appreciation. "Y'all cops?"

Nick flashed the badge. She nodded and kept on digging ice out of the bin for a huge mixed drink in a go-cup.

"He got here earlier than usual. Like about two o'clock. He was upset because some old car of his quit running. He was drinking harder than usual. I would have cut his drinks, but you can't do that when he's drinking straight booze on the rocks."

"When did he leave?" Steve asked.

"About five. Y'all looking to arrest him? I thought he was tied in with the police."

Steve looked at his watch. Almost seven.

"Naw. But we do need his help. Did he say anything about where he was going?"

"Uh-uh. But I might know where he went. He left with Monica, the barmaid that just got off shift. They go out sometimes. He's about the only one around here that'll take her to nice places. They must have taken a cab. Monica doesn't have a car. My guess is the St. Regis."

On the way out, Nick and Steve made a pact to include the joint on their list of regular stops.

The dew had set in early and it promised to be another foggy night. Nick had to turn on the wipers to clear the already abused windshield. The birds had been unmerciful while they were gone, and the wipers mixed the windshield contents into a gross paste that reminded Steve of nothing so much as diarrhea.

Known for steaks, the St. Regis was located in an old mansion in the Carrollton area, off St. Charles Avenue. Although the building had become slightly seedy, the steaks were huge. The restaurant elected to serve "choice" instead of "prime' steaks, and it wasn't unusual for a porterhouse to be slightly larger than the sizzling platter that tried to contain it. Typical of New Orleans, it had been owned by the same family for the better part of a century.

# XLIV

The St. Regis was having a slow night. The Lenten season in New Orleans is tough on steak houses, but you have to stand in line at the seafood restaurants, thanks to all the Catholics who can't eat meat during Lent. They were greeted at the door by the head waiter, who was obviously relieved to see a few more customers.

"Two, gentlemen?" He reached for menus.

"Not just yet. Just a couple of drinks at the bar," Nick said as he steered in the direction of the dark lounge area. It was filled with overstuffed chairs, and cherry red velvet wallpaper; a painting of a partially nude twenties-era flapper hanging behind the bar.

"*There*. Over there." Steve nudged Nick. LaRose was sitting on one of the overstuffed sofas with a middle-aged woman of obviously Creole descent. They went over.

LaRose spotted them approaching and waved towards the overstuffed chairs on each side of the sofa.

"I would normally say it's a pleasure to see you gentlemen, but judging from the scowls on your faces, it is my guess that you are here on business. Is that not true?"

Nick and Steve sat but remained tensed, leaning forward on the edges of their chairs.

"Monica, these are a couple of gentlemen that I work with from time to time. I believe they wish to discuss something with me. Be a dear and go powder your nose for about ten minutes."

Monica nodded at Nick and Steve, and took a stool at the bar, ordering a fresh drink. LaRose looked at Steve.

"So. Obviously there is something new. Yes?" LaRose leaned back into the sofa and sipped his drink, waiting.

Steve filled him in on the events of the day.

LaRose nodded somberly. "Everything you are telling me fits what the FBI likes to call the 'profile.'" He put his drink down. "So you need to know if the Claibornes have property in eastern New Orleans? Let me think."

A waiter came by, but Nick and Steve didn't have any interest in drinking. He walked away a little sullen about the lack of business.

"You know, the mind is amazing in its ability to retain knowledge obtained decades ago. Things that really were not very important at the time but somehow got lodged in the catacombs and chambers of the brain are able to somehow be washed back into your conciousness with the right stimulus. Or stimuli, for that matter."

Nick wasn't in the mood to listen to LaRose's ramblings. "*Goddam* it, Doc. We're already behind the eight ball on this, for letting Bridgette get caught by Jeremy. I just hope she's still alive. *Is* there such a place?"

LaRose raised his hand. "Calm down, Nick. Let me think for a minute."

"I seem to remember that the Claibornes *did* have a place in the east. The land was something passed down through the Claiborne family, purchased by their ancestor, W. C. C. Claiborne, shortly after he was appointed governor of the territory by Thomas Jefferson some time around 1804."

Nick and Steve looked at each other. "That's gotta be *it*. Where is it?"

LaRose held up his hand again. "I'm thinking."

"We used to have fraternity initiations out there. It's a strange place. It's on the edge of the swamp, and occasionally you'd see these balls of luminescent swamp gas floating in the ooze. Really scared the pledges, especially the ones from up East who knew nothing about swamps." LaRose chuckled. "I believe I can take you there."

"Just tell us where it is, Doc. You don't need to be caught up in this," Steve said.

"I'm not sure I can give you directions with any precision. You may waste too much time trying to locate it. Better I come with you." LaRose stood up. "Besides, if you need to deal with Jeremy, it might be better to have me there."

LaRose walked over to the bar. "Monica, I'm afraid I have to accompany these two gentlemen on a mission. Go ahead and get whatever you want to eat. I'll tell the waiter to leave my tab open for you. Hopefully, I'll catch up with you a little later."

# XLV

By that time, the fog had set in, and Nick cursed as he turned on the wipers which at first only continued to smear the bird crap around. He knew the fog would only worsen as they headed out into the eastern swamps. LaRose sat up front so he would have a better view of where they were. Steve, much to his dismay, had no choice but to sit in the back seat.

"Where to, Doc?" Nick asked.

"Get on Gentilly Boulevard. That's the only way I'll know where I am. I'm not real familiar with the Interstate out through the east. *My* God, what *have* you boys been driving through?"

"Don't ask," Steve replied. "What kinda place is this, Doc? I mean, are we talking about a mansion, a camp, what?"

"No, it wasn't a mansion. Picture an Acadian cottage with a sort of West Indies style roof. It had a fishing pier around back, and there was a bayou that meandered around through the property. I believe they call it Bayou Bienvenue," LaRose answered.

Nick let out a low whistle. "That fits *perfectly*. Bayou Bienvenue is where Collette Prejean's gator was caught."

LaRose scanned the road as they headed east on Gentilly, which was old U.S. Highway 90.

"All of this is so populated now. None of it looks the same. But keep on going. It was quite a ways out. I'm sure we haven't passed it. I remember it being near the lake. We'd go over the levee and throw out shrimp nets, then boil the shrimp right there in the yard. Of course, there'd always be a couple of kegs of beer."

"*Pay attention*, Doc. You can ramble on about old memories later."

"Calm down, Nick. I'm paying very close attention."

LaRose suddenly sat up straight. "Slow down. This is it. Turn left here." He indicated Downman Road. "Now go all the way back to the lake."

Nick turned the flashing grille lights on, but didn't use the siren because he had no idea how close they might be to Jeremy's place, and didn't want to alert him in any way, if he was out there with Bridgette.

"Well, you *can* slow down some," LaRose said, nervous at all the red traffic lights Nick was ignoring as he sped toward the lake.

"Seconds might make a difference, Doc. Hang on."

"Yes. Yes, this is the right direction. Turn right up here and drive alongside the levee. It's still a ways yet."

They headed east on Haynes Boulevard alongside the levee towards the old fishing camp area known as Little Woods.

The fog on Haynes was rolling down the levee onto the road like swirls of cotton candy. Nick cut the flashing lights and slowed to a crawl, at times barely able to make out the white stripe on the right side of the road edge.

"Slow down. This is starting to look like the right area," LaRose said.

"*Shit*. I'm already at a crawl. I'm only doing ten miles an hour."

"*Stop*," LaRose yelled.

They were at a gravel driveway. LaRose got out and walked up it a few feet, then returned to the Crown Vic.

"Not it. Very similar, but not it. Seems to me that there was some kind of wrought iron decoration on both sides of the drive. Of course, that may not be there any more."

They cruised about a half mile further.

"I think we've passed it," LaRose said.

Nick cursed and found another driveway a short distance up. He backed the Crown Vic into it, the left rear tire spinning free for a moment as it dropped partially into a ditch when Nick pulled back onto the road. He swung the car hard to the left and gunned it.

"Not so goddam *fast*." LaRose tugged on Nick's sleeve. "Slow down. This fog's too thick... *There*. What's *that*?" He was pointing to the left.

Nick stopped and swung the spotlight over to where LaRose was pointing.

"I believe that's it," LaRose said. "I *thought* I could find it."

"I'll be damned," Nick muttered.

They were looking at what was obviously at one time a gravel drive, with a rusted wrought iron gate post on each side. With the passage of time and lack of maintenance, the posts had gradually begun to lean away from the driveway, and were now at a forty-five degree angle to the ground. They had apparently been painted white at one time, and some flecks of white paint still held desperately to the rusted metal, as if knowing that they would never again be seen if they fell to the ground. The gravel had long been overgrown with weeds.

Nick killed the lights and sat for a minute, letting his eyes adjust to the total darkness. Then he pulled into the driveway and killed the engine.

"How far down this drive is the house?" he asked LaRose.

"About a hundred yards."

They all got out and started to walk slowly up the drive. Fortunately, the wet grass muffled their steps. Although he had brought his flashlight, Nick tried not to use it, relying instead on the feel of the gravel under his shoes to ensure they stayed on the drive.

About half way down the drive, a halo appeared in front of them which turned out to be a single naked bulb on the front porch, dimly visible through the fog.

"Well, its got electricity," Nick noted.

They continued on toward the house, staying on the drive as it wound around the house to the rear. The rear porch light was also on.

"Guess who's here," Steve said in a whisper as they spotted Jeremy's probation office van parked behind the house. "What a surprise."

"Yeah, no shit," Nick agreed. He started to go around the van to put his hand on the hood to see if it was still warm when he heard something. He turned and motioned to the others to be quiet. "I thought I heard something out there." He waved toward the rear of the property.

They all listened intently.

"*There*. Did you hear *that*?"

It was faint, like a stifled moan. Definitely coming from the rear of the property.

Then there was a *shriek*. A *female* shriek. Followed by the sound of something thrashing around in water.

Realization dawned on all of them simultaneously. They moved as quickly as they were able to the rear of the property, stopping at the edge of the bayou.

Nick flashed his light up and down the bayou. They saw a familiar sinister shape glide across the water, dragging a large object.

"Jesus goddam *Christ*." Nick pulled the Magnum and took aim, but there was too much danger of hitting the alligator's prey. He handed the flashlight to LaRose.

"Keep this on that fuckin' gator so I can *see* him!"

"You're not going *in* there. There might be *more* of them," Steve shouted.

"*Crap* on a crutch. Christ, I *hate* cold water!" Nick said, and jumped in, swimming after the gator.

The bayou was about fifty feet across, and Nick caught up to the gator about ten feet from the opposite bank of the bayou. Fortunately, the beast had its mind focused on its task and didn't pay much attention to Nick, as he neared from behind. As he got closer, he could tell that the gator was in fact dragging a woman by the leg, with the rest of the body submerged. He got as close as he could and put the gun up to the animal's skull, firing twice at point-blank range. Eerily, the boom of the gun seemed to bounce off the fog itself.

The animal began a series of violent death throes, its tail striking Nick in the head, momentarily dazing him and knocking him under. As he sank slowly to the bottom of the bayou, he inhaled some of the slimy water and choked back into full consciousness, fighting back to the top of the inky black water. As he emerged, he could hear LaRose calling out to him.

"Nick, *goddam* it. Are you *alright*?" The old man was waving his arms frantically, trying to spot Nick with the flashlight.

Nick waved and looked around. The gator had stopped thrashing and was sinking to the bottom of the bayou. The woman's body was partially submerged up against the bank. He grabbed it by a leg and swam back to the opposite bank, to where LaRose was standing.

"Let me help you." LaRose reached out and grabbed Nick by the collar. Together, they hauled the woman's body onto the grass.

LaRose put the light on her face. Nick felt like puking. It was Bridgette Griffin. He checked carefully for vital signs, but she was gone. He shook his head and sank to the ground, kneeling alongside of her.

"Steve went after Jeremy," LaRose said.

Nick looked at him, startled out of his guilt. He hadn't realized Steve wasn't there. "*What? What the fuck are you talking about?*"

"Just after you shot the gator, Jeremy took off in the van, down the drive. Steve ran off behind it and I heard a loud crash about the time you went under water. It may be that Jeremy ran into your car in the fog."

Nick stood up and let out a horrifying primal scream.

"Stay here, and don't let anything *else* get her!"

He took off down the drive, reaching for his gun but realizing he must have lost it in the bayou when the gator whacked him with its tail.

Sure enough, the probation van had hit his beloved Crown Vic head-on and the unit was making all those painful sounds of a vehicle whose major arteries are leaking their vital fluids. Steve was trying to open the van's driver door, but it was wedged from the impact. Nick went around to the passenger side, which hadn't been damaged. It opened easily, and the interior light revealed Jeremy Claiborne, passed out with a gash on his head. He hadn't been wearing a seat belt, and had kissed the windshield with his forehead.

Nick reached in and yanked Jeremy out of the van, throwing him to the ground.

"*Rodent*. You fucking *maggot*." Nick started to kick him, until Steve finally stopped him.

"*Don't*. You can't do it that way." Steve tried to restrain Nick. "You know, if you kill him, there'll be an autopsy, and they're gonna know how he died. If he's gonna die from his injuries in this collision, that's cool. If he's not, then we'll deal with it. But there's no sense in your getting put away for this piece of garbage."

Nick stopped struggling.

"Was that Bridgette?" Steve asked. "Is she dead?"

Nick nodded.

"Sorry, dude. I know how you felt about trying to save her."

Nick was silent.

"*Now* what do we do?" Steve asked. They looked at each other.

"Well, we're gonna need transportation," Nick said.

He retrieved his radio from the car and called Mike Faust, still at Jeremy's house in the Quarter.

"Faust, 10-99 over to channel 3." Cops normally switched off of the main monitored channel to a lesser channel for conversations they didn't want taped by the communications room. "Mike, I can't give you any details over the radio, but I need you to transport your prisoner to your station's pokey, and then meet me on Haynes Boulevard, almost to Little Woods. *Hustle* it."

"Dat's a 10-4. Be right dere."

"Mike, I also need the meat wagon."

"Oh, man. Sorry ta hear *dat*. I'll take care a' it."

Nick turned to Steve. "Now, go back and get LaRose to come up here and examine Jeremy to see if he needs to go to the hospital. Hopefully, he doesn't. You stay with Bridgette's body to make sure *nothing* else gets to her before the coroner comes."

Steve took off down the drive, and LaRose appeared a few minutes later.

"Did you check for a pulse?"

"I didn't *touch* the creep, except for a few well-placed kicks."

LaRose bent over.

"His pulse is strong in his neck, and he's breathing regularly. I don't think anything's broken, but he could have internal bleeding from the steering wheel. That's a nasty gash on his forehead. Could be a concussion. We do need to get him to a hospital."

Nick reached down and handcuffed Jeremy, then walked over and looked at the Crown Vic, surveying the damage. Definitely a candidate for a new front cap and radiator; hopefully nothing else had been damaged. He called motor pool for a wrecker.

"Doc, you got any friends at a hospital who can keep it quiet if this creep shows up in their emergency room?" Nick asked.

"Why? What are you thinking?"

"What I'm thinking is that if Jeremy is taken to the hospital, they might try to contact next of kin, and his father could remove him to some place where we couldn't find him, which would likely be a major first step in any attempt by his father to block prosecution of his beloved son, who, of course, is also his grandson. But if we have Jeremy stashed somewhere under a phony name, it might give us enough time to get this thing in front of the public so he has to play on our field, instead of us playing on his."

"I see what you mean. I believe we can accommodate you. The emergency room at Charity is the best place for that. Not that they are careless, mind you. Just the opposite. It's the best emergency room in town. However, the charge nurse is a *very* close personal friend. I believe she could probably find a place in one of those labyrinthine hallways where they always have to store people waiting for beds. It's not uncommon for many Charity patients to be labeled as 'John Does.' I'll ride with him in the ambulance, and call her en route. In fact, I also have a few friends operating ambulances... They might enjoy a little excitement. I'll just tell them this is an undercover operation, and they'll write it up anyway we need."

"*Out*-fucking-standing." Nick got back on the radio and had Faust contact the ambulance service LaRose named.

"10-4 on that. I'm headin' fer da station wit' da prisoner. Everythin's copascetic. You OK?"

"Not really," Nick answered. "Come on out when you finish at the station. You got the meat wagon coming?"

"10-4. Body snatchers are already on their way."

Nick went back to the bayou where Steve had stayed with Bridgette's body. Steve was nervously shining the flashlight around the bayou as much as possible, given that the fog limited visibility over the swamp even worse than it did where he was standing.

"You *do* know that you can't hear them when they come out of the water for you, don't you?" Nick said in a low voice as he crept up on Steve.

Steve jumped.

"*Goddam* it. Don't *ever* sneak up from behind when I'm worried about swamp creatures all around me. *Shit. Douchebag.*"

"Give me the light."

Steve handed the light over to Nick, who had knelt alongside Bridgette's lifeless body again.

"Let's see what we got here."

Even in the poor light, Bridgette's lips were obviously blue from lack of oxygen. Her eyes were closed. Although Nick had tried to be gentle when he put her on the ground, her legs were contorted at angles that made them appear to be broken. The same seemed true for her arms. Her left leg was severely mangled where the gator had clamped down and dragged her through the water. Nick noted what appeared to be rope-burn marks on her wrists, and the same type of marks that would be left by the hand-and-foot screws on the torture rack in Jeremy's house.

Nick lifted her left arm and found what he was looking for.

The black orchid stood out ominously on the glare of her milky white skin.

Nick had never before experienced the grief and guilt of not being on time to save a life. It surpassed anything he had ever felt. He could feel his guts start to twist as he slumped over Bridgette's lifeless form.

"I promised her she would be safe. I told her someone would be looking out for her. This kid wouldn't be dead if I had been more careful about protecting her." Nick was beyond anger.

# XLVI

*"Ambulance is coming."*

It was LaRose yelling. Steve went up front to help him. They watched while the EMTs loaded Claiborne; LaRose got in the passenger seat, where he could talk to the hospital on the way.

"I'll call you at the hospital," Steve told LaRose. LaRose waved, and the ambulance left.

Steve waited up front for Faust and the coroner's unit. They arrived almost simultaneously. He guided them around back to where Nick was waiting.

"Dey'll take care a' da bartenda until ya decide what ta do," Mike told Nick, indicating the district station personnel.

Nick nodded. "Good deal."

They watched while the coroner's crew did their thing, and then checked out the house after the unit left with Bridgette's body.

The back door of the house was open, and there was a light in a hallway. It must have been a nice place at one time, meant to be a place of good times and good friends, with a large front room and full-length windows that opened out onto a porch that ran completely around the house. The furniture in the house appeared to be the original furniture from the time when LaRose said he had visited the house. The overstuffed chairs were raggedy and gave off a musty smell. The paint was peeling off the walls in large sections. The bedrooms were bare, as were the closets. There was nothing to be gained from any further inspection of the place at night. Nick would send a crime scene team the next day to go over it.

They closed the back door and got into Faust's unit.

"*Now* what da we do?" Faust asked. They all looked at one another.

"Seems to me the first thing we do is figure how to keep Thomas Claiborne, or his daughter for that matter, from trying to stop us from prosecuting Jeremy," Steve said. "You know what they say? About the best defense being a good offense? Seems to me that we have to go on the offense."

"What 'cha got in mind?" Nick asked.

"I'm thinking we need to have a face-to-face meeting with the honorable Thomas Claiborne. In private."

"Oh, *great*. Let's go straight to the enemy, why don't we? He'll have us skewered like those meat things they slice to make gyro sandwiches," Nick said.

"Well, maybe not. Think about it. We got one hot item to use for leverage. What is the *one* thing that might throw fear into Thomas Claiborne?"

Nick was silent.

Steve continued. "What about the loss of his reputation with his society cronies? Not to mention likely being forced into retirement from his cushy federal job?"

"You mean..." Nick started.

"*Right*. No way Thomas Claiborne's gonna want the city to know he's guilty of incest, *and* that he fathered his own grandson."

"So..." Nick started again.

"So, we make a deal with the devil. He doesn't block Jeremy's prosecution, we don't make the scandal public. That means he's only got to deal with the public on the fact that his son is a serial killer. The public won't know the *reason* his son turned into a serial killer, and he gets to keep all his laurels."

Silence for a minute.

"I don't know, man. That bastard's so egotistical, he might think he can bluff his way through the incest thing," Nick offered.

"He might think that. But then, he's gotta realize that the feds have no sense of humor when it comes to shit like that. He's a goner if that becomes public. He'll have to resign his federal position."

"So how do we do this?"

"We got Jeremy covered for tonight, at least. Bridgette will have to undergo her autopsy tomorrow, which will be handled as simple routine by the coroner. Mike has the bartender stashed for at least twenty-four hours, so I suggest we get to Claiborne in his chambers *tomorrow*. Just you and me. Mike doesn't need to be with us."

"And that gives us a little breathing time to think about any contingencies we might overlook tonight," Nick added.

"And now..." Steve started.

"You're right. We need a stiff drink."

Mike started the car, and they headed back to Nick's place so he could bathe and change clothes, then they went downtown, to the Devil's Den.

# XLVII

The next morning, Steve met Nick at the coffee shop, as they had agreed the night before. Both were bleary-eyed.

"I called LaRose this morning and asked him to meet us here. He ought to be along any minute," Steve said. Nick just grunted and sipped on his coffee.

About ten minutes later, Steve spotted LaRose crossing the street towards them.

"So how's our little Charity case?" Steve asked. LaRose sat down and nodded gratefully when the waitress showed up and poured a stiff cup of coffee. Steve and Nick accepted refills.

"I'm sorry to say he's going to be OK," LaRose replied. "Nothing broken. Slight concussion on the forehead. I have a friend there who is keeping him mildly sedated until we decide what to do."

"What we have to do is pretty obvious," Steve began. "We've decided to go straight to Thomas Claiborne and take the wind out of his sails before we talk to anybody else, especially the D.A. I think the three of us should go there together. Once Claiborne is taken care of, the D.A. won't be any trouble. But if I go to the D.A. first, he'll go overboard trying to cover his ass with Claiborne, and then we'll be in trouble."

The other two thought about it for a couple of sips of coffee, then agreed.

"My thought is that we should go to Claiborne's chambers around noon, after he's finished with his morning docket."

"Cool," Nick agreed. "In the meantime, I'll go by the coroner's office and pick up the results on Bridgette's autopsy."

"Let's meet in the lobby of the federal courthouse at about 11:45, then," LaRose offered.

# XLVIII

Nick had already arranged for the Crown Vic to be repaired and he swung by New Orleans Body and Fender Works to make sure his car had arrived. He was amazed to find that they had already removed the busted front cap and sent the radiator out to be repaired. That put him in a little better mood.

He returned to the crime lab to watch the technicians swarm over Jeremy Claiborne's van. They were thorough, removing hair samples from the carpet, and bagging pieces of upholstery and carpet that appeared to have stains.

His next stop was the Coroner's Office, where Bridgette's body was still on the stainless table, her chest already stitched up.

"What 'cha find, doc?" he asked the pathologist who was just completing his dictation.

"Death was caused by asphyxiation from drowning, Nick."

"Yeah, no surprise. I was there."

"I understand you had to shoot an alligator to get to her. He really made a mess of her leg. Oddly enough, the leg was actually pulled out of its hip socket, but not by the alligator. Both of her legs and both of her arms were pulled from their sockets. There's also strange markings on her hands and feet, as if someone tightened some sort of screw mechanism down on them."

"Torture rack," Nick said.

"*What?*"

"She was on a torture rack before being taken to the area where the gator got her."

"No kidding. *Kinky*. Rather gruesome, I'd say." The pathologist shuddered slightly. "Then there's this strange tattoo on her left inside forearm. It looks amazingly fresh. Almost a homemade thing—very crude."

Nick nodded. He didn't feel a need to go into the entire story at this point in time. The pathologist had told him what he needed to know. He checked his watch. It was time to meet Steve and LaRose at the courthouse.

As he entered the front door, Nick flashed his I.D. and went through the metal detector to the safe deposit boxes where he stashed his revolver. Steve and LaRose were already there, and he joined them.

"Claiborne is on the third floor," Steve said as they headed for the elevators.

At Claiborne's chambers, Steve rang the buzzer for admission. After a few seconds the door buzzed and they walked down a narrow hallway lined with poster art, arriving at the secretary's window.

"Good morning, gentlemen," she said, somberly. "May I help you?"

Steve handed her his business card, and introduced Nick and LaRose.

"We need a few minutes with Judge Claiborne on a personal matter," he said.

"Goodness. So *many* of you? I'll check with Judge Claiborne."

She left and returned ten minutes later.

"Judge Claiborne will see you now, but I'm to advise you that it will have to be brief, as he has a luncheon meeting." She escorted them back to chambers.

Steve entered first, with Nick and LaRose behind them.

He hadn't seen Thomas Claiborne in many years, and was impressed with the man's appearance and bearing. Steve took in the height, wavy white hair, and iceberg blue eyes with a steely expression that somehow didn't go with the bow tie the judge was wearing. There was no smile on his face. Steve's impression was that this was a man who was not to be fooled with, and was glad he had brought LaRose. Somehow he felt that Claiborne would listen to an old college chum before he would agree with anything Steve or Nick told him.

"Jack LaRose." Claiborne walked around Steve and extended his hand to LaRose. "You're running around in strange company. Who are these folks?"

"Meet Steve Chaisson, Assistant D.A., and Nick Saladino, one of homicide's finest." LaRose made the introductions.

"Well, have a seat." Claiborne waved towards the seating area in front of his massive desk and returned to his chair. "Jack, I haven't seen you in years. I hope this is a social visit, but I must assume from the demeanor of your companions that it is not."

"That's correct, Tom. You will not be pleased with the news we bring," LaRose began. "Your son is under arrest and being held at Charity Hospital.

"*Jeremy*? Under arrest?" Claiborne sat back in his chair and folded his hands across his chest. "Whatever for? Why is he in Charity? What's wrong with him?"

LaRose continued. "First, let me say that Jeremy is essentially alright physically. He was involved in a small car accident last night and suffered a minor concussion. He will be fine. That said, let me start with the tough part first. Jeremy is a murderer, of the worst sort. A serial killer."

"Jeremy?" Claiborne almost choked at the beginning of a horse laugh. "A *serial* killer? *My God,* Jack. You really have lost your mind." He sat forward, leaning towards the three. "Are you people demented? *Jeremy?* Jeremy doesn't have the balls to *kill* anything. He's wound tight, and he's got as much personality as a Mexican fruit fly, but a *killer?*" He chuckled.

"I am dead serious, Tom. We caught him out at your old place on Haynes Boulevard last night, with a hooker. She's dead." LaRose told Claiborne the whole story of Bridgette Griffin and her predecessors.

"You're telling me that Jeremy has been torturing hookers at his home?" Claiborne repeated, shaking his head in disbelief. "I know my old friend Jack LaRose didn't come down here to tell me lies, but I have been in that home many times, and I can't imagine *where* Jeremy would have a medieval torture rack, of *all* things. Not in his home. That is *not* a large home."

"Your honor, it's there. I assure you," Nick said. "Off of Jeremy's bedroom is a bathroom. Go through the far bathroom door and you will enter a small, dark room that apparently has served as a dungeon."

"I can't imagine anything like that," Claiborne said confidently as he looked at Steve and LaRose.

"It gets *worse. Much* worse. Jeremy not only tortures his victims on the rack, he also tattoos each of them," LaRose went on. "We found a small tattoo gun with inks and stencils on a table near the rack."

"Before you go any further, tell me, on what *authority* did you enter and search Jeremy's home?" Claiborne was starting to emerge from his initial shock; his legal expertise had started to kick in.

"Exigent circumstances," Nick answered. "I had reason to believe that he was holding Bridgette Griffin hostage in his home. As it turned out, he *was* in fact torturing her there, but had left before we arrived. He took her to your place in the east and fed her to the alligators when he was through with her.

"I might as well tell you now," Nick continued. "This investigation got started when our office discovered an alligator from the Bayou Bienvenue area with a partially digested human arm in its belly. That arm had a unique tattoo on it. We were able to trace the fingerprints on that hand to a hooker assigned to Jeremy's probation case load. As it turns out, the tattoo stencils in Jeremy's room are of the same unique tattoo."

Claiborne sat back in his chair and crossed his hands over his chest. "Gentlemen, what leads you to believe that I would actually sit back and allow you to prosecute my only son for murder? I have only to call the D.A. and the Chief of Police, and *both* of your jobs are history. As for you, Jack, I don't understand why you're mixed up in this, but everyone believes *you're* already out to pasture. I'm not *about* to let the good name of Claiborne be tarnished with a murder prosecution." He was starting to turn red—beet red. "I haven't heard you tell me that you have *proof* that Jeremy actually killed these people. And I can tell you right now that I can easily have your entry of Jeremy's home ruled illegal, and *any* evidence obtained from that entry ruled inadmissible."

LaRose raised his hand and shook his head, as if dealing with a child.

"*Tom*. Tom. You really don't want to *do* that. It is not in *your* best interests, I assure you."

"What the hell are you talking about? Are you *threatening* me? You don't know *what* the hell is in *my* best interests." Claiborne was bright red, and starting to lose control. "You think

I'm going to allow a Claiborne to be prosecuted as a goddamn serial killer? Think of my *reputation*. Think what that would do to my standing as a federal judge."

"We have thought of that. We spent a good deal of time trying to determine a course of action that would cause you the least public embarrassment, my friend." LaRose was trying to calm Claiborne down. "You haven't heard everything yet, and you need to. Desperately so."

"*What?* What the hell *haven't* I heard?" Claiborne's pompous demeanor was starting to re-emerge.

"You haven't heard *why* Jeremy is a serial killer, and *why* he is tattooing and torturing hookers, then killing them," LaRose continued. One of the crucial pieces of evidence is the tattoo that Jeremy etches on the left inside forearm of each of his victims. It is a tattoo of a black orchid, and he uses a black cherry color for the tattoo. Does a tattoo of a black orchid sound familiar to you?" LaRose was leaning forward now. "*Think*, Tom."

Claiborne's fluffy white eyebrows arched. He looked at his own left arm.

"That's right, Tom. Let us see it. We *know* you got such a tattoo during the war. On your left forearm. We even have the tattoo artist who placed it there. He ended up in New Orleans after the war. We also have the photo published by the *Times-Picayune* when you returned to New Orleans. Your tattoo shows up in the photo," LaRose said.

"All right. So I have a tattoo on my left arm. It's some kind of goddamn flower from the Philippines. What the hell is the significance of that? Most returning servicemen in World War Two had tattoos. Are you telling me the design has some kind of hidden meaning or something?"

"No. The only thing sinister about it is the manner in which Jeremy has used it," LaRose said.

"Then I don't get it. What the hell is the significance of Jeremy *allegedly* putting a similar tattoo on his *alleged* victims?" Claiborne stressed the word "alleged."

"The significance, Tom, is that Jeremy's use of the tattoo is his way of expressing his hatred of you, and the female victims are his way of expressing his hatred of his mother," LaRose explained.

"Hatred of *me*?" Claiborne was incredulous. "That boy has no reason to hate me. I provided a good life for him. He *never* wanted for *anything*."

"That's not where I'm going with this," LaRose continued. "Tom, we know that Charysse is Jeremy's mother."

"Of *course* she is. You *knew* my wife Charysse. We all hung together. You knew what a *saint* she was."

"No, Tom. The charade is over. We know that your *daughter* Charysse is Jeremy's mother, not your *wife* Charysse." LaRose was becoming animated. "We have Jeremy's birth certificate from Massachusetts, which indicates that Charysse was a *teenager* when she gave birth to Jeremy. And that is why your wife Charysse died a short time later. She was *heartbroken* over the incestuous birth. You hid it very well at the time. Even *I* accepted your story back then. *None* of your friends thought to question it. Unfortunately, it also explains your daughter's attitude toward the world in general, and men in particular."

Claiborne sat back and exhaled loudly.

"Jeremy *also* knows that his sister is his mother," LaRose said. "And his *obsession* with it is apparently the source of these murders, and the manner in which they are committed."

"So. You plan to make all of this public, I assume," Claiborne said quietly. "The purpose of your visit is to dethrone Thomas Claiborne?"

"No. At least, not necessarily. That truly depends upon you, my old friend. We came prepared to make you a deal, so to speak," LaRose replied.

"I'm listening."

"You let Jeremy go through the system without interfering in any manner whatsoever with his prosecution, and we keep the incest quiet," Steve said. "*If* you interfere with Jeremy's prosecution, the incest will be all over the front page of the *Times-Picayune* the next day. *That's* a guarantee. We certainly have *no* interest in embarrassing Charysse, who is an innocent victim of yours, but Jeremy *has* to be removed from society."

"It is extremely unlikely that Jeremy would go to trial," LaRose explained. "I can tell you definitively right now that Jeremy is in fact *insane*. A sanity commission will be ordered at arraignment, and the court will have no choice but to commit him to Jackson, the hospital for the criminally insane."

"And, considering that the sentence for his crimes, if he were *sane*, is either death or life imprisonment," Steve added, "Jeremy may spend the rest of his days at Jackson, without release."

Claiborne got up and went to the wet bar at one end of the office, and poured a straight Scotch. He turned and took a pull on it, then motioned to the bar. "Anyone else?"

No one took him up on the offer.

"Judge Claiborne," Steve said, "You *also* need to know that there is one other person, a police officer, who knows the entire story and who will also maintain silence, unless you break your word. Each of us has the documentation of the incest locked away in safe deposit boxes, so it will do no good to harm us. Finally, we would expect you to agree *not* to retaliate against our jobs or careers."

Claiborne returned to his desk and sat. "Does Charysse know any of this?"

"She does not," LaRose replied. "We do not plan to talk to her, and hope that you will inform her of our agreement. It is expected that she will also cooperate."

"It sounds as if you leave me little choice, gentlemen. I will think about it," Claiborne said, wearily. "Now, if you will leave me, I have a great many things to take care of."

# XLIX

Nick arrived at Charity Hospital early the next morning to transport Jeremy Claiborne to Central Lock-up for processing. He went straight to the room where a guard was posted. Claiborne was in street clothes but disheveled, a pathetic-looking figure with what was left of his hair standing out like spikes around the sides of his head, not unlike the crown on the Statue of Liberty. His ferret-like black eyes were narrow, dark slits. Looking at them, Nick felt as if he were looking into the very depths of hell itself.

"You know that my father will have you skewered for this. He will never permit a Claiborne to be prosecuted for a crime." Jeremy's voice was thin and reedy but somehow sibilant. Nick put him in the car.

"Not this time, douchebag. We've already talked to the good judge and told him that if he keeps his hands off, it won't be necessary to let the press know that you are the bastard product of his incestuous liaison with your sister. I don't have to tell you that his precious name is more important to him than you are."

Nick checked him into a holding cell and completed the paperwork to book him on two counts of first-degree murder, totally unaware of the events that were surfacing around the arrest of Jeremy Claiborne.

"*1251.*" It was a male dispatcher on the radio. Nick had a fleeting twinge of regret, hoping that the chick with the sultry voice hadn't left the police department.

"1251," he replied.

"Watch commander says you are to report to the D.A.'s office *immediately*. See the D.A. himself when you get there."

"10-4."

*Not good*, Nick thought. *It's already hit the fan.*

L.

That same morning, Steve was actually surprised to find that the D.A.'s office was already surrounded by a herd of trucks used by the TV stations when they broadcast live from a remote location. He had to walk through a group of talking heads rehearsing their names and sign-off blurbs in order to get in his front office door.

"The D.A.'s looking for you," Melanie told him when he walked into his office. "He wants you upstairs the minute you walk in. Didn't sound like he was in a good mood. In fact, it was more like a steady stream of obscenities."

Steve wasn't surprised. He had assumed that Claiborne would contact the D.A. as soon as they left his office, but he couldn't imagine why the reporters were circling. He grabbed a cup of coffee and headed for the elevators.

"Sit down, Chaisson." The D.A.'s face was beet red, like someone with chronic high blood pressure.

Steve noted a small prescription bottle on the desk next to a tall glass of water.

"*What* in God's name have you *done*? You have been investigating Jeremy Claiborne in connection with a *murder*? You *know* that Thomas Claiborne is a close friend and a political ally of mine. *Sweet Jesus*. Why the hell wasn't I informed of this investigation?"

Steve sat back and let him run on. He knew that any answers would be of no interest to his boss. His only thought was in the form of a hope that Thomas Claiborne would take the deal that had been offered to him, which would be the only thing that would keep the D.A. from firing him on the spot.

"*Jesus*, Chaisson. You and Saladino and Jack LaRose actually had the *balls* to confront Tom Claiborne with *this*? That's like Curly, Larry and Moe calling on the pope, for Christ's sake. I should fire your ass *now* for this. The only reason I haven't is that Judge Claiborne specifically asked me not to. And I am at a loss to understand why." The D.A. looked at Steve with a genuinely puzzled expression. "I don't know what dirt you've found on Tom Claiborne, but for now, I'm respecting that request in order to help Tom, even though it's against my better judgment. I can't have any loose cannons on my staff. What if I'd gotten a telephone call from the goddam press asking for details about the arrest of Jeremy Claiborne, and *I* didn't know anything about it? *Christ*. I may *still* fire you."

Steve breathed a sigh of relief. Claiborne had taken the deal.

"I've ordered your playmate, Saladino, up here to meet with us. Stay put right there. I want both of you together."

Steve heard the secretary's voice over the intercom as the D.A. stopped to take a breath.

"*Detective Saladino is here.*"

Steve hadn't expected the D.A. to confront Nick, whom he imagined would have to face off with the head of the homicide division at N.O.P.D.

Nick was equally surprised to see Steve sitting there when he walked in. Considering the circus going on outside the D.A.'s office, he had assumed that his law enforcement career was over. He looked at Steve with a quizzical look, and Steve gave him a thumbs-up signal when the D.A. looked out the window for a moment. Nick's expression relaxed, and he sat down.

"Detective Saladino," the D.A. began, glowering at Nick. "It is my understanding that you and Mr. Chaisson here have been off on your own little investigation, and have placed me in a potentially embarrassing and politically damaging position. I don't have to tell you how *intensely* I dislike such distasteful positions."

"Tom Claiborne has advised me that you plan to charge his son with multiple homicides, and that you believe that Jeremy is actually a *serial* killer, for Christ's sake. As if that weren't one of the most shocking things I have ever heard, what I find more shocking is that he has asked that I not kick Mr. Chaisson's ass out on the street for this. Judge Claiborne has also asked the police superintendent not to relieve you of your badge."

"I know Tom Claiborne well enough to know that he is a very vindictive man when he is not pleased. Tom Claiborne has the power to wipe you two off the face of the earth if he so chooses. He is *not* the type of person to forego the use of that power when he is pissed. I have been around him long enough to know that the only reason he would restrain from taking action against you two is that you have something very powerful over him. Something so powerful that he is willing to take these steps to avoid having that *something* become public."

"Although I have to confess that I have an overwhelming curiosity as to what Judge Claiborne could *possibly* fear from you two, I have an even stronger feeling that I may be better off not knowing. I am one of Tom's closest allies, and I've always assumed that if *I* don't know about something in Tom's life, no one does. He has been in the public arena for decades, and literally *no one* has ever slung dirt at Tom Claiborne."

"I must say that I *have* developed a new respect for Mr. Chaisson, as I never suspected that he was capable of striking fear into the heart of a person such as Tom Claiborne. You, of course, Detective Saladino, are well-known as a fearless street fighter. You face physical confrontation many of the days you are on the job. You will be happy to know that I have been advised by the Superintendent of Police that he also intends to comply with Judge Claiborne's request not to dump you from the force, at least for now."

"Now, I expect you gentlemen to fill me in on how this investigation came about and what led you to Jeremy Claiborne, and do it fast. We have a press conference in twenty minutes."

Steve and Nick told the D.A. the essential details, omitting only the significance of the tattoo and its relation to Jeremy's killings.

"My *only* concern at this point is to assist Judge Claiborne in presenting an appearance to the public that he has cooperated in the investigation and arrest of Jeremy." The D.A. swallowed a pill from the container on the desk and gulped some water. "He has called a news conference for ten a.m. in our briefing room. He has specifically requested that the three of us, along with the Superintendent of Police, attend that conference with him, because he intends to participate in the announcement of Jeremy's arrest in order to maintain the public's confidence, to assure the public that he and the Claiborne family are not above the law. He will announce that he has cooperated with the investigation and criminal proceedings against his son."

The D.A. stood up and preened in the mirror on one wall, then turned to walk out the door. "I will expect both of you to keep your goddam mouths absolutely shut while we are in front of the rodents from the press."

He stopped at the door and looked back at Steve and Nick.

"*Jesus Christ.* You two are more insidious than the fucking *mafia.* Did Claiborne wake up with a goddam horse's head in his goddam bed?" The D.A. was shaking his head as he walked to the conference room with Steve and Nick on his heels, swapping smiles behind his back.

# LI

The D.A.'s conference room was on the third floor of the building and was occasionally used by the Grand Jury for some of its sessions, because the Grand Jury room in the Criminal Courts Building was dismally small. The D.A. frequently used it for press conferences, set up with one long table facing a number of folding chairs that were reserved for the press. It was the practice of the D.A. to have the First Assistant D.A. and a few division chiefs sit to his left and right, to assist in fielding questions from the press.

As they approached the room, Judge Claiborne was standing in the foyer just outside it with the Superintendent of Police. They both greeted the D.A., but did not acknowledge the presence of Steve and Nick. Claiborne turned and entered the room with the four others behind him. As the judge moved to the center of the table, the press turned on their lights and cameras, looking at the five men with vapid, bored gazes. It was apparent that the press assumed that they were going to report some type of political announcement.

Steve looked around and noted that the only reporters present were the locals; apparently no wire services had been notified. That didn't come as a surprise to him. Claiborne would have made certain that only those reporters he had an acquaintance with would be present. There would be fewer questions, and the locals would be grateful to make the national network news with a story like this.

The D.A. stood up.

"It is with sorrow that I announce to the citizens of New Orleans that my office, in cooperation with the New Orleans Police Department and Judge Thomas Claiborne, has identified and arrested a person suspected of multiple homicides in this city."

There was a buzz in the room as the reporters perked up and leaned forward, scribbling furiously in their little notebooks. It reminded Steve of a herd of hyenas, circling for the kill.

"I have mixed feelings about this arrest, because it is the son of a dear friend of mine and a person who is greatly respected by our community. The person arrested is Jeremy Claiborne, son of Judge Thomas Claiborne." The buzz got louder. Some of the reporters started to ask questions, but the D.A. held up his hand for silence.

"One of my assistants, Steve Chaisson, seated here with me, assisted Detective Nick Saladino, seated next to the Superintendent, in interpreting and developing some of the first clues of this case for this office, and, needless to say, this office is proud of Mr. Chaisson for his help in solving a case of this magnitude before the city was aware that a series of related homicides had occurred." The D.A. waved in the direction of Steve and Nick. "And now, Judge Thomas Claiborne."

Claiborne stood up, his arrogant bearing conflicting with the look of humility on his face; a look apparently practiced before a mirror the night before. Claiborne chose his words carefully.

"All of you know me as a member of this community who has always been concerned with truth and justice, a person who has at all times striven to provide an excellent example of moral strength and values in our city. As you are aware, my daughter Charysse Claiborne has followed that example and is one of our finest criminal court judges, also sworn to defend this community from those who would destroy it through their criminal acts and moral depravity." Claiborne stood with his head held high, ensuring that the camera lights would highlight his silver hair.

"I am heartbroken to inform you that my son, Jeremy Claiborne, has in fact been arrested as a suspect in multiple homicides, and is currently incarcerated. I have been informed by the District Attorney that it is believed that Jeremy is suffering from a severe mental condition that makes him unable to distinguish right from wrong. If that in fact turns out to be true, it is a condition of which neither his sister, Judge Charysse Claiborne, nor I, was aware. It is a condition of the type and severity that would require Jeremy to be hospitalized for the remainder of his life.

"I was brought into this investigation early on by the District Attorney and the Superintendent, in the hope that I could assist in securing an amicable arrest, without endangering either Jeremy or any member of the community. Although Charysse and I have suffered unbearably throughout the resolution of this matter, we have both devoted our full cooperation to these outstanding law enforcement efforts, as we would expect others in our positions of responsibility to do. We are simply devastated at the possibility that a member of our family could have been engaged in the crimes being alleged, but we will not fail to fulfill our obligation of cooperation to society and the citizens of this town, even though, of course, we will retain defense counsel and provide a proper defense to Jeremy in these matters. If, in fact, Jeremy is deemed insane, as we understand it, we will see that he obtains the most effective state of the art treatment."

Claiborne was a master of press manipulation. Steve could see the change in the reporters, all of them now listening quietly to Claiborne with a look of reverence, much the same as a cobra responds to the snake charmer.

"I have come to you personally to be part of this initial announcement to stress to you that, regardless of the fact that Jeremy is my son, he will be treated as any other person charged with a crime, and no information or facts will be withheld from you. I am here now personally to tell you of this, and I will remain available at all times to discuss the matter openly. We are simply one family in this wonderful city of families, and we are also subject to the same human frailties that bind all of humanity.

"Finally, let me say that, if these allegations are true, it is our wish to make known to the relatives of the victims that they have our sincerest sympathies and concern for the loss of loved ones. And now, I must leave to resume my day on the federal bench. The Superintendent will fill you in on the allegations against Jeremy."

Claiborne walked out the door and drove off in a black federal Suburban parked outside the back door of the D.A.'s office.

# LII

Channel 31 interrupted normal programming to announce Jeremy's arrest with only the sketchiest of details, simply stating that the son of federal Judge Thomas Claiborne had been arrested for multiple homicides, possibly as many as nine.

By five o'clock, all of New Orleans's channels were ready, and they gave it their all, including full coverage of the press conference conducted in the D.A.'s office.

Channel 5 started with their lead story: *"It has been announced today in this breaking story that the son of a respected New Orleans family of jurists has been arrested and charged with being a serial killer."*

Channel 7 was right there, too: *"At least nine people suspected dead at the hands of one of New Orleans's bluebloods."*

Channel 13, not to be outdone, added: *"We will have a special on tonight at 9:00, with more in-depth coverage into this story, including interviews with a psychiatrist, a criminologist, a criminal defense attorney, and a retired prosecutor. Be sure to stay tuned."*

*Typical*, Steve thought. The Superintendent of Police had passed out a written statement of the charges against Jeremy, which contained the barest set of facts, in order not to interfere with the state's case against Jeremy. The reporters were wasting no time filling in the missing blanks with the sheerest of speculation, their stock in trade.

# LIII

Within a few days, the crime lab people had finished their work, and Nick met Steve at the Devil's Den.

"So what did you guys come up with?" Steve asked.

"Turns out Jeremy had cameras in the bedroom and the dungeon. They found his stash of videotapes of his victims. The bedroom had two cameras, one overhead and somewhat to the side, and one on the wall facing the foot of the bed. There was a tape for each victim with her name on it. It appears that Jeremy had a ritual that was virtually the same with each one. The tape starts off with the bartender tying the victim to the bed, then cutting and ripping her clothes off. You can see the bartender's raggedy ass pumping up and down on each one of them, and you can hear Jeremy telling him what to do next. Then Jeremy starts cursing the bartender and tells him to get out. A few minutes later, Jeremy comes back into the room and binds her with some of that bondage shit we found, including one of those latex ball gags. He gets in the bed on top of her and starts rubbing himself on her face, then he jacks off, coming on her face and rubbing it all over her face and hair. Oddly enough, he almost never touches them with his hands.

"Then Jeremy drags the victim into the dungeon and puts her on the rack. We found one camera and a couple of standing Klieg-type lights in the dungeon. You can see that, after he's got her bound to the rack, he does his tattoo thing to her. By this time, the drug's wearing off, and she's moaning and talking, slurring her words. Jeremy starts cursing the victim and proceeds to turn the crank on the rack, and the victim starts to scream, which seems to excite him even more. You can hear what sounds like bones cracking on the tape, and the victim passes in and out of consciousness. That's pretty much where each tape ends. And we know the rest... *except...*" Nick had a puzzled look on his face.

"OK. I'll bite," Steve said. "Except *what*? Don't leave me in suspense, cocksucker."

"Well, what I thought was odd, and no one in the crime lab had an explanation for this, was these strange small coins in an inlaid box on the table with the tattoo equipment. They actually looked to be old, even ancient. The coroner actually found one in her stomach."

"Maybe the guy had an odd way of storing his coin collection," Steve ventured.

"No. Not a collection. There were no other collector-type coins in the house."

# LIV

Nick, Steve and Jack LaRose sat in the back of the courtroom, and watched the proceedings of the sanity hearing on Jeremy Claiborne. Claiborne himself sat next to his attorney, Beau Celeste, the darling of the uptown crowd. LaRose was ethically unable to participate in Jeremy's mental status examination, since he had participated in the investigation that led to Jeremy's arrest. LaRose hadn't been surprised when Steve told him about the unusual coins found in Jeremy's dungeon. For some reason, LaRose speculated that they might be Greek, but Steve hadn't had time to press him for more information.

An artist from the *Times-Picayune* was feverishly drawing the courtroom in pastels, and there were a number of reporters scattered around the room. Judge Max Oser had ruled that there could be no cameras present. Neither Thomas Claiborne nor Charysse Claiborne were there.

Dr. Henry Scribner droned on about his examination of Jeremy, under questioning by Jeremy's defense attorney. It was Dr. Scribner's opinion that Jeremy was legally insane at the time he committed the murders. As it is common practice in New Orleans for two forensic psychiatrists to examine a defendant for a lunacy commission, Dr. James McKenzie took the stand next. His testimony was the same as Dr. Scribner's.

When he stepped down, Judge Oser had the prosecutor read a brief synopsis of the factual basis for the charges against

Jeremy, and then Beau Celeste made a perfunctory argument to the court, pressing Jeremy's insanity defense.

Judge Oser's booming voice filled the courtroom. "Jeremy Claiborne, this court finds that you were insane at the time of the commission of these offenses, and sentences you to the Feliciana Forensic Facility for the rest of your natural life."

As Jeremy was escorted out the rear of the courtroom, he stared icily at the three. When their eyes met and lingered, Steve shivered; he felt as if he were looking straight into a dark abyss. As they were getting up to leave, they heard a loud, strangely sibilant voice and looked back toward Jeremy, who had twisted away from the guard and was staring at them.

"I am *Charon*. I *will* be back for you."

# THE END

# ABOUT THE AUTHOR

Bill Culver is an Assistant Parish Attorney for the Parish of Plaquemines, the southernmost parish in the State of Louisiana, having retired from the Louisiana Department of Justice, Office of the Attorney General with nineteen years of service as an Assistant Attorney General in the Litigation Division. He has tried approximately three hundred jury trials in state and federal, civil and criminal courts in Louisiana and Texas. He was an Assistant District Attorney and Division Chief in New Orleans for almost a decade, where he prosecuted every type of violent and white-collar crime, including numerous capital murder cases.

Culver has been an Adjunct Professor of Law at Tulane University School of Law for the last thirty-five years. He holds a B.S. in Business Administration from Louisiana State University, and acquired his law degree from Loyola University New Orleans College of Law in the evening division while an Assistant Vice President at a local bank.

# Acknowledgements

Many thanks to Kathryn Galán for her assistance in moving this book beyond the manuscript stage. Without her advice and guidance, it would still be lurking in my computer archive folder.

Credit also goes to the criminal justice system, which requires coming to terms with one's limitations and making the best of them under extremely adverse conditions. There is no more fertile ground from which to create scenarios.